"It's a little late for apologies, don't you think, Joel?"

"No, Mari. Not when I really mean it. I regret all the times I got you into trouble with your dad."

He could tell from the doubt in her eyes that she didn't believe him. He couldn't blame her. He'd done nothing in his life to earn her trust. In fact, just the opposite. He'd thought cigarettes and booze gave him a grown-up image. Wearing muscle shirts made him look tough and attractive. Other girls liked him. But not Mari, the one girl he wanted most.

Now he realized how little he'd really known Mari. Pure, honest and hardworking. She wanted a good man, not a rebel who defied everything holy.

He'd just have to prove himself to her. Prove that he wanted nothing to do with his old lifestyle. If she could see inside his heart, she'd know that he'd changed.

Books by Leigh Bale

Love Inspired

The Healing Place
The Forever Family
The Road to Forgiveness

LEIGH BALE

has won multiple awards for her inspirational romance, including the prestigious Golden Heart Award. A member of Romance Writers of America and Phi Kappa Phi Honor Society, Leigh also belongs to the American Christian Fiction Writers and various chapters of RWA, including the Faith, Hope and Love chapter and the Golden Network. She is the mother of two wonderful adult children and lives in Nevada with her professor husband of twenty-nine years. When she isn't writing, Leigh loves playing with her beautiful granddaughter, serving in her church congregation and researching her next book. Visit her Web site at www.LeighBale.com.

The Road to Forgiveness
Leigh Bale

Steeple Hill®

Published by Steeple Hill Books™

STEEPLE HILL BOOKS

Steeple Hill®

Recycling programs for this product may not exist in your area.

ISBN-13: 978-0-373-87600-6

THE ROAD TO FORGIVENESS

www.SteepleHill.com

Printed in U.S.A.

For with what judgment ye judge, ye shall be judged: and with what measure ye mete, it shall be measured to you again. And why beholdest thou the mote that is in thy brother's eye, but considerest not the beam that is in thine own eye?

—*Matthew* 7:2–3

This book is dedicated to Marjorie Baird, my dearest girlfriend, teacher, conspirator and mentor. I adore you down to the ends of my pinkie toes. You told me, but I didn't believe. I'll listen next time.

And many thanks to Craig "Tinx" Anderson, for answering my greenhouse questions.

Chapter One

Marisol Herrera awoke with a jerk. She widened her eyes, peering through the shadows above her bed. Moonlight cast a dim haze through the slats in the window blinds. Her eyes drooped wearily and she rolled, scrunching the pillow beneath her head.

"Mari?"

She glanced toward the doorway and rubbed one eye. Olivia, her seven-year-old sister, stood beside the dresser, wearing one of Dad's old T-shirts. The garment sagged to her ankles. The night-light in the hall silhouetted her long, dark hair and thin legs. Her pale, oval face gleamed in the darkness.

"Mari, are you awake?"

Biting back a groan, Mari propped herself up on her elbows. "I am now. Where's Mom?"

"Asleep."

Which is what Mari wished she was doing right now. "What time is it?"

"I don't know." Livi shrugged.

Mari peered at the clock radio on the bedside table. Six twenty-eight in the morning. Stifling a wide yawn, she sat up. As usual, she'd worked late, transplanting petunias from seed trays into four-inch pots. Four measly hours of sleep and now this.

"Max is barking out by the basket houses," Livi said.

The basket houses. The three greenhouses where they grew hanging baskets of colorful vine geraniums and fuchsias. The dog had probably found another rabbit. Somehow the varmints kept shimmying their way under the heavy polyethylene of the greenhouses, eating their fill of cauliflower and pepper plants. "All right. I'll go check."

Mari flung her pillow aside, once again missing Dad more than she could say. At age twenty-five, she should be finished with college and starting her nursing career, not worrying about the family business and a mountain of bills.

She reached for the worn T-shirt she'd tossed aside earlier. As she thrust an arm through one sleeve, an explosion shook the house, rattling the windows. Olivia screamed and fell to the floor.

"Livi!" Mari bolted from the bed, her legs tangling in the covers.

She clasped her sister's arm and helped her stand. Cool night air wrapped around her bare arms and she shivered. Confusion fogged her mind. What had just happened?

"I'm okay. Was that an earthquake?" Livi's voice wobbled, her eyes wide with fear.

"No. Wake up Mom and call 9-1-1." Mari stumbled as she jerked on her blue jeans.

With a short nod, Livi turned and scurried down the hall. Mari yanked on her socks, then sprang for the door, passing Mom as she came out of her bedroom. When Mom flipped on the hall light, Mari blinked her eyes. Mom's short, gray-black hair stuck up in places, her plump face pinched with alarm as she pulled the folds of her bathrobe around her.

"Mari says we have to call 9-1-1, Momma." Livi scurried down the hall behind her mother.

Elena Herrera's brows drew together. "What on earth is going on?"

"I don't know, Mom. Can you keep Livi inside?" At least they didn't have to worry about Matt, who'd stayed the night at a friend's house.

"But I want to come with you," Livi whined.

"No! I need you to take care of Mom," Mari called as she raced outside.

"Aww!" Livi grouched.

On the front porch, Mari thrust her feet into her knee-high rubber work boots before sprinting toward the greenhouses. Her pulse pounded in her head and she drew cool air into her lungs to settle her nerves.

The new dawn painted the eastern sky with a haze of pink and gray. Frost covered the lawn. Mari preferred that to snow. You didn't have to shovel frost or rain. The March weather had been unseasonably warm, but Mari knew winter wasn't over.

She ran past the three-car garage, the mulching huts and rows of long, industrial-sized greenhouses. The heavy blanket of sawdust on the ground muffled her footsteps. At the end of the row, billows of smoke rose from one of the sheds next to the bedding plant greenhouse where she'd worked late last night. Her heart beat madly in her chest.

No, no! All her hard work. The variety of annuals she'd planted would have been a bumper crop. Her family couldn't afford to lose the flowers. Not if they wanted to eat and pay their bills.

Flames darted from one of the twenty-one-foot-wide press-wood end walls on the south greenhouse. The blaze created a clear, red glow in the sky.

Fire!

The air smelled of propane and her breath stalled, her hands clammy and cold. Had the tank exploded? No! Common sense told her if the 2,000-gallon tank had blown, the whole place would have gone up. This must be caused by one of the small propane heaters leading to the older greenhouses to keep them warm. She'd adjusted all the heaters last month. With the cool March temperatures, the danger of frost could destroy their plants. So, what went wrong?

The two tall mercury vapor yard lights came on, bathing the dirt road in blue light. Mom must have turned them on, bless her.

Mari came to a halt at the end of the rutted road and scanned the last greenhouse. Their dog, Max, stood barking at the fire. A Border collie and Australian shepherd mix, the black and white mutt had proven to be a good, but noisy watchdog.

The polyethylene siding of the greenhouse melted, curling back and evaporating in the heat of the fire. Flames engulfed the wooden trusses of the structure, licking at the long benches where thousands of potted seedlings waited for sunshine, water and time to turn them into beautiful flowers in someone's garden.

Tall galvanized steel pipes supporting the structure in high gothic arcs appeared like the skeletal remains of a dead giant. Several pipes had given way in the blast and the elegant fuchsia baskets crashed to the ground in a ruined melee of dirt, hemp and limp plants. The explosion had blown out the propane heater and pressboard wall on the west end of the greenhouse. Flames ate at the end wall and baseboards, scorching the tender plants and incinerating the white PVC pipes of the automatic watering system.

Horrified by the sight, Mari pressed a hand to her mouth. They had no insurance. The premium had been too steep, so she'd let the policy lapse.

In the smoky haze, she sprang toward the water hose hanging on the side of another garden shed. Max ran after her, barking and jumping on her.

"Down, boy!" If she hurried, she could put the fire out before it spread to the outbuildings and other greenhouses.

Before it destroyed their entire livelihood.

With quick twists of her hand, she cranked on the tap and jerked the hose free of the wall hooks. Squeezing her index finger, she depressed the trigger on the spray gun and directed the water in a high-velocity stream at the fire. Compared to the flames, the piddling spray didn't have a chance. She persisted, hoping to contain the blaze until the fire trucks arrived.

More pipe supports collapsed and the other large end wall creaked and swayed. What on earth—?

Mari screamed as the fifteen-foot wall slammed toward her. She lunged, trying to get out of the way. She wasn't quick enough and it struck her hip, knocking her flat. As she hit the ground, the air whooshed from her lungs and her face and arms scraped in the dirt. She gasped for breath, trying to scramble away. The wall landed on her legs, pinning her to the ground. Pain forced another scream from her throat.

Mari lay on the ground, shocked and panting as agony washed over her in shattering waves. She clawed the earth, fighting to pull herself free of the heavy wall, but she couldn't get loose.

In a change of tactics, she twisted her body and grasped the edge of the wall to push it aside. It didn't budge. She only needed a few inches to squeeze free, but the heavy lumber held her tight.

Looking up, she saw the fire traveling along the baseboards, moving nearer. She grit her teeth against the nauseating pain, fighting off the darkness threatening to swallow her up. She couldn't faint now. Not with the fire so close. She had to stop the flames before they reached more propane heaters.

Before they reached the wall pinning her down.

She clawed at the wood, fighting for her life. Splinters stabbed her fingers, but she ignored the pain. If they lost their crop, they'd face bankruptcy and scandal. If she were killed, who would take care of Mom and her brother and sister?

Please, God. Please help me.

A dark shape appeared overhead. A man! He bent near her shoulders and placed his hands on the edge of the wall. Large, strong hands that lifted the side of the pressboard with seeming ease.

Where had he come from?

Max kept up a shrill litany of barking, snapping and snarling at the stranger.

"Shut up, Max!" Mari yelled in a hoarse voice. The dog quieted for a few moments, then started barking again.

"Can you move?" The man's deep voice mingled with the dull roar of the fire. He grit his teeth against the strain of holding up the wall.

Breathing in wheezing pants, Mari pulled herself free. She locked her jaw, fighting the urge to cry.

The man dropped the wall. A whoosh of dust sprayed her in the face and she coughed.

Who was he? And what was he doing here?

In a glance, she took in his eyes cast in shadow, his dark, shaggy hair and heavy denim jacket. Threadbare blue jeans molded his long legs, his scuffed work boots covered with dust. He might be a homeless person who had sought shelter for the night in one of their sheds. But what was he doing so far outside of town?

The stranger crouched over her and she tried to think clearly. To sort out what was happening.

"You okay?" he asked, his voice low and soothing.

He looked vaguely familiar. "Who are you?"

He didn't answer as he reached out and removed her rubber

boots, then pressed his palms against her shins. He squeezed gently along her calves, checking for damage. She drew in a startled breath, more from shock than pain.

"You're lucky. I don't think any bones are broken." His gaze never wavered from hers, his eyes hard. Again, she had the impression that she knew this man from somewhere, but the darkness kept her from seeing his face clearly.

As the early morning sunlight blazed behind the greenhouses, a brief spark of sympathy flashed in his eyes. Blue eyes, so bright and clear they reminded her of the beautiful topaz necklace Mom kept buried in her jewelry box. Dad had given Mom the piece when they had first married and Mari sometimes took it out and wore it when no one was watching.

A lock of black hair fell over the man's brow, adding to his dangerous aura. She opened her mouth to speak, but choking smoke made her cough. He stared at her, a glint of rebellion in his eyes.

"There might be more explosions. We should move back." Bending at the waist, he scooped her into his arms and carried her a safe distance away from the ruined greenhouse. Her weight didn't seem to hinder him in the least and she had no time to react before he propped her against the small tractor by the side of the toolshed.

Sirens pierced the air and the red glare of lights whirred overhead as two big engines loomed into sight. Max tore off toward the fire engines, barking at these new strangers.

The man grasped the garden hose and sprayed the pressboard with water, wetting the wood before the flames could spread. If not for him, Mari shuddered to contemplate what might have happened when the fire reached the wall where she'd been trapped.

"Mari! Are you okay?" Mom came running down the lane, now dressed in blue coveralls and knee-high boots. She grasped Max by the collar and leashed him so he couldn't chase after the firemen.

Livi slogged behind, wearing blue jeans and Matt's oversized boots. The child shadowed Mari everywhere and she couldn't contain a smile of endearment as the girl screamed at the top of her lungs. "Mari! We called 9-1-1, just like you said."

An ambulance bounced down the narrow road behind the fire engines. A host of firemen wearing heavy yellow suits and helmets descended on the greenhouse like ants on a birthday cake. Mari prayed they didn't cause more damage with their axes and tromping boots.

As if in slow motion, she watched the men unwind a thick hose. Within minutes, powerful jets of water extinguished the blaze and soaked everything in sight. The dry earth churned into mud, but the rest of their precious greenhouses were safe. Thankfully, the thick poly covering held against the strong blasts of water, protecting the delicate seedlings and flowers inside. Too bad it wasn't as effective against little cottontail rabbits.

"I don't think anything's broken, but you should go to the hospital for some X-rays," an EMT told her.

Thinking about the expense, Mari flexed each of her legs before bending them at the knees. They felt bruised, but solid and she decided they didn't need any additional medical bills. "No, I'm fine. Really."

Instead, they gave her oxygen and wrapped an elastic bandage around each of her calves and knees. When they finally left, Mari pulled herself up and Mom helped her. "Mari, I want you to go to the hospital. I can't lose you, too."

Knowing she was thinking about Dad, Mari reached out and cupped her mother's cheek with her hand. Mom had been through so much, losing her husband and trying to raise Mateo and Livi on her own. Her eyes crinkled with concern, her face lined with fatigue. Mari felt compelled to reassure her. "I'm okay, Mom. Just a bit sore."

Mom smiled, but lines of worry creased her forehead. They huddled together with Livi, watching the firemen work.

Sometime later, Larry Henderson, the fire chief, came to speak with them, his face streaked with dirt. "Looks like you had a small propane leak. Probably a simple valve failure. I'm guessing the igniter on the heater clicked on and created a spark that caused the fuel to ignite. My men have checked your other heaters and they seem secure."

Mari shook her head with disbelief. She'd checked each propane heater herself. Or so she thought. Lately, she'd been pushing too hard to get the seeds planted so that they germinated in time for the family to meet their contracts. Exhaustion burned through her body. She must have missed one heater. Maybe—

"Wait! Where's the man who rescued me?" She craned her neck, trying to find him in the crowd of firefighters. He seemed to have disappeared.

"What man?" Mom asked.

Mari caught no sight of him. Surely she hadn't imagined the tall man who'd saved her from the fire.

Mom frowned as she faced the fire chief. Although Elena had lived in the United States for twenty-nine years, fear and fatigue caused a hint of a Spanish accent to lace her words. "Can we start cleaning up the mess now?"

"Not yet. I know the debris is bothersome, but it'd be best if you ignore it for a couple more days. We should finish our investigation and have a report ready by Tuesday."

"Okay, thanks for all your help."

"You're welcome, ma'am. I'm just sorry you had this trouble." Tipping his head, Larry turned and walked away.

Mari wondered what a report mattered when they had no

casualty insurance to cover the faulty heater. Right now, she felt incredibly stupid for letting the policy lapse. They'd have to work harder to make up for the loss.

"We have a lot to be grateful for. This could have been much worse," Mom told her.

"Yes, you're right." Mari's throat felt like sandpaper. She silently gave thanks to her Heavenly Father for protecting her tonight.

Livi crowded close, leaning her head against Mari's shoulder. Mari hugged her sister, overwhelmed by tender feelings for her family. And yet she'd never felt more alone.

They watched as the firemen wrapped the site with yellow tape and packed up their equipment. By the time the engines pulled away, the morning sun blazed high. And that's when the stranger returned. Mari lifted her head and saw him standing by the burned-out shed. He'd removed his denim jacket, his arm and shoulder muscles tightening like heavy knots of rope as he stacked plastic crates that had been knocked over by the blasts of water.

"That's him. That's the man." Mari pointed.

Mom gasped. "Oh, dear. I didn't expect him until next week."

Mom walked to the stranger and embraced him. At first, the big man's eyes widened and he kept his arms by his sides. Then he gave Mom a stiff hug, the color of his face brightening. When Mom released him, he brushed a hand against the stubble on his chin, looking around as if he didn't know how to react. Elena clutched his arm and led him to the tractor where Mari sat on the torn cushioned seat. "Mari, you remember Joel Hunter, don't you?"

Joel Hunter—?

Mari groaned as recognition blazed across her brain. He'd certainly changed in the eight years since she'd seen him last. A vague memory of a handsome, dark-haired, seventeen-year-old boy, wearing a crooked smile and an Oakland A's baseball cap, flitted through her mind. His mother had lived in Oakland, California, until her death three years earlier. She and Mom had been best friends since childhood.

In the past, Joel had spent numerous summers working here at Herrera Farms, returning to Oakland in the fall, in time for the new school year. As children, they'd been the best of friends, even when Joel had teased her constantly, yanking on her braids and drinking her apple juice. But something changed as they got older. By age thirteen, Joel became more rebellious. When he turned fourteen, he wore black clothes and spiked chains. He'd hid behind the greenhouses to smoke cigarettes. Mari tattled on him, but Dad had patiently responded that Joel didn't have a father of his own and they needed to be supportive. Mari had doubts.

When Joel started chasing after the wilder girls in town, Mari decided he was a bad boy and she wanted nothing to do with him. Gradually, she came to dislike and reject him.

"When did you get in?" Elena asked, trying to untangle her legs as Max circled her with the leash.

Joel shot Mari a look, a frown of agitation tugging at his brow. "My bus got in to Reno late last night."

"But how did you get down here to Gardenville?" Mom brushed dust off his sleeve and Mari wished her mother wouldn't fuss over him.

"I hitched a ride to Gardenville and then walked out here to your place."

Mom grimaced. "That's a five-mile walk and hitchhiking isn't safe. Didn't you have our phone number?"

His gaze rested on Mari like a ten-ton sledge. "Yeah, I have your number."

"I don't understand why you didn't call us. We would have driven to Reno to get you. It's only sixty miles."

His eyes didn't waver and Mari felt like squirming. "It was late and I didn't want to bother anyone. I decided to walk out and wait until morning. Then I heard the explosion."

Elena hugged him again, breathing a sigh of relief. "You've never been a bother to us, Joel. We're just glad you're safe. I can't believe how grown-up you are."

Grown-up was right. Muscular, lean and handsome. And wild as ever. Mari felt dwarfed by his height. She stared at her mother, her ears ringing. A sick feeling settled in her stomach as one question hammered her thoughts. Why? After all these years, why had Joel Hunter returned to Herrera Farms? And why hadn't Mom told her that he was coming to visit?

Chapter Two

"Are you okay?" Joel managed a vague smile. Mari's beautiful brown eyes widened. Even with her long, dark hair tangled around her shoulders and dirt smudging her dainty face, she looked lovely. After all these years, seeing her again brought him a sense of relief. Only this woman could make his heart race.

She pinned him with a quiet gaze. "What are you doing here?"

"Mari! Don't be rude," Elena exclaimed.

Mari rotated her head, weary frustration etched in her features. Joel couldn't blame her. She'd been injured and lost a valuable source of income and now faced a lot of work to clean up the mess. He intended to help.

Joel lifted a hand and inclined his head toward the red brick house at the end of the dirt road. "I didn't mean to cause a problem. Maybe we can talk about this after Mari's had a chance to rest."

He hadn't seen Mari in eight years, yet he felt like he'd never left her side. Memories of their childhood came flooding back. Pushing Mari in the swing, her sweet laughter surrounding him like Christmas morning. Mari dressed in red silk, her hair pinned up in loose flowing curls as she waited for the captain of the football team to pick her up for the spring dance. Joel had stood watching them in the doorway of her living room, feeling out of place, his hands clenched, his heart wrenching with jealousy.

Mari raised one of her perfectly arched brows. "Talk about what?"

"Oh, nothing. It can wait." Elena laughed nervously.

She helped Mari pull on her boots, then clasped Mari's arm and helped her to her feet. Elena wouldn't meet Mari's eyes and a sick feeling settled in Joel's stomach. If he guessed right, Elena hadn't told Mari he was coming or that Elena had offered him a job.

The first step Mari took, she stumbled, a low cry bursting from her lips.

"Let me help." He cupped her elbow.

She tensed. "I can make it on my own."

"Yeah, I know. But it'll take less time and hurt a whole lot less if you let me help."

She sucked in a harsh breath and he met and held her stare. He hated her disapproval, but when had he let that stop him? No doubt she noticed how his long hair curled against the nape of his neck. She'd never seen him appearing this rough and he was highly conscious that he needed a serious haircut and shave. Crude and untamed, like the last time he saw her when they were still teenagers. She'd come to hate him, which was a curse for him. He'd always adored Marisol, from the first moment he laid eyes on her when they were no more than ten years old.

As he slid his arm around her waist, he realized she didn't want him here. In spite of all the time they'd spent together as kids, shoveling dirt, planting flowers and fishing in the stream, they now seemed like strangers.

Mari had hurt him that last summer he'd worked for her father. They'd been seventeen and he'd scared her with his brash talk of running away together. She'd thought him forward and reckless. A hooligan. Not the type of boy she wanted to be with. Never quite good enough for her. Not that he held that against her. He agreed.

Mari loved the Lord. She was dedicated, disciplined and decent. Everything he was not. But he'd changed since then. Now he wished he could be a man of God. For her. He just wasn't quite sure how to go about it. Too much time had passed and they no longer knew each other. Which might be a blessing. If Mari knew what he'd done and what he'd become, she'd probably order him to leave immediately.

She tried to withdraw her arm, but he held on, his mouth twitching with a suppressed smile. "I take it you still haven't forgiven me."

Every muscle in her body tightened. "For what?"

"For decking your boyfriend."

She stared straight ahead, limping toward the house. Elena and Livi trailed behind with Max panting at their heels. "I've forgotten all about it."

"Yeah, sure."

"He's not my boyfriend anymore."

"I'm glad to hear that."

Her face darkened. "You always were jealous of Troy Banks, though I'll never understand why."

Nothing had changed. She still read him like an open book. He wasn't about to explain his jealousy. Instead, he chuckled, his veins pulsing with happiness. He couldn't explain it, but being near her again, talking with her, brought him exquisite joy. "Ah, come on. You almost gave in and went out with me that last summer I spent working here with your dad."

She snorted. "I never came close to doing any such thing. Dating you would have given me a reputation as a fast girl."

No, she was too busy trying to save him from himself. He'd been aware of it and used her compassion against her, trying to win sympathy so she'd date him. It hadn't worked. "I'm sorry about that."

Disbelief filled her eyes and her mouth dropped open. "It's a little late for apologies, don't you think?"

"No, Mari. Not when I really mean it. I regret all the times I got you into trouble with your dad."

He could tell from the doubt in her eyes that she didn't believe him. He couldn't blame her. He'd done nothing in his life to earn her trust. In fact, just the opposite. He'd thought cigarettes and booze gave him a grown-up image. Wearing muscle shirts made him look tough and attractive. Other girls liked him. But not Mari, the one girl he wanted most.

Now he realized how little he'd really known about Mari. Pure, honest and hardworking. She wanted a good man, not a rebel who defied everything holy.

He'd just have to prove himself to her. Prove that he wanted nothing to do with his old lifestyle. If she could see inside his heart, she'd know that he'd changed.

If only he didn't care. If only he could forget that last summer when he'd called her *sunshine* and she'd taught him how to slow dance. She'd refused until her father insisted. Joel had felt so grown-up with her in his arms. Like he could fly to Jupiter. She'd been repulsed by his bad boy image. Even then, he'd been a troublemaker involved in fighting and drag racing. She might never approve of him, but he couldn't help hoping.

"I always cared for you," he confided.

"Trina thought you liked her, too."

Yeah, he remembered once how Mari caught him kissing her best friend. *Eye candy,* Trina had called him. He'd felt flattered, knowing he was good-looking in a dark, dangerous sort of way. But he'd never impressed Mari.

"I kissed Trina to make you jealous." His plan had backfired. Mari had hated him all the more.

She released a harsh laugh. "It wasn't very nice and you didn't succeed."

"You can't blame a guy for trying."

She shot him a glare. "You were trying in the wrong way. Trina never spoke to me again."

"I'm sorry. I hope you'll forget the stupid things I did as a kid."

"I'm smart enough to know if you play with fire, you get burned. I'm not a child anymore, Joel."

He met her eyes, liking the way her mouth curved in a satisfied smile. "So I've noticed."

Her lips thinned in disapproval. "You're just as rude as ever. Always self-assured."

"Not lately." He spoke under his breath, wondering if he'd ever feel sure of himself again.

"What?"

"Nothing." He laughed it off, catching her glower and praying she didn't sense how her words cut deep into his soul.

"You never were the type to feel sorry for anything or anyone, except yourself."

Ah, that hurt. "You might be surprised how I've changed."

"If you've changed, you're right. I would be surprised."

Under her perusal, he squirmed beneath his denim jacket. He'd always wanted her approval, yet done everything contrary to win her affection. Throughout his life, there'd been only two people he really cared about hurting. Mari and her father. No one else mattered. Not even his mom, and he'd hurt her most of all. Now he was determined to make amends.

"You do seem a bit different," she said.

He lifted one brow. "You think? How so?"

"Your eyes seem…haunted."

"Haunted, huh?" He could feel her looking at him, trying to see into his mind.

"Yes, like a caged tiger after it's been freed and can go anywhere it wants, except it doesn't know where that might be."

How perceptive. Even though he was free, he felt incredibly lost. Searching for something he didn't completely understand. Intuitively he believed Mari and Herrera Farms could help him find the answer.

"When did you eat last?" she asked.

"It's been awhile, but I can wait for breakfast."

A flicker of sympathy flashed in her eyes, then was gone. Maybe he imagined it. When she spoke, her voice quavered. "Something has changed about you that I can't quite put my finger on. You're definitely older and have filled out, but you seem even more worldly and sad."

Great! He should have known she'd see right through him. She always did. Straight to his soul. And yet she saw that side of him that he longed to hide. A niggling doubt filled him and he realized with blazing insight that who he had been and who he wanted to become were inseparable. He stood at a crossroad, wondering which way might lead him home.

A part of him longed to confide in Mari what he'd been doing the past eight years. To tell her everything and get it off his chest. Another part of him hated to disappoint her even more and he wished he'd never returned to Herrera Farms.

Weary to the bone, he felt in no mood to fight with the only girl he'd ever loved. Conscious of the weight of her slim fingers wrapped around his arm, he veered off the main road. He could hear Elena and Livi padding after them as he led them on a shortcut across the field. Señor Herrera would never have let the brown grass grow so tall before mowing it down.

"I planned to trim the grass after I had the seedlings transplanted," Mari said.

"I'll take care of it today."

"You're here on vacation, not to work."

Vacation? Obviously Elena hadn't told her that she'd offered him a job. He sure didn't want to be around when Mari found out.

"I want to help, Mari. I won't take no for an answer."

She bit her bottom lip, looking frustrated. No doubt she couldn't afford to be laid up for even one day or she'd fall behind in her work. Seeds must be planted, the hothouse tomatoes watered and pansies transplanted. One day of sloth could mean the loss of thousands of dollars. The thought of helping Mari brought him joy. Finally, a way to bless someone else's life after all the chaos he'd caused. He'd work hard and make sure the Herreras met their contracts this season. He owed that much to Señor Herrera. As soon as he had something to eat, he'd get to work.

When they reached the house, he helped Mari hobble across the lawn and step up on the porch. Elena hurried ahead and opened the screen door so they could go inside.

Livi stood hugging the doorway, her eyes crinkled with apprehension. "Are you gonna be okay, Mari?"

Mari laughed, but Joel caught the quiver of tears in her voice. Her legs must be pounding like bass drums. "Of course, sweetie. I'm just tired. Don't worry."

Livi smiled, then scurried off to her room, her long, black hair whipping behind her.

The rumble of a car and loud music came from outside. Joel stood in the living room, gazing out the picture window as a blue pickup truck parked out front.

"Mateo's here. Looks like Dallin Keats brought him home." Worry lines creased Elena's brow. She shook her head and went into the kitchen where she took out a pan to make breakfast. Joel tried to read between the lines. From what he gathered, Elena didn't like Dallin very much.

In spite of the chilly air, Dallin rolled down his window by the driver's seat and braced his left arm along the outside edge of the door. The breeze across the fields tossed his long ponytail over the shoulder of his black sleeveless T-shirt. Colored tattoos covered the boy's bare arms, and in each ear he wore an enormous studded earring. Loud rapper music blared from the truck, the bass thudding in Joel's chest.

The passenger door swung open and Joel caught a glimpse of Matt, Mari's seventeen-year-old brother, as he hitched up his baggy pants. He clutched the waistband with one hand as he slammed the door closed. Joel couldn't imagine why today's kids thought such loose clothes looked cool, walking with their legs slightly spread so their pants didn't fall down around their ankles. To Joel, they looked like they wore a baggy diaper.

Joel understood Elena's concern for Matt, but withheld judgment. Since Señor Herrera died, Elena wrote to tell Joel that Matt had dropped off the football team, his grades had plummeted, he'd become less helpful around the farm and more rebellious. He now hung out with reckless kids like Dallin Keats, a boy known to be involved in car theft and illicit drugs. Matt insisted he was behaving. That all he did was hang out and have fun. But Joel knew better. If Matt was hanging out with kids like Dallin, it was only a matter of time before he got into trouble.

Shaking his head, Joel turned and watched as Mari limped down the hall to the back of the house. Her slender shoulders drooped, as if they carried the weight of an elephant.

"Can I get you something?" Joel called after her.

"No, thanks. I'm going to rest for a while."

He let her go, staring at the closed door long after she'd gone into her room. A bereft feeling settled over him, like he'd lost his best friend. And then he fully realized what he'd always known. It'd been in the back of his mind, slowly simmering, but he'd been too preoccupied to let it take root until he saw Mari again.

He loved her still, he couldn't deny it. During the past eight years, he'd spent a lot of time in isolation. He'd thought of nothing but Mari. Her long silky hair, dark eyes, quick wit and firecracker temper. She was all that had kept him from going insane. All that kept him alive and gave him hope for the future.

When he'd come here, he'd planned to hide out and recover his semblance of humanity. Instead, he had the crazy notion he'd run smack into trouble. He still loved Mari and she still detested him. Maybe her hatred was God's punishment for what he'd done.

Chapter Three

In her bedroom, Mari closed the door, then swallowed two aspirin before lying back against her pillow with a sigh of relief. She let her body relax, promising to rest only an hour or so. She could deal with her problems later.

As she closed her eyes, she ached for sleep, but it wouldn't come. She couldn't stop thinking about Joel and his swift actions to save her life. Or the brooding, lonely hurt in his eyes.

What was he doing here? If he wanted a handout, he could find it somewhere else. Dad was gone, and they had nothing to offer him.

She thought about his apology and his confession that he'd kissed Trina just to make her jealous.

"Ha!" she called out to the empty room. Did he really expect her to believe such things?

She thought of him helping her walk back to the house, his strong arm wrapped around her waist. A cloying reminder of all the times she'd tried to save him from himself, and failed.

Now she had her hands full helping her family. She had no energy and resources left to expend on Joel Hunter. She just prayed he didn't cause any problems for them while he was here. With any luck, he'd stay a few days, get bored with the drudgery of work, and move on.

Joel sat at the kitchen table, gulping a glass of orange juice. The tantalizing aroma of frying chorizo wafted through the air and his mouth watered. His stomach rumbled as he fingered the edge of his plate. With just enough money for his bus ticket to Reno and a pack of gum, he hadn't eaten in two days. He tried to be patient as he listened to Elena explain to Matt about the explosion.

"You might not remember Joel Hunter, *mijo*. You were about Livi's age when he was here last. He'll be working for us again." Elena reached over and removed the baseball cap from Matt's head before propping it on a hook by the door. "He and Mari grew up together."

Well, not really. Throughout his youth, Joel had spent every summer working at Herrera Farms, but he'd never actually gone to school with Mari. Each summer when he returned, he felt surprised by the changes in her. Over the years, she'd gone from pigtails to homecoming queen. But now, things were different. They weren't kids anymore.

Matt slouched in a kitchen chair, taking Joel in with a hint of caution. "Yeah, I remember. Hi, man."

"Hi," Joel returned.

"I remember you, too." Livi gave him a smile that lit up her eyes and reminded him of a younger Mari. He noticed the child had not a single hint of a Spanish accent, a legacy of being born and raised in the United States.

"You couldn't remember him, sweetheart. You weren't even born yet," Elena said.

"Oh." Livi frowned with disappointment.

Joel brushed the tip of her nose with one finger. "But we'll get to know each other now, okay?"

"Okay." The girl beamed from ear to ear, then faced her brother. "Joel saved Mari's life."

Livi spoke dramatically, her smile zinging straight to Joel's heart. It'd been a long time since anyone had praised him for a good deed and it felt mighty good, even coming from a guileless child.

Matt studied him, his brows drawn together as though he stared at a stinkbug. "Is that so?"

Joel met the boy's gaze head-on. "I just happened to be at the right place at the right time."

"What did you and Dallin do last night?" Elena ruffled Matt's disheveled hair before returning to the stove.

Matt tossed a glare her way and gave a sullen shrug. "Nothing."

"I thought you said you were going to a movie." She placed two bagels in the toaster and pressed the lever. Joel thought she was doing an admirable job of trying to find out what her son had been up to without making it a big deal.

"We changed our minds and hung out over at Dallin's place." The boy didn't look at Elena, keeping his eyes downcast as he waited for his breakfast.

From the slump of Matt's head, Joel thought the kid was lying. How many times had Joel done the same thing when his own mother had questioned him? Lying about hanging out with bad crowds, racing cars, smoking and drinking. All the things a good mother dreaded her child might become involved in.

Observing Matt, Joel felt as though he were seeing himself years earlier, before he nearly destroyed his life. He narrowed his eyes, wondering what the boy had really been doing last night.

"Mari's going to need help today. Do you have much homework?" Elena persisted.

"Nah, it's done."

"You sure? Mrs. Carter said you've been turning a lot of assignments in late."

"I've got it caught up, so you can stop worrying." Insolence laced the boy's words.

Elena pursed her lips, but didn't press the issue. Joel tried not to watch her as she stood at the stove, stirring eggs. A restless feeling that had nothing to do with hunger settled over him. After what he'd been through, relaxing and chatting about homework felt strange and wonderful all at the same time. It felt normal. And he hadn't done normal things for almost eight years.

"I was sorry to hear about Frank," Joel said.

Elena gave him a sad smile. "I know. Thank you for your letter. We all miss him. He kept this place running like a top. But Mari's been doing a good job."

The room went silent for several moments, with everyone lost in their own thoughts. Joel remembered the last time he saw Frank Herrera like it was yesterday. Joel had been Matt's age, frightened and sitting in a jail cell in Oakland. Frank had driven all the way from Nevada to be with him. He'd promised when Joel got out, he could have a job at Herrera Farms. Frank had followed up on that vow by sending Joel a hand-written letter every week until his death.

"You'll like working here again, Joel. I know you want solitude and a fresh start. Herrera Farms will definitely give you that." Elena placed a basket of *pan dulce* on the table and Joel almost pounced on the sweet bread. The enticing aroma of *huevos rancheros* made his stomach growl.

"I appreciate the job. Are you sure Mari's okay with this? She didn't seem too excited to see me." Steam rose from the hot *papas fritas* as he popped several into his mouth before chewing with relish.

"Yes, she'll be fine. She'll get used to the idea."

An uneasy feeling gnawed at him as he scooped up several more pieces of bread. "You haven't told her, have you?"

Matt looked up, a curious expression on his face.

Elena gave a nervous laugh. "Not yet, but I will as soon as we have a moment to talk. We're so shorthanded right now, she'll be glad to have your help. And Frank wanted you here."

Great! Mari didn't know about the job Elena had offered him or about his past. The last thing he wanted was to add to Mari's worries. He should leave right now, before she awoke. Before she found out the truth and hated him even more. But where would he go? He couldn't return to Oakland. Not if he wanted any kind of a future.

The truth was he needed this job. Badly. No one else would hire him, unless he lied about his past. And he wouldn't do that. He'd promised both Frank and the Lord that he'd be honest in all his dealings and he intended to keep his word no matter what.

Matt reached for the butter. "I can't wait to get outta this place. Why would you want to work here?"

The teenager sat beside Livi, who munched on a piece of chorizo. The little girl hummed a happy tune, swinging her legs back and forth on her chair, seemingly lost to the conversation around her.

"Maybe here isn't such a bad place. I can think of some places a whole lot worse." Joel didn't smile as he dug into the plate of eggs Elena slid in front of him.

Matt's mouth pinched and he stared at Joel like he'd lost his mind. "You gotta be kidding. I'm getting outta here just as soon as I can."

"Where you gonna go?" Joel asked between bites.

"Traveling. Maybe to Los Angeles or Oakland."

Joel grimaced. "What about college?"

"Nah, I'm sick of school. Some of my buddies and me want to start a rock band."

"You got some musical instruments?" Joel noticed the lines of apprehension drawing Elena's brows together as she listened to their conversation.

Matt looked doubtful. "Not yet. We gotta make some money first."

"And you can do that by helping your sister with some chores," Elena said.

"Stop nagging, will you?" Matt glowered at his mother.

Elena bit her lip and Joel saw the hurt in her eyes. He regretted hurting his mother the same way. How he wished she were still alive so he could take her into his arms and apologize. He couldn't help wondering why so many teenagers became rebellious and cruel to the people who had given them everything.

"Don't be rude to your mother, Matt," Joel chided gently.

Matt's face tightened with anger, then flushed red and he hung his head over his plate as he ate his food in silence.

Joel had no right to reprimand the boy, but he couldn't help himself. When he was Matt's age, Joel had put his own mother through so much pain and he now regretted it more than he could say. He hated seeing Matt traveling down that same road.

"How's Mari?" Matt asked.

Joel liked the protectiveness he detected in Matt's voice. It meant the boy hadn't become completely selfish, which meant they still had time to save him from Joel's fate.

Elena frowned as she chopped onions and green peppers. "She seems okay, but I'm worried about her. She works too hard and she was injured today."

The scowl on Matt's face deepened. "Did she see a doctor?"

Joel took another bite of *pan dulce,* then licked crystallized sugar from his index finger. "Nope. You know Mari."

"She says it doesn't hurt and she told me not to worry," Livi supplied in a happy tone.

Joel forced a smile, his insides clenching. Strong, in control Mari would never show any weakness or allow her baby sister to worry about her.

"Has Mari got any boyfriends?" Now why did Joel ask that? The question slipped out before he could think to call it back.

Everyone at the table stopped and stared. How foolish of him. A beautiful woman like Mari ought to have a trail of men standing outside her door, with Joel at the head of the line. He felt suddenly inept and jealous, and he didn't even know whom he was jealous of. All these past years, he could have been working and going to college, to make something of his life. To be the kind of man Mari wanted and deserved. Instead, he'd made an ugly mistake that had cost him and his family dearly.

How he wished he could go back in time and change things. All he needed was fifteen seconds to alter his decision and save a man's life. But he couldn't go back. He could only go forward. God had given him a second chance and he was determined not to blow it.

"Mari doesn't date. She just works," Livi supplied.

An unexplainable sense of relief flooded Joel. Mari didn't have a boyfriend and for some crazy reason that knowledge made him incredibly, deliriously happy.

Elena leaned near and whispered to Joel. "Mari will find a good man when the time is right. Someone she can respect and admire, who'll treat her right and love the Lord."

Matt snorted and scraped back from the table. "I've got things to do."

He sauntered out of the room with an impatient huff.

Livi spread strawberry jam on her bagel. "How long you staying with us, Joel?"

"Indefinitely." Joel longed to say permanently, but didn't

feel he had the right to be that forward. "I'll be working through the summer. After that, we'll see."

Joel didn't know why he bothered giving so much information. He couldn't explain it, but he wished he could stay forever.

"You knew my daddy?" Livi asked.

"Yes, very well."

The girl frowned. "I miss him."

"I know, honey. Me, too."

Not one to dwell on the topic for long, Livi hopped up from the table and ran to the living room where she clicked on the TV and plopped onto the couch to watch cartoons.

Mari came out of her room and hobbled down the hallway before sinking into a kitchen chair. Every nerve in Joel's body buzzed with awareness. Her dark eyes looked puffy with sleep and he hoped they hadn't woken her with their chatter.

"Feeling better, *niña?*" Elena reached out and caressed her daughter's cheek.

"Yeah, but my legs feel like they've been squeezed in giant vises."

"They're bruised. It'll take time for them to heal."

Joel studied Mari, her flushed cheeks and mussed hair. Her smile didn't quite reach her dark eyes. A strand of long black hair fell across her pale face and she tucked it behind her ear. She wore a pair of denim overalls, the pants rolled up to her slim calves. He stared at her bare feet, mesmerized by her pink-painted toenails. Right then and there, Joel decided she was the most beautiful woman he'd ever seen.

"Maybe this will help make you feel better." Elena opened a drawer and pulled out two tickets before waving them in front of Mari's nose. Mari snatched them up with a squeal of excitement. "Oh, Mom! The Sierra Philharmonic Orchestra. I thought they were sold out. How did you get tickets?"

Elena shrugged, looking pleased with herself. "Mr. Macon

is on the board and we're providing all the bedding plants for the Heritage Theater in Reno, so I pulled a few strings. These are VIP seats."

"How wonderful. You'll go with me, won't you?"

"No, you and your father loved classical music, not me. The only thing you need to decide is what you'll wear and who you're going with." Elena tossed a suggestive smile in Joel's direction.

He almost choked on his orange juice. For some reason, he no longer felt hungry. He set his fork down and pushed his chair back before standing and nodding at Elena. "Thanks for breakfast. I think I'll get to work."

Mari's mouth dropped open in surprise. "Work? What do you mean—?"

He walked into the other room, desperate to escape. He paused beside the sofa, long enough to ruffle Livi's hair. The child giggled and he moved to the door, still able to see the occupants of the kitchen, his hand squeezing the doorknob.

"What's he doing here?" he heard Mari whisper. Joel's gaze locked with hers and a waver of uncertainty filled her eyes.

"I invited him." Elena's voice sounded terse. "I didn't know I needed to ask permission before I invite an old friend into my own home."

Joel didn't want to hear this. With a nod, he stepped outside and pulled the door closed behind him. Max lay on the front porch, sunning himself. The dog ignored him as Joel stood drawing in the pungent scent of damp soil. The wind cut through him and he buttoned his jacket, gazing at the dirt road leading to Highway 395. He was half-tempted to start walking and never look back.

No! He shook his head, knowing if he walked away now, he'd be running away the rest of his life. It wouldn't be easy, but he had to stay. He had to fight to make things right in his life.

To the south, the mountains sheltered the small valley, shutting off the view of town. To the north, rows of long, white greenhouses, work sheds and wooden bays of dark, rich soil lined a field of rabbit brush, sand and sage. A small orchard of apple trees bordered the east side of the house with a cluster of quaking aspen on the west, their green branches shivering in the breeze. Joel had helped Frank plant them fourteen years earlier. The prim front lawn, shrubs and flower beds showed impeccable grooming, in spite of the cold weather. Joel expected nothing less from Elena and Mari.

Joel had always loved Herrera Farms. Memories of this place were all that had sustained him over the past years. Señor Herrera had been the father Joel never had. He'd welcomed Joel with open arms, treating him like a son. Right now, Joel missed Frank Herrera more than he could explain. When he'd heard Frank had died, he'd felt the pain of loss deep in his heart, but he hadn't felt like crying.

Until now.

He stepped down off the porch and headed for the back of the garage where he'd seen the riding lawn mower. He had a second chance to make his past right. To redeem himself at least a little.

A man like him didn't deserve a second chance, but the Lord had worked a miracle for him. Here at Herrera Farms, he could forget his past and begin anew. He could find quiet and solitude, but he doubted he'd ever find peace.

Chapter Four

❧

While Mom tossed a load of clothes into the washing machine, Mari tucked a pair of work gloves into the pocket of her jeans and limped outside. She climbed onto one of the four-wheelers they used to get around the farm more quickly. Turning the key, she started up the motor and drove down the dirt road at a slow pace. Max trotted alongside the machine.

The pungent aroma of freshly cut grass filled the air. Scanning the fields, she saw Joel sitting on the riding mower, bouncing gently in the seat as he mowed long, even trails.

Emotions of gratitude and resentment warred inside her. She appreciated Joel's help, yet couldn't understand what he was doing here. Didn't he have better things to do with his time? Surely he had a life of his own.

Joel hadn't been here one full day and already he'd stepped into the work like he belonged here. Some vacation. Maybe he wouldn't stay long. Part of her wanted to see him, to talk and ask how he'd been. She hadn't trusted him since they were fourteen years old, but they'd shared their childhood and an odd sort of unique bond she couldn't explain. Her father had loved Joel and she loved her father.

She also feared Joel. His presence dredged up old feelings she thought she'd long forgotten. Anger and resentment. Jealousy over her father's fondness for a boy who lived recklessly just to spite God. She'd never understood why Dad loved Joel, and she'd competed for her father's affection.

No one ever challenged her like Joel. His blunt candor usually left her open and vulnerable, a feeling she disliked and couldn't afford. He brought out the animosity in her like no one else could. Her feelings made her ashamed. It wasn't Christian for her to hold a grudge against Joel, no matter what he'd done. It wasn't her place to judge him, yet she couldn't seem to help herself.

She remembered the last summer he'd worked at Herrera Farms when he'd snuck out of her parents' house in the middle of the night. He'd told her he was going drinking with his buddies. Even then, she was still trying to save him and she'd begged him not to go. At peril of being grounded by her parents, she'd tried to follow, to bring him back. She'd heard a sermon in church on being your brother's keeper and had made Joel her mission in life. To save him from depravity and wrongdoing.

She ended up tripping over the garden hose and lying flat on her face in the grass. Hearing her cry out, Joel had returned to her side, waving his friends off as he took her back to the house. She remembered how he'd brushed the long hair out of her eyes and bandaged the scratch on her elbow. No matter how hard she chastised him, he never raised his voice to her. He'd laughed when she told him what he was doing was wrong and would only bring him ruin. He had never listened, but told her not to worry because his soul was already lost anyway.

She'd been aghast. How could he say something so sacrilegious? How could he live his life so recklessly and offensively?

She shook her head, wishing he hadn't returned. Wishing she could stop thinking about him. He was no good and would only bring them trouble.

In the petunia greenhouse, she popped a CD of orchestra music into the boom box sitting on the table. She turned it up just loud enough so the vibrant music could be heard throughout the room. Then she went to work, transplanting flats of seed packs into four-inch pots. Elena joined her and hooked up the garden hose.

"The lawns are mowed."

Startled, Mari turned and smacked her head on the PVC pipe leading to the drip hoses.

"Ouch!" She rubbed her temple and squeezed her eyes closed.

"I'm sorry. Are you okay?" Joel stood beside her, his eyes filled with concern as he lifted a hand to touch her face.

"I'm fine." Surprised and breathless, Mari brushed his hand aside, wondering how she'd become such a klutz. It didn't help that he moved so silently and she reached to turn the music down.

His smile crinkled the corners of his blue eyes. "I didn't know I had such a dramatic effect on you."

She snorted. "I see you still have an ego."

Shaking her head, she tried to look anywhere but at him. It did no good. Her gaze returned to his face, a compulsion she couldn't deny.

He stood too close for comfort, smelling of cut grass and peppermint. Memories of Dad flooded her mind. He'd smelled the same way.

Mari stepped back. She couldn't get used to him being all grown-up and tall. It made him seem even more dangerous.

"What are you listening to?" He wrinkled his nose and contemplated the room, as if searching for the source of music.

"Mari believes the music helps the plants grow." Mom

chuckled as she pulled a work apron over her head and reached her hands behind her back to tie it in place.

"You and I need to talk," Mari interrupted, unable to control the tinge of reproach in her voice.

"Okay, shoot." He folded his arms, his blue eyes unwavering.

Mom reached for another pack of seedlings, her head bowed over her work. Mari wasn't fooled. Mom listened to every word.

"I don't know what you're doing here, but I won't tolerate any of your pranks. If you're up to no good, rest assured, I'll pack your bags for you and have you carted away. Dad isn't here to go down to the jail and bail you out again." Okay, she'd said it more harshly than she intended, but she could tell from the widening of his eyes that he'd gotten her point.

His eyes went hard as iron, piercing her to the bone. "I understand. And let me assure you that you will not have one moment of trouble from me. I will never be taken to a jail cell again as long as I live, and that's a promise."

She blinked, wondering what to believe.

"I don't suppose it'd do any good to ask you to go into the house and rest until you're feeling better," he said.

His considerate suggestion angered her and she couldn't explain why. She turned and reached for a hand shovel before digging into a bucket of soil. "Leave me alone. I feel fine."

"Sure you do. And I'm the Easter bunny."

She ignored that. "Thanks for mowing the field. It helps keep the rabbit brush under control. And we have a lot of rabbits to deal with out here."

"No problem. I'll get you some more mulch." He grasped the handles of an empty wheelbarrow, then steered it toward the door.

"Aren't you supposed to be on vacation? You don't need

to help us work," Mari called after him, but he didn't reply. She turned and found Mom leaning against a bench watching this exchange, her arms folded.

"What?" Mari asked.

Elena frowned as she picked up several plastic flats before setting them on the benchtop. The heavy polyethylene of the greenhouse drew the rays of the sun inside, warming the soil so the petunia seedlings would grow large and bud out by mid-April when they opened their farm stand. "You don't need to be rude to Joel."

"I wasn't rude." Mari tried to appear natural and composed, like nothing bothered her. With the hand shovel, she scooped loamy soil into a quart-sized planting cup, swallowing a big gulp of guilt. She plopped a petunia into the dirt and pressed the roots down tight with her fingers.

"He's not a stranger, Mari. He's my best friend's son and your father loved him."

Did she have to bring Dad into this? The reminder bothered Mari. Dad once told her that he would have brought Joel here to live with them permanently if he could, but Joel's mother couldn't stand to be away from him that long. Oakland was no place for a boy without a father in his life. Too many gangs crowded the city, leading good boys and girls into a life of drugs and crime. Mari's father wanted to get Joel away from that influence and help him find a better, happier life. So he brought Joel here each summer, giving him a job, teaching him the family business right alongside Mari.

Dad had demanded just one thing from Joel in return. He went to church each Sunday with the family. And Joel never argued that point, although his sullen attitude had spoken volumes.

"He's not a member of our family, Mom. And he's not a kid anymore. He could cause some real problems for us. We haven't seen him for years." Mari hated the judgmental tone of her voice, but couldn't seem to help it.

"Your father kept in touch with him, up until the day before he died."

Mari paused, her fingers coated with dirt. "He did? I never knew."

"He knew how much you disliked Joel, so he saw no reason to tell you."

Ah, that hurt. Dad knew she'd rejected Joel every time he'd asked her out on a date. Even when she told her parents about Joel smoking and cursing, Dad asked her to befriend the young man. Mari never understood why. What did Dad see in Joel? As far as she was concerned, Joel had been a lost cause. And here he was, right smack in their lives again.

"Remember how you played baseball with Joel when you were a kid? You were such a tomboy and he couldn't catch you to save his life, although he sure tried." Elena chuckled as she picked up another six-pack of seedlings and placed them on the wooden counter so Mari could reach them more easily.

"I don't know why Dad kept in touch with him."

"They were very close, Mari."

"Ha! If they were so close, why didn't Joel come to Dad's funeral?" Mari's voice sounded grumbly with resentment.

Mom popped another sprout into a dirt cup. "Joel wanted to attend, but he was indisposed at the time. He sent flowers instead."

Flowers? Mari scanned the greenhouse where a myriad of colorful plants lined the benches in tidy, even rows. The last thing they needed was another flower. She didn't care to hear Joel's excuses. Dad had been kind to Joel over the years. What could keep Joel so busy that he couldn't even attend the funeral? "This isn't much of a vacation. What's he really doing here, Mom?"

Elena took a deep breath and let it go. "We need to talk about that."

Something in Mom's tone caused Mari's spine to stiffen. A bad feeling overwhelmed her, like she was about to get slugged in the gut. "Mom, I hope you didn't—"

"Mari, you want me to bring up some more four-inch pots?" Netta, one of their full-time employees, stood in the doorway, pulling on her work gloves.

"Yes, would you, please?" Mari called.

With a nod, Netta disappeared from view and Mari turned to face her mother. "Okay, tell me what's going on before we have another interruption."

"Nothing's going on, *niña*. I simply offered Joel a job working for us."

Mari's breath caught in her throat. "What?"

"I said, I offered Joel a job and he accepted—"

"I heard you, Mom. I just don't understand why."

"Because he needs a job and we need his help."

"Oh, Mom. Where will he stay? He's not a kid anymore. He can't stay in the house. We don't have room."

"I know that. I figured he could stay out back in the old caretaker's cottage."

Mari laughed. "That old hut? It's filled with junk and the roof leaks. If we have another rainstorm, he'll need a raft to keep his head above water."

"Don't worry. I've been cleaning it out for several days now. Matt helped me haul all the junk off to the garbage dump. It's tidy and clean."

A lance of surprise speared Mari's brain. The farm was a big place, but she couldn't believe she hadn't noticed Matt and Mom cleaning out the caretaker's cottage or hauling a truck-load of garbage away. "Matt helped you?"

"Yes, and I'm sure Joel can repair the roof before it

rains again. Remember how handy he was with a hammer and nails?"

Yes, he'd built the farm stand and several sheds. By day, he and Dad had been inseparable. At night, Joel did whatever he wanted.

Obviously Mom had been planning this for some time and hadn't said a word to Mari. "I hope you haven't been lifting heavy things or working too hard. You know what the doctor said."

"I haven't overdone."

"Why didn't you tell me about this before?"

"We just haven't had a chance to talk. You've been working sunup to sundown."

True, but Mari knew better. Mom hadn't told her about Joel because she knew Mari wouldn't approve. "I don't know how we'll pay him a salary. We're barely making ends meet as it is."

"I'll work for room and board."

Both Mom and Mari whirled around and found Joel standing in the doorway. His gloved hands gripped the handles of the wheelbarrow, which contained a mound of rich, dark mulch. How much of their conversation had he heard? And how had he filled the wheelbarrow and returned so quickly? It always took Mari so much longer.

"We don't employ slave labor," Mari spoke tartly.

He pushed the laden wheelbarrow inside and set it down beside her. "You feed me and give me a place to stay and I'll work hard for you. That's all I need."

Mari hesitated, held captive by his brooding gaze. Something about his words deadened her heart. He seemed as desperate to stay here at Herrera Farms as she was for him to leave. And yet something about his expression seemed so anxious, calling out to her like a cry for help. She couldn't say no. "All right. But we'll pay you a fair wage for a fair day's work."

He opened his mouth to speak, but she turned away before he could argue with her. What did she care about his life? He meant nothing to her. He would be just another employee. Just another workman. If he got out of line, she'd fire him. Which would be difficult since even their employees were also their good friends.

They had nine greenhouses with three full-time employees, two part-time employees and one deliveryman who worked as needed Tuesdays thru Fridays. They needed two more full-time employees, but couldn't afford the payroll. Mari worked late to pick up the slack. If they could sell their spring and summer flowers and vegetable plants, they'd be able to pay off the new tractor and hire more help.

She remembered Joel was a hard worker, strong and fast. And yet having him here seemed a constant reminder that Dad was gone and they were all alone, fighting to keep Herrera Farms afloat.

Elena tossed a reassuring smile at Joel. "Yes, we can afford to pay this boy."

"Boy? How old are you?" Mari stuck a plastic name tag with growing instructions into a flowerpot and set it aside with the other transplants.

"Twenty-five. The same age as you."

Mari huffed. "I'd hardly call you a boy."

"No, I'm no boy." His eyes darkened, glinting with a mixture of laughter and annoyance.

"Of course not." Mom busied herself with the watering pot, not meeting Mari's eyes. Which meant she wasn't telling Mari everything.

What else could they be keeping from her? Mari wasn't sure she could take many more surprises.

The next seedling lay limp and forgotten in Mari's hand. She stared at her mother's face, watching her expression. A smear of dirt marred Mom's right cheek, the edge of her collar lopsided and curled under. Mari reached out and smoothed the collar. For some reason, Mom's slight disorder endeared her to Mari. Elena gave freely of her time and trusted so easily. Livi was just like her. Sweet and loving to everyone. Mom's heart attack five months ago had scared ten years off of Mari's life. They'd already lost Dad. They couldn't lose Mom, too. Livi and Matt deserved to have at least one parent around to see them raised to adulthood.

She glanced at the doorway, surprised to find Joel had disappeared, taking a stack of empty crates with him. He seemed to know exactly what she wanted done before she even asked.

A deep sigh of relief slipped from her throat and she spoke in a slightly louder tone. "Mom, what were you thinking to promise this guy a job?"

Mom's spine stiffened. "This *guy* is practically family. He knows our routine and how to work hard. You leave him to me, sweetheart. If he bothers you so much, he'll be under my supervision."

Which meant he'd get away with anything and everything. "Mom, this isn't a good idea—"

"I mean it, Mari. I've hired Joel. Now let it go." Elena met Mari's gaze and pursed her lips together, looking stern. They'd reached the end of their discussion. Very rarely did Elena put her foot down, but when she did, Mari deferred out of respect.

She reached for another pot before scooping soil and slapping another plant into the cup. "Why would he want to work here? Surely at his age he can get a better job somewhere else."

"I want to work here."

Mari thumped against the workbench, startled by Joel's reappearance. "Why do you keep doing that?"

"What?"

"Sneaking up on us."

He shrugged. "I'm working."

And startling her into oblivion. He moved his tall body with the quiet grace of a cat. "You could clear your throat or something, so we know you're here."

A sarcastic smile curved his handsome mouth. "I'll try to make more noise in the future."

"What have you been doing since high school?" Okay, very blunt, but she saw no reason to beat around the bush. As his new employer, she had a right to know.

His eyes twinkled with amusement. "I've taken some college classes and worked a few odd jobs."

"How many college classes?"

"Quite a few."

She lifted her eyebrows. "Enough for a degree?"

"Yes, I have a bachelor's degree in business."

A feeling of envy speared her heart. How she wished she could return to college and finish her nursing degree. It didn't sit well with her that the wild kid from her past had earned his education while she was still here working at the family farm. He'd never made very good grades in high school, so she doubted he'd qualified for a scholarship. And his mother never had much money. So how had he paid for his education?

"What kinds of jobs have you had?" She tried to sound disinterested, which was far from the truth.

"What does it matter what he's been doing?" Elena asked.

"I've been a dishwasher, worked in a laundry and did some simple landscaping."

Not much information. At his age, he should be busy with a career and a sweetheart. She longed to ask him if he had a girlfriend, but couldn't bring herself to say the words. He might take the question wrong and she didn't want him to think she cared in the least.

"You see?" Elena interjected. "He's got plenty of work experience. He's been very busy."

"If you have a business degree, why would you want to work here at the farm?"

"Hi there, tall man!" Netta appeared at the end of the greenhouse, carrying a box of empty four-inch pots. She set the box on the graveled ground and hugged Joel. "Elena told me you'd be coming to work with us again. It's sure good to see you. My goodness, but you've grown into a big man."

The same age as Mom, Netta studied Joel with motherly affection. She reached out and brushed her fingers against the stubble on his face and laughed.

Joel scrubbed a hand against his cheeks, his face reddening. "Hi, Netta. It's been a long time. I've been traveling quite a bit, but I'll shave later tonight, after my work's done."

She rested her hands on her thick waist and eyed him critically before winking at Mom. "Actually, I kind of like the scruffy look. Although it makes you appear older and that reminds me of my own advancing age."

"Nah, you'll always be twenty. How's your husband?" Joel asked.

"The same. Still working for the state road crew."

Mari couldn't believe Mom had told Netta about Joel, but neglected to tell her own daughter. Mari's emotions whirled as she stood there for several moments, her mouth hanging open while Joel made small talk with Netta.

Finally, they ran out of steam and Netta sighted Mari. The irritation must have shown on her face because Netta's cheeks flushed red before she stammered a farewell. "Guess I'd better get back to work."

Joel hesitated and Mom interceded. "Come on, Joel. I'll show you the caretaker's cottage. I've put fresh towels in the bathroom and clean sheets on the bed. There's even a small television set, although reception isn't the best. You'll have to adjust the rabbit ears antennae. There's no cable out here, but I think you'll find it comfortable. Of course, you'll take all your meals at the house with us."

Mom took Joel's arm and steered him back past the rows of flowers as she took him to the caretaker's cottage. Mari stared after them, grateful Mom hadn't insisted he live in the main house. She was in no mood to share her bedroom with Livi.

As she watched Mom and Joel leave, she longed to tag along, still curious about what he'd been up to for the past eight years, but she resisted. Her legs ached from standing too long. She sat on a tall stool while she worked, letting the rich, loamy soil sift through her fingers, soothing her frazzled nerves. Funny how her work seemed to relax her.

Later, she'd peek in at the caretaker's cottage, to see what work Mom had done there. Knowing Mom, she'd probably cleaned the place from stem to stern and made a comfortable place for Joel to stay.

A feeling of remorse settled over Mari. She had her hands full running the farm and helping care for her younger siblings. She didn't need further aggravation by having Joel here. She should trust her mother's judgment and be glad for the extra help.

Mari would say no more. It'd do no good. Whether she liked it or not, Joel Hunter would now be working at Herrera Farms. But something didn't feel right. Mom seemed too secretive. Too nervous. As though she were keeping something from her. Something big.

Chapter Five

As Joel stood in the doorway of the caretaker's cottage, his throat tightened. He gazed about the three-room structure, feeling overwhelmed by emotion. He hadn't enjoyed such comfortable surroundings in years.

The cottage resembled a studio apartment with the kitchenette, living room and bedroom all part of one big room. The strong odor of cleanser came from the small bathroom where he knew from past experience the family often washed their hands before they went up to the main house.

Soothing pictures of fenced pastures and snowcapped mountains covered the freshly painted walls. Comfy throw pillows rested on the sofa. A pretty vase of yellow tulips sat in the middle of the coffee table. After where he'd been living for the past eight years, he felt as though he'd walked into heaven. He couldn't believe he got to live here, in such nice accommodations.

"You like it?" Elena asked, a wide smile plumping her rosy cheeks.

He nodded, too overwhelmed to speak.

Elena rested a hand on his arm. "Welcome home, Joel. You don't ever need to leave, unless you want to."

"Thank you," he croaked, his voice vibrating.

He turned away, so she couldn't see how her words affected him. Big, strong men didn't cry. And he'd been strong for so long. He'd stood up to other bigger men who'd have loved nothing more than to shoot, stab or strangle him while he slept. Now in the face of this small, dark-haired woman's generosity, the burn of tears and his gratitude almost reduced him to the state of a trembling boy.

"Well, I'll leave you to settle in. Come on out to the greenhouses when you're ready." Elena stepped outside, leaving the front door open. A breeze swept past, laced with the pungent aroma of sage.

Joel watched her go, wondering how he could ever repay her and Señor Herrera's generosity. More than ever, Joel was determined to try, even if it meant facing Mari's disapproval.

"Hi there." On Joel's way to the greenhouses, he met Livi, who accompanied him.

"Hi, Joel." The girl took his hand, her lack of guile reminding him that he wasn't a complete monster if a little child could still trust him. He smiled as she skipped beside him, calling to the dog. "Here, Max."

Max came running and Livi let go of Joel's hand, shrieking with delight as the animal jumped up on her. "Down, Max."

Inside the greenhouse, the dog found a sunny corner and grunted as he slumped on the ground by the door.

"Are you all settled in?" Mari looked up from her work, a smudge of dirt along her jawline.

Joel shrugged, his fingertips tingling with the urge to wipe the dirt away. "I didn't have much to settle."

Netta appeared at the end of the greenhouse. "Royce just called from the Flower Box. He wants fifteen flats of lilies.

Between Easter sales and a last-minute wedding, they need the flowers pronto."

"We don't have a delivery man today. Can't he come here to pick them up?" Mari asked.

"Nope. He's working alone in the shop and can't leave the cash register. I'd take them in to town, but I've got to pick Timmy up from school in fifteen minutes."

Mari eyed her mother. "Where's Matt? He could drive the lilies in if we help load them."

"Dallin drove him to town to buy groceries. We're out of milk, bread and eggs," Mom supplied.

"Great! That means we won't see Matt for the rest of the afternoon. I don't know why a trip into town has to take three hours."

"He's just a normal kid," Joel said.

"Yeah, and he has to finish his last year of high school, if I don't strangle him first." Fatigue and frustration dripped from every word.

"I can take the lilies into town," Joel offered.

"Oh, would you?" Mom slipped her hand into the pocket of her apron and withdrew a set of keys. "Take the green truck parked in the garage. The van has a major oil leak."

She tossed the keys to Joel and he snapped his hand around them, catching them in midair.

"I better help load the flowers so you take the right ones." Mari headed for the door.

Elena frowned at Mari's limp, which had eased slightly. "Why don't you stay here and I'll go?"

Mari kept walking. "No way! The doctor said you're to do no heavy lifting. Not unless you want another heart attack. I'll be back as soon as I can." She smiled at her mother, as if to soften her reprimand.

"Can I come with?" Livi asked.

"Sure! As long as your mom says it's okay." Joel reached into the cooler sitting by the door and tossed a bottle of water to the girl. She caught it with both hands, flashing him a gape-toothed grin. She hadn't been born yet when he used to work for her father and he wanted to get to know her better.

"Can I go, Mom?"

"Yes, but don't get in the way," Elena said.

Mari spoke very little as they retrieved the truck. Joel wondered what she was thinking as they pulled the vehicle up to the greenhouse and parked close to the door.

"How you liking school?" Joel asked Livi.

"Fine, I guess. Except for math."

"Why's that?" Following Mari, he retrieved flats of lilies with delicate white blossoms from the greenhouse before sliding them into the bed of the truck.

"I'm not too good at math. Especially take away."

Joel removed a crate from Mari's arms, set it into the truck, then wiped his brow with the back of his hand. "Maybe we can do something about that later on. I'm pretty good at math."

"Really?" Livi gazed at him with adoration.

Joel patted the little girl's cheek. "Sure, you just have to concentrate. Once you understand the basics, there's nothing to it."

Reaching for another heavy load, he caught Mari watching him, her brows drawn together in perplexity.

"I envy your strength," she said.

"No need. I'm here to help." If only he could convince her that he meant no harm. That he really wanted to lend a hand.

After he climbed into the truck and buckled Livi's seat belt, Joel picked up a class schedule for the local university lying on the dashboard. He perused it for just a moment, then tossed it aside. "Is that yours?"

Mari's face flushed red as she climbed into the truck. "Yeah, it's mine."

"You still in college?" He liked the thought of her going to school. As soon as he had enough money, he planned to take more classes, too. He'd gotten his degree entirely online and longed to sit in a stuffy classroom with a professor up front giving him a boring lecture. For a fleeting moment, he imagined him and Mari as college students, falling in love, graduating and building a life together.

"No, I had to drop out."

Surprising. "What about nursing school?"

She looked startled. "How did you know about that?"

He hitched one shoulder. "Your dad wrote and told me you were in nursing school. When we were kids, you used to bandage all your dolls. Then in high school, you talked about becoming a nurse all the time."

"That was a long time ago. I attended a few semesters, but had to drop out when Dad became ill." She stared out the windshield, her entire body rigid.

He should have taken a hint from her short, curt answers, but he pressed on. "Why don't you go back?"

"Lots of reasons."

"Such as?"

She threw him a glare over the top of Livi's head and snapped her seat belt in place. "It's none of your business."

True, but her brusque response surprised him. "Why so defensive?"

She released a deep sigh. In the depths of her eyes, he saw a shadow of frustration and he longed to give her a hug of encouragement. Maybe she'd feel better tomorrow, after a good night's rest.

"I'm sorry," she said. "I don't mean to be rude, but can we please talk about something else?"

"Sure, whatever you like." He sensed a deep-seated longing within her and wondered what kept her from going to school.

The obvious reasons came to mind. Time, lack of money, fear of failure. Was it that simple? Or did her dilemma run deeper than that? Somehow, he planned to help her overcome all the obstacles. She obviously wanted to take classes. So, what was holding her back? He didn't dare ask at this moment. Maybe later.

He chewed on a toothpick, holding it between two fingers. He felt Mari's gaze boring a hole in him like a two-inch drill.

"You still smoking?" She nodded at the stick.

"No, just when I was a stupid kid." He used the roller to lower the window before tossing the stick out.

A slight smile curved her pretty mouth. "I'm glad to hear you gave it up. Livi couldn't take it with her asthma and smoking isn't good for you, either."

"So I hear."

"You used to smoke, Joel?" Livi sat between them, a hint of shock in her wide, brown eyes.

Joel nodded. "Until I smartened up. I hope you'll never try it."

"Not me, but I saw Matt do it once." She crinkled her nose with repugnance. "Dad grounded him for a whole month."

A subtle tension filled the cab of the truck. Joel wasn't surprised to hear that Matt had tried smoking. The boy reminded Joel of himself when he'd been seventeen.

"Has Matt decided where he wants to go to college yet?"

Mari gave a sarcastic scoff. "Are you kidding? All Matt can think about right now is being free of us and doing whatever he wants. He just hasn't figured out how he's gonna pay for it. He's used to living off Mom and Dad and hasn't realized it takes work to support himself."

"I'm sorry to hear that. Sounds like you've had your hands full." His heart went out to her and the load she must have been carrying since her father died. He couldn't blame her for feeling tired and cynical. He just hoped it wasn't too late to remind her of all the joy life had to offer.

He turned on the motor and shifted the truck into gear before pulling out of the yard. Classical music came from the CD player, a soft romantic melody that caused Joel to stare at the dashboard for several seconds. "What is that?"

"Mari's music," Livi said.

Joel quirked one brow. "Since when did you start listening to classical in place of country-western?"

Mari reached across Livi and turned off the CD player. "Dad loved classical music."

"Yeah, but classical music is for—" He didn't finish his thought out loud. He was about to say stodgy, old men, but reconsidered. Señor Herrera had been anything but dull. Mari worshipped her father and had obviously come to appreciate his taste in music. Joel couldn't blame her.

"Classical music is for what?" Mari asked, lifting her chin higher in the air.

"Never mind. I just remember how you used to hate your dad's music and asked him to turn it off."

"I've come to appreciate the sophistication Dad tried to give us."

"Remember how he'd gather us in the living room and read the classics almost every night after work?"

She flashed a dazzling smile that caused his breath to hitch in his chest. "And then we'd have family prayer. You were so irreverent, making faces at me from across the room."

He chuckled. "If you didn't want to see my face, why did you have your eyes open?"

Her smile faded. "Funny how hard parents work to try to help their kids become better people and how hard the kids fight against doing anything more than necessary. Only when their parents are gone do the kids realize how much they appreciate what their folks tried to do for them."

Not him. All Joel could remember about his own father was his mother's screams. The man had never given them anything but fear and loathing. He regretted that he hadn't been there when his mother died. He'd sent her a letter, apologizing for everything he'd put her through and telling her how much he loved and appreciated her, but it wasn't the same as being there in person. "Your dad was the only father I ever had."

She glanced sharply at him before sympathy filled her eyes. "I think he knew that, Joel. Dad always thought of you like a son. I just wish I had a few last minutes to tell him thank you for all he tried to do for me."

"Yeah, me too. I know he wanted you to go to college."

She frowned, a troubled expression covering her face. As she stared out the window, Joel wished he could say something to comfort her. Instead, he reached over and flipped the CD player on. The soft vibration of violins accompanied by the sweet trill of flutes filtered over the air.

"It's beautiful," he agreed.

"Yuck!" Livi clasped her hands over her ears and puckered her lips like she'd eaten a sour pickle.

Joel chuckled, driving down the dirt road, a billow of dust following their passing. "Just be glad it's not opera."

"Even worse," Livi said, but she didn't try to turn off the CD. In fact, she hummed along and Joel realized she recognized the tune, which meant she'd heard it often before.

"Remember how your dad insisted we all get college degrees? He said there was nothing wrong with being educated farmers," Joel said.

Mari took a deep breath and released it. "I keep thinking I'll have time tomorrow to apply for readmittance, but things keep getting in the way."

Ah! Now they were getting somewhere. He decided to act casual and let her do the talking. "Like what things?"

A harsh laugh slipped from her throat. "Nothing important. Just work, paying the bills and running the farm. Dad's health wasn't very good for several years before he died and Mom's health isn't good now. Matt's been hanging out with a drug dealer and we just lost one of our greenhouses. I've had a few things on my mind lately. It seems like school is just a wish that can never become a reality."

He nodded. "I understand, but be careful. Tomorrow is today. It passes by too fast and then you're stuck with regrets."

She tilted her head and laughed. "Why, Joel, you've become poetic."

"Nah, just smarter."

"You sound like you've got a few regrets yourself."

"I have. More than I can say."

He could feel Mari silently watching him and longed to confide his regrets, but feared she'd be repulsed. If she asked, he'd pour out the entire story to her, and he feared her reaction. He couldn't stand to see disgust or pity in her eyes.

"Do you know where to go?" She faced forward, watching farmhouses zip past as they drove into town.

He flashed her a grin. "Of course. I've been there many times before. Has it moved?"

"No, it's in the same place."

Fields sprouting new spring grass spread out before them. Cattle grazed in fenced pastures. A skiff of snow hid from the sun beneath shade trees.

As they drove down Main Street, Mari didn't speak. They passed a series of old buildings with tidy green lawns and flower boxes filled with purple and yellow pansies. Joel turned onto Johnson Lane, which led to the Flower Box Florist Shop in Gardenville. At the shop, Joel pulled around back and parked in the alley, then hopped out of the truck. While he lowered the tailgate and began carrying crates into the store, he whistled the classical tune he'd heard in the truck. He felt so free and happy to be here, yet his heart was leaden with concern for Mari and her family.

Livi slid out of the truck and followed Mari inside.

"Hi, Royce. We got here as quickly as we could," Mari called. "You want us to put the lilies in the back?"

A squat, neckless man leaned across the counter at the front of the store, a silly grin on his face. At first sight, Joel recognized Royce Howell. The man had changed very little over the years. He still wore a pair of black spectacles, which slid down his nose and made him appear fifty years old instead of twenty-eight. Strands of thinning hair fell over his brow and he slicked them back with pudgy fingers. "Howdy, Mari. Yes, that'd be great. Thanks for bringing the flowers in."

Royce smiled at Olivia, then reached beneath the counter and pulled out a jar of assorted lollipops. "Hi, Livi. You want a treat?"

Livi looked at Mari. "May I?"

Mari chuckled. "Okay, but just one."

The child dipped her hand into the jar and pulled out a yellow lollipop. After removing the plastic wrapper, she stuck the candy in her mouth. She knelt down to pet Sadie, Royce's golden retriever that lay panting on the floor beside the counter.

"Royce, you remember Joel Hunter, don't you?" Mari made the introductions.

Royce peered at Joel through the thick lenses of his glasses. "Yeah, weren't you that kid that got arrested for shoplifting over at the general store a few years back?"

Mari coughed, her face flushing red. "More like ten years. That was a long time ago, Royce, when we were all kids. Didn't you ever pull some stupid pranks when you were young?"

Royce gaped at Mari, a blank expression on his face.

"I guess not," she mumbled under her breath.

Joel clenched his fists, something inside him hardening. He'd known when he returned to Gardenville that he might face some censure from people he'd offended as a kid, but he still wasn't prepared for the continued feelings of shame that washed over him. He'd paid his debt to society and longed to be free of the guilt, but wondered if that were possible. The road to forgiveness wouldn't be easy, but he'd made a promise to God and resolved himself to making amends, no matter what it took.

"Yeah, I'm sorry to say I got in a bit of trouble when I was younger. But I've grown up and changed since then." With a nod, Joel turned and went outside to the truck, conscious of Mari following behind.

He peered over his shoulder. She stood watching him quietly. A momentary flicker of compassion filled her eyes, then she reached for a flat of flowers.

"Don't mind Royce," she said. "He never did have any manners."

He took the flowers from her, a blaze of happiness burning through him. She didn't make a big deal out of it, but she'd defended him and just offered him encouragement.

Together, they carried the flowers inside. Joel worked double-time, trying to take the heavy flats of lilies from her arms, unwilling to let her carry the plants if he could help it. He rushed back and forth between the truck and shop so fast that she could do little more than watch and get out of his way.

"How are your legs feeling now?" He ignored her frown and smiled as he passed by.

"Nothing's changed in the past thirty minutes. I'm still just fine. I'm not an invalid, Joel." She shook her head and laughed, the sound like a gentle breeze across an open field of wildflowers. He caught a hypnotic whiff of her perfume. A pretty floral scent that left him weak in the knees.

Back inside the shop, she handed an invoice to Royce, who produced a check. She tucked it inside her pocket as Joel brought in the last load of flowers. He couldn't help noticing how Royce hovered over Mari, grinning in a sheepish sort of way. His balding head glimmered with a sheen of perspiration, his nose overlong and hooked on the end. Joel realized the man was attracted to her. She reached for the empty crates, seemingly oblivious to Royce's attention.

"You been to the new diner that just opened up on Main Street last week?" Royce asked her.

A curl of hair came free from Mari's long ponytail and she tucked it behind her ear. "Nope, have you?"

"Not yet. Actually, I was wondering if maybe you might want to go with me for dinner Friday night?"

Joel shook his head, a blaze of jealousy twisting in his gut. He stood beside the back door, feeling like an outsider and wishing he were anywhere but here.

"Um, I'm sorry, but I'm busy Friday night." She made a beeline for the door.

"What about Saturday night?"

"Sorry, I'm busy then, too."

"Oh, well, maybe some other time."

"Perhaps. Come on, Livi. We've got to get back to work. Thanks, Royce." Mari hurried outside.

Livi jumped up and skipped toward the door, oblivious to what had just transpired. Mari barely spared the shop owner a second glance. Joel watched her go, feeling sorry for Royce, yet elated that Mari had turned the man down. Royce wasn't too smart and Mari deserved better.

Then Joel reconsidered. Mari had put off too much of her life. School, dating and friends. What life did she have of her own? It seemed all she did was serve others and left nothing for herself. He admired her sacrifice, yet he also worried about her. He wanted to see her happy and he sensed deep inside that she wasn't. He cared for her, no matter how hard he tried not to.

Caring meant he still had a heart that could be broken.

Chapter Six

The drive home didn't go much better. Joel's constant scrutiny made Mari uncomfortable and she braided Livi's hair to keep her nervous fingers busy.

"You should go out with that man."

"Who? Royce?" Mari stared with incredulity at Joel, trying to absorb what he'd just proposed.

"Yeah, you should have accepted his invitation and gone out on a date."

She snorted. "He's too old."

"No, he's not."

"Well, he seems too old. Royce is one of our clients and nothing more. His mother owns the flower shop. He works there and does whatever she tells him. A pure momma's boy. Besides, he was rude to you."

She was unprepared for the flood of compassion that washed over her when she thought of what Royce had said to Joel. And yet a part of her believed Joel deserved what he got.

"You don't have to marry the guy, Marisol. Just go out with him."

Marisol! He said her name so smoothly, rolling the *R* with

a Spanish accent, just like Dad used to say it. As though she were his best friend and he had a right to worry about her.

A shrill laugh broke from her lips. "What on earth would I do with Royce?"

"Relax and have fun for a change?" It was a question, not a statement.

"I have fun."

"Doing what?"

"I...I..." Her mind whirled for something. Anything! But it did no good. Besides work, church and family responsibilities, she had absolutely no social life or outside interests. Listening to Dad's old CDs of classical music didn't count.

For the past year, she kept stopping by the university to pick up class schedules and catalogs. She even met with a counselor once. But she never made the plunge and actually reapplied. She longed to finish her education. She loved science and the art of healing, but life kept getting in the way. She had a long list of excuses.

Joel's reminder made her defensive. "I can guarantee I'm not going to have fun with Royce. He's not my type."

A slight smile curved his mouth and she got the feeling her confession pleased him. "What is your type?"

"Not Royce. The thought of dating him gives me the creeps." She shivered with repulsion to make her point.

"He could be worse. Remember Philip?" Joel chuckled.

Mari sucked in a breath. "Phil Taylor? You have got to be kidding."

Joel draped his right arm along the back of the seat behind Livi and smiled. His handsome, quirky smile reminded her of the endless times he'd teased her. "I'm dead serious. Good thing I scared him off when I told him you were my girl or he would have kept asking you out."

"Okay, yes. I admit he was a nuisance." Mari covered her

heated face with her hands, remembering the love poems Phil dedicated to her and had published in the school newspaper. She'd been mortified and taunted by everyone in school. If it hadn't been for Joel arriving at the end of the school year and threatening Phil with dire consequences, she feared Phil would never have stopped. Even though Phil had been scared, she'd felt grateful Joel had interceded at the time. "I feared Phil's mom was going to get a restraining order against you."

Joel shook his head with disgust. "The most obnoxious kid I ever met."

Mari pursed her lips and frowned. "I can think of one other."

"Who?" he asked innocently.

She laughed in spite of herself. "You, maybe?"

"What'd I do?"

"Don't go there, Joel." She waggled a finger at him, conscious of Livi looking back and forth between them, taking in every word of their conversation. "Troy Banks was an honor student and the quarterback of the football team and you cornered him out back of the school gymnasium and threatened him, too."

Joel's eyes narrowed. "He deserved it."

"Why?"

Several pounding moments passed before Joel answered. Mari got the feeling he was trying to pick his words carefully. "You'll just have to trust me on this, Mari. Troy Banks was after one thing only. I didn't want him to hurt you."

Hurt her? Joel must have discovered Troy's proclivity for taking advantage of women. It had taken Mari years to find out the truth. Thankfully, she no longer had any interest in Troy and didn't care to hear more stale gossip. Not from Joel Hunter.

"Ha! That's fascinating coming from you," she said.

His countenance seemed to drop on the floor. "I never disrespected any young ladies."

That shut her up. Even when they'd been kids, he'd brought her field flowers or shared half his candy bar with her. No matter how much trouble he got into, he had always said *please* and *thank you* and treated her with respect. And it infuriated Mari that she had actually felt flattered by his effort. "Joel, I became a pariah at school because of you."

"You were head varsity cheerleader. I wouldn't call that a pariah."

"A cheerleader without friends. I ended up with no date for my junior prom. No one dared ask me out." Mari took a deep breath, wishing they hadn't dredged up these old memories.

"I should have returned from Oakland and taken you to the prom myself," he said.

What? Mari stared at his handsome profile, his stubborn chin and high forehead. And yet there was a maturity in him now that she didn't detect in other men his age. A maturity filled with worldly experience she wasn't sure she wanted to contemplate.

Shaking her head, she let her breath out in a slow exhale, wishing she could ignore him. Not in a lifetime would she ever have agreed to go to the prom with Joel Hunter.

Livi pulled the lollipop out of her mouth, her dark eyes wide. "Are you guys fighting?"

Joel dropped his hand on Livi's arm and gave her a comforting squeeze before looking at Mari. "Of course not, but I owe your sister an apology. I'm sorry."

Mari's mouth dropped open. She studied Joel's face, finding nothing but sincerity in his eyes. No! She wanted to yell. No, no, no!

"That's nice of you," Livi said. "Mommy says you shouldn't hurt anyone's feelings and you should always say you're sorry when you're rude."

Mari bit her tongue. Now he even had Livi buying into

his charm. Mari tried to think of anything besides Joel and how he'd turned her world topsy-turvy by walking back into her life.

"Whatever became of your old boyfriend, anyway?" he asked.

A choking cough rose in Mari's throat. Troy Banks had always been a thorny issue between them and it irritated her that Joel had been right about Troy all along. "Not much. He went to UCLA where he played college football and got a Master's degree in education. Afterward, he married his college sweetheart."

Okay, so she omitted the part about Troy bloodying his wife's lip and blacking her eye so she had filed for divorce six months ago.

"He's happily married?" Joel asked.

She couldn't bring herself to lie. "No, I didn't say that. Actually, he's in the middle of a divorce."

He threw her a questioning stare, then his face darkened. "I'm sorry to hear that. You're not still interested in him, are you?"

Not in a million years. "And if I were?"

"Who?" Livi asked.

"You never mind. Let's change the subject," Mari said.

"Do you mean Troy?" Livi continued with the tenacity of a dog with a bone. "Matt told me that he was doing drugs, drinking and chasing after anyone wearing a skirt."

Mari's breath hitched in her throat. "Livi! Don't talk like that. I can see I need to speak with Mateo about his conversations with you."

Joel glanced at Mari. "Did you know about Troy?"

"Yes, it's a small town and people talk. Troy played football for UCLA, but he was kicked off the team for using steroids."

Joel gave a low whistle. "I'm sorry to hear that. Looks like I'm not the only one who messed up my life."

Wow! She never thought she'd hear him say that.

"What are steroids?" Livi asked.

Mari hesitated, picking her words carefully. Livi wasn't too young to know about drugs or that they could destroy her health and her life. "They're a drug used by some athletes to make them stronger, but it also can damage their health."

"So they're not good to use, right?" The girl's nose crinkled.

"What do you think?"

Livi studied the vinyl seat, her forehead creased with thought. Good! Mari wanted her sister to formulate her own opinions, the earlier the better.

"No, I don't want to take drugs," Livi said.

"Unless you're sick and the doctor prescribes some medicine," Joel said.

They drove in silence for several minutes, but some unfinished business hung in the air.

"Let's get back to what you do for fun," Joel continued.

"She teaches Sunday school," Livi piped in.

Thank you, Livi! "That's right. I teach Sunday school every week."

Okay, she was grasping at straws here, but she couldn't stand to let Joel think she had no life of her own, even if it was true. All her friends had gone to college, gotten married, started careers and even families. Deep inside, she felt somehow deficient and left behind. She wanted so much more.

Joel reached forward and clasped the class schedule before tossing it into Mari's lap. "Why don't you take another nursing class? Just one to start with."

She grit her teeth. "Maybe I will, but it's none of your business."

"Wooee, girl! You still have a temper, I see. You're still a hot taco."

She studied him, her mind racing to understand his meaning until she realized he'd said it wrong. "The expression is 'hot tamale.'"

"Yes, you're definitely a hot tamale."

She laughed, unable to help herself. He'd muffed the saying and she found it more than comical. Pursuing this line of dialogue would only lead to trouble. She knew it instinctively. In spite of their differences, he'd always been easy to talk to. She didn't want to like this man, and yet she couldn't help feeling downright comfortable around him.

"Mari, I don't like school. You can do my homework if you want to," Livi invited in a happy voice.

Mari chuckled and tugged on Livi's braid. The little girl's sweet laughter filled the cab of the truck. "No, sweetie. I think you need to do your own schoolwork. Otherwise, how will you learn what you need to know when you become an adult?"

"Ah." Livi's mouth pulled downward in a pout.

"And what about you?" Mari gazed at Joel.

"What about me?" He shifted gears and pressed the accelerator.

"With your education, you could do so many things, yet you came here to Herrera Farms. It almost seems like you're hiding from something."

His jaw locked hard as iron.

"Did I say something wrong?" she asked in a sweet voice, knowing very well she'd needled him.

He didn't respond, his demeanor tight and forbidding. Even with the heater running, the air turned cold as a frozen pond.

She couldn't sort out the riot of feelings going through her mind. Joel was right. She needed to get out more and have some fun. If she wanted to go to school, she should do it now, before she got older. The years would pass by no matter what. And what would she have to show for it?

Mom had gotten her two tickets to the philharmonic. Joel was the only man she could think of to go with her that wasn't totally repulsive or already involved with someone else. And that didn't make sense. She didn't like Joel. Right? Of course, right!

Chapter Seven

Maybe coming to Herrera Farms wasn't such a good idea after all. Joel stood in the dark of the garage, breathing in the musty scent of peat moss. He pinched the bridge of his nose.

Mari's words haunted him. She'd defended him to Royce Howell, something he never expected. He thought when he chose to come here that he could make a fresh start, but people had long memories and didn't quite trust him. What if he couldn't overcome their prejudice? He didn't want to become a liability to the Herrera family.

One day at a time.

The thought filled Joel's mind with peace. If he were patient and long-suffering, he'd be able to prove himself to the people of this community. He'd be able to prove himself to Mari, too.

After retrieving the shovel hanging on a peg by the door, he walked to the compost pile and began filling a wheelbarrow. Maybe he could get an early start on the second crop of hothouse tomatoes and peppers they planned to transplant. Work provided an outlet for his inner demons and helped salve his guilt.

He tried to ignore what was really bothering him, but his thoughts kept coming around to Mari's accusations about chasing off her boyfriends. He remembered Troy Banks buying alcohol and illicit drugs from one of Joel's friends in town. Troy had bragged about his plans to spike Mari's soft drink and then take advantage of her. Without thinking, Joel had decked Troy, almost breaking the other boy's jaw in the process. The only reason Troy hadn't called the cops was because he'd been underage when he bought the booze and drugs and would have gotten kicked off the football team and possibly done some jail time.

Joel had tried to protect Mari, but he'd earned her animosity in the process. He'd chased off her boyfriends because he didn't consider them good enough for her. No one was good enough for Mari.

Not even him.

Mari got up early in the morning to fertilize the broccoli and cabbage plants. When she found that Joel had already done the chore, she felt a mixture of gratitude and irritation. More and more, his work eased her load. She didn't want to feel beholden to this man, but maybe it wouldn't be so bad to tell him *thank you* for his efforts.

Carrying a bucket of vine-ripened tomatoes from the hothouse, she rounded the corner of the garage and heard Joel yelling football calls to Mateo in the front yard. Max barked, chasing after the two men as they sprinted across the lawn.

"Okay, here it comes. Go long!" Joel called to Matt.

Mari peered around the lilac bush as Joel wound up his arm and threw the football in a straight, fast arc. Matt darted after the spinning ball, his head tilted up to the sky.

Joel had shaved and trimmed his hair in a short crop. Mari wondered if Mom had helped him with the chore. Regardless, she approved of his smooth face. He looked great in a pair of faded blue jeans, shirt and tennis shoes. The morning sunlight glinted off his dark hair. Instead of looking wild, he appeared like any normal man, taking a break from the work of the day to toss a few balls to his younger brother.

Matt reached out his arms, catching and almost dropping the ball.

"Great catch, but you don't want to fumble." Joel trotted over to Matt before taking the football.

Joel tossed the ball high in the air, then caught it and pulled it close to his chest, cradling it tight with both hands. "See how you have better control if you place your hands like this? If you're tackled, you cup your body around the ball and go down, protecting it like this." In example, Joel fell to the ground, using his body to shield the ball as he showed Matt what to do. "The other team will have difficulty getting the ball away from you."

Matt nodded as he studied the technique and a smile of discovery lit up his face. "Yes, I see what to do. I sure wish my coach had explained it that way."

"You have a lot of natural ability. I wish you'd try out for the team again. They could use you next fall."

"I'll think about it."

Joel tossed the ball back to Matt, then playfully head-locked the boy briefly with his arms.

"Hey, dude!" Matt laughed and struggled to get free before Joel released him and the two pretended to box for several moments. Then their play ceased as abruptly as it began.

"You ever work on a car engine?" Joel asked.

Matt inclined his head. "A little bit, with my dad."

"Your dad taught me, too. Come on. I could use some help getting the van up and running." Joel jerked his chin toward the garage as he clapped his hand on Matt's shoulder.

Matt hesitated for a fraction of a moment and Mari expected him to refuse. She swallowed a cough when Matt headed in that direction with Joel. She noticed the happy jaunt in Joel's stride. He seemed to fit right back into their life. Like he'd never left.

The two talked in muted tones and she wished she could hear the rest of their conversation. She studied her brother, really studied him. His dark, handsome features reminded her so much of Dad. The muscular definition of his arms, chest and shoulders. His long legs and jubilant laugh. Even though he was her brother, she could appreciate his good looks. No wonder the girls called him on the phone. Their forward behavior drove Mom crazy. She didn't think a girl should call a boy. Mari had to agree.

As the boys disappeared inside the garage, Mari couldn't help wondering if Joel was a good influence on her brother. Joel seemed different and yet she couldn't stop being suspicious of his motives. If he fixed the van, she'd owe him big-time and yet she resented him being here. Why?

The answer came clear as a bell. Because of what he made her feel. Old emotions she thought were long dead.

No, she didn't want him here. So, why did the thought of him leaving make her feel so empty inside?

That afternoon, Mari walked up to the house in time to see Joel driving the van as he pulled out of the driveway.

"Where's he going?" she asked Mom, who stood on the front porch waving goodbye.

Mom turned to go inside and Mari followed. "I don't know. He asked to borrow the van for a few hours. Can you believe he got it running?"

No, it didn't surprise her that Joel had repaired the van. He'd always been good with engines.

"And you let him go?" The screen door slammed closed behind them.

"Of course."

"Have you forgotten all the trouble he used to get into whenever he borrowed Dad's truck in the past?"

Mom frowned. "That was a long time ago. Joel's a grown man now. Besides, he's been working hard and is entitled to some free time of his own once in a while."

Hmm. Mari didn't know what to make of this. "If he gets himself into trouble, I won't be going into town to bail him out like Dad always did."

Mom dipped her hands into the sink of hot, sudsy water to wash the supper dishes. "You judge Joel too harshly. He's not the same person he used to be. He's changed, can't you see that?"

Yes, Mari had noticed. And yet she couldn't help feeling skeptical. What did they really know about him now? He hadn't been here long enough to prove he'd really changed.

"There isn't much to do in town, unless you're getting into trouble. You really don't know where he's going?" She picked up a dish towel and dried a plate before setting it inside the cupboard.

Mom pursed her lips, obviously not wanting to talk about this. "I think that's Joel's business, don't you?"

"Of course, but I thought you might know."

Mom paused as she wrung out the soggy dishcloth, then wiped down the countertops. "Why don't you ask him when he returns?"

Mari tensed. She would, if she got the nerve. Part of her didn't want to know. Her insides warred with her curiosity and what was right. Joel was now a grown man and had a right to make his own decisions. She didn't want to insult him. Deep inside, she knew Joel had not had a good time in life over the past few years. Not if he was willing to come here to Herrera Farms to work.

The hour was late when Joel returned, the house quiet with everyone gone to bed. Mari sat up and peeked through the blinds on her bedroom window, watching as he got out of the van and walked back to the caretaker's cottage. She studied him for any furtive movements, the telltale signs that he'd been up to no good. Instead, he walked straight and tall, his hands slung low in his pockets as he whistled a classical tune he'd heard her playing on the CD in the greenhouse earlier that morning.

Knowing he was home safe and sound brought her ease and she finally fell asleep. The next morning, she longed to ask him about his Thursday night foray, but couldn't seem to muster the courage. Instead, she decided to let the subject drop. Maybe Mom was right. Joel had worked hard. Within one week, he'd cleaned up the majority of the mess from the explosion, repaired the van, reroofed the caretaker's cottage, and almost finished bunny-proofing two greenhouses. He had a right to some free time.

She just hoped he was behaving himself.

On Saturday evening, Joel came up to the main house to borrow Mom's iron. Sitting at Dad's rolltop desk while she prepared some invoices, Mari watched in silent curiosity as Mom walked to the hallway closet. She returned momentarily with the iron in hand.

"Hi, sunshine." Joel greeted her with a wink.

Mari's throat went dry. She couldn't explain the warmth flooding her chest. "Hi. You know that's for ironing clothes, not making toasted cheese sandwiches, right?" She nodded at the iron he gripped in one hand.

"Yep, I know." His mouth twitched, indicating he remembered the time he'd used Mom's iron to make himself lunch. He didn't seem the least bit flustered by the sarcasm dripping from her voice.

"Thanks for fixing the van." Okay, not too flowery, but at least she'd said the words.

"You're welcome." He flashed a devastating smile that left her breathless.

Without further comment, she turned back to her work, trying to ignore him. In the back of her mind, she was dying to know why he needed the iron.

The following morning, she got her answer. He showed up in the driveway just as they all walked out onto the front porch to go to church. Mom must have invited him and Mari felt guilty for not thinking to do so. She'd assumed he'd say no.

He stood leaning against the van, clean-shaven, his dark hair combed back and tidy. He'd pulled down the crisp collar of his white oxford shirt over one of Dad's old ties. Mari recognized the tie. She'd given it to Dad for Father's Day several years earlier.

She expected to feel resentment toward Joel for wearing her father's clothing. Instead, a strange, happy contentment bubbled inside her.

He crossed his long legs at the ankles, wearing clean but faded dress slacks. Each shirt sleeve and pant leg showed an impeccable crease. He'd obviously put Mom's iron to good use.

"Good morning." He spoke to them all, but his smiling gaze rested on Mari.

"You're looking very dapper this morning," she said.

"And you look beautiful." His gaze traveled down her legs and high heels.

A flush of heat seared her face and she smoothed a hand over the front of her blue skirt. Why his words would cause such a reaction, she couldn't say. As he opened the rusty van doors, Mari caught his spicy scent along with a hint of pep-permint mouthwash. He smelled as nice as he looked.

She slid past him to climb inside and whispered for his ears alone. "You know you may see several people at church who recognize you from the past."

A thoughtful frown tugged at his brow. "That won't be a problem. It's time I make amends."

Impressed by his comment, she sat down, swung her legs inside and snapped on her seat belt.

Matt grumbled as he climbed into the van behind Livi. "I don't know why I have to go."

Joel clasped the boy's shoulder and smiled. "To worship the Lord. Church service teaches us respect for God. There are many good lessons to learn from the Scriptures, too."

"I don't learn anything from them," Matt groused.

Joel slid the back door closed and climbed into the driver's seat, his voice sounding jovial. "I felt the same way once. Then I discovered I had to put some effort into it to get some-thing out of it. If you'll open your heart, you'll see it, Matt."

"Your father always said that church gave him a peaceful feeling after a long, hectic workweek," Mom added.

Matt wasn't buying any of this. He threw an ugly glare at his mother. With another indistinguishable murmur, the boy slouched in his seat and closed his eyes.

Mari's heart plummeted. She hated Matt to act this way. His belligerent attitude made it difficult for the rest of the family to feel close to the Spirit. More and more, he reminded her of Joel when he'd been a teenager. A heavy weight rested on her heart as she wondered how to get through to her brother. She didn't want to lose him, physically or spiritu-ally. She loved him and wished he wouldn't have such a hard heart.

As they entered the redbrick church in town, Nancy

Granger and her parents stood in the main foyer. Seeing them, Nancy bustled over to Mari.

"Hi, Mari. Who's your new friend?" Nancy eyed Joel with a wide smile. Her crimped blonde hair hung across her right eye, her red lipstick stark against her flawless, pale skin.

Mom disappeared into the chapel, trailed by Matt and Livi.

"This is Joel Hunter, an old family friend." Mari gave a stiff smile and made the introductions, but she couldn't deny a hollow emptiness in the pit of her stomach. Nancy was attractive and just two years younger than Joel. Mari couldn't explain why she felt territorial around him, but she did.

"Hi, Joel. Are you staying in Gardenville permanently or just visiting?" Nancy shook his hand, lingering overlong before he tugged to disengage his fingers.

"I'm staying." He stepped back, his gaze darting to the chapel doors.

"Have you been here before?"

"Yeah, I spent my childhood summers here, working for Mari's dad. I've known the Herrera family for years." His voice sounded detached.

Nancy moved closer, blocking his path to freedom. Mari shifted her weight, wondering if she should rescue him or join her mother.

Nancy gave a toss of her long hair. "I moved here three years ago with my folks. It's a great place to raise a family."

"Yeah, it is." He stunned Mari when he brushed past Nancy, placed his hand at the small of Mari's back and urged her into the chapel.

For some reason, his touch brought Mari a deep sense of satisfaction. Out of her peripheral vision, she saw the frown on Nancy's face as she watched them leave. Then Mari felt uncharitable for her unkind thoughts. Nancy was a nice enough girl. Maybe Joel should go out with her some time.

Soft organ music filtered over the air as they took their seats on a padded bench beside Mom. Mari watched with surprise as Nancy passed by, going to her parents who sat up front, and made them get up and move closer to where Joel sat. Nancy turned her body so she could peer back over her shoulder at Joel. He didn't seem to notice, but then Mari heard his deep sigh of irritation.

"Is she one of your friends?" He leaned his head down to Mari and she caught his clean, spicy scent.

"No."

"Then you won't be insulted if I ignore her?"

Definitely not! "You're a grown man and it's not my business. I don't care who you hang out with."

Yeah, right.

She glanced at him in time to see a hurt expression cross his features, so fleeting that she thought she must have imagined it.

Orson Gates and his wife, Millie, sat in the pews just to their right. Orson bumped Millie with his elbow and jerked his chin in Joel's direction. The two turned and stared with open surprise, which quickly melted into dark outrage.

Mari groaned. Joel and his friends had once smashed all the pumpkins in Millie's garden, reducing the woman to tears. Millie always entered her enormous pumpkins in the county fair, but that year, she had nothing to enter.

Mari leaned over to whisper a caution to Joel, but he didn't give her the chance.

"Take it easy. I see them. Hopefully Millie has forgiven me for that childish prank."

Not likely. From the indignant scowl on Millie's face, she remembered every detail and wouldn't forgive Joel anytime soon.

"I have a feeling they still remember," Mari whispered, trying to keep her gaze pinned on the front pulpit.

Word of Joel's presence seemed to spread throughout the congregation. A low buzz of chatter filtered over the crowd as more and more people turned around to look, bending their heads together as they glared at Joel. So much for Christian charity.

Joel smiled and nodded with respect to Millie and only Mari heard his quiet murmur. "Don't worry, I'll make it right with her."

"What do you intend to—?"

The meeting began, cutting Mari off. Thank goodness. Everyone except Nancy turned around to sing the opening hymn. The sermon focused on Mark 11:25-26 and forgiving those who trespass against you. How appropriate, yet the message seemed to rub salt in many old wounds. Several people's jaws hardened as they gaped at Joel and it occurred to Mari that forgiving others could be as difficult as receiving forgiveness.

Mari listened intently, forgetting everyone else in the room and all the troubles haunting her back at home. She felt strangely comforted as she heard Joel's deep bass voice during the hymns. After the meeting, she tried to stay close to Joel, to run interference in case someone decided to get confrontational about his past.

She lost track of him by the end of Sunday school. She found him standing outside in the sunshine with Orson and Millie Gates, and several other people. Nancy hovered close by Joel's side, showing a simpering smile and brushing her arm against his. Except for a tightening of his jaw, he paid her no mind.

As Mari pushed open the glass doors and stepped out on the sidewalk, Millie gave Joel a hearty hug. Mari coughed, wondering at this change. They actually laughed together.

"You come on over to the farm tomorrow and pick up those pumpkin plants," Joel said. "They're hybrids and I can practically guarantee they'll produce the biggest pumpkins you ever saw."

"That would be lovely," Millie gushed. "We'll see you bright and early tomorrow morning."

Mari stood beneath a shade tree, watching this exchange with amazement. Somehow, Joel had made amends for what he'd done. A mixture of pride and shame battled inside of her. Pride in Joel's efforts and shame because these people could forgive him so easily when she had difficulty offering him the same concession.

"You giving away all our vegetable plants?" she asked when he joined her a moment later.

"Just a few. I have a plan."

They walked toward the van, waiting for Mom and her siblings to join them. "And what is that?"

"Pumpkins."

"Pumpkins?" She angled her face in his direction, unable to resist a smile of amusement.

"Yeah, I planted lots of extra pumpkin plants and they've just started to sprout. I hope that's okay."

At her doubtful expression, he hurried on, "I've already told your mom to take the expense out of my first paycheck."

"Of course it's okay. If it helps mend your relationship with Millie, then it's worth it, Joel. You don't need to pay us for it. Just give Millie the plants." And she meant it.

"Millie's also planning to buy some tomato and bedding plants when she comes out to the farm to pick up her pumpkins. I figure the free pumpkin plants will make her happy, but she'll also give you some extra business in the process."

She made a tsking sound. "You're so mercenary, Joel."

He shrugged one shoulder and took her arm as they stepped off the curb into the parking lot. "That's not my intention. I just want to make amends. I'd feel bad if my presence here at the farm drove away any of your customers. Maybe we can bless people's lives while we earn a living."

His words made her stop and think. When was the last time she'd done something good for someone else just because she could? Just because she wanted to bless their lives? Maybe she could learn a lot from Joel's example.

The following day, Mari couldn't help bristling when Nancy showed up at the farm. The girl insisted Joel wait on her. He pulled along one of the red wagons they provided to their customers as she pointed out what she wanted. Without a word, he filled the wagon with an array of bedding and tomato plants. He didn't seem to notice her calf-eyed gaze or the veiled suggestions she made about going out together. And whenever she tried to touch his arm, he moved away.

By the time Nancy left with the trunk of her sedan filled with plants, Joel clenched his jaw tight as a drum.

"You don't seem to like her very much," Mari observed as she stood in the front yard, fighting with the nozzle of the new sprayer she'd bought for the garden hose. She tried to keep the happy lilt in her voice to a minimum.

He dusted off his hands and reached for the hose. "She's pushy and forward. Girls should wait for the guy to ask them out. What's the problem with the nozzle?"

"The trigger is jammed." She tossed her hair out of her eyes. "I never knew you were so old-fashioned when it comes to dating."

"No man likes to be hunted, unless they're interested in the woman." He removed the head of the nozzle and reset the rubber washer inside.

"She seems plenty interested in you." This was the first time she'd seen Joel brush aside a pretty girl and she couldn't help teasing him.

He grumbled something unintelligible as he screwed the sprayer back onto the hose.

"What was that?" she asked.

He handed her the sprayer. "I'm not interested in Nancy Granger."

He reached down and turned on the water with quick twists of his wrist. "Okay, try it now."

"Why aren't you interested in Nancy? She might be lots of fun." She depressed the trigger. Water shot forward, spraying Joel in the chest.

He gasped, his mouth dropping open in surprise. Mari released the hose and it fell limp to the ground. Joel's eyes widened as he lifted a hand to wipe at the wet splotch saturating his shirt.

Mari covered her mouth, trying and failing to suppress her laughter. "I guess it works great."

His eyes narrowed. "You did that on purpose."

"No, I didn't." She shook her head, backing away.

His brows lowered, warning her to run while she had the chance. She turned and sprinted toward the house, but not quick enough. Joel caught her, hooking his arm around her waist, dragging her back. She squealed with laughter, fighting for her freedom. When had he picked up the hose? He aimed the sprayer at her nose.

"No, Joel! Please! Don't get me wet," she shrieked.

His deep laughter mingled with her shrill yells. "Tell me one good reason why I shouldn't let you have it, sunshine."

She tripped and fell to the grass, staring up at him as he bent over her, holding the sprayer inches from her face. He flashed a smile wide enough for her to see his even, white teeth. His lopsided grin reminded her of his fun sense of humor. Memories of playing hide-and-seek and hunting for pollywogs down by the stream zipped through her mind. They'd had fun once, before he became an unruly teenager.

She raised her hands in self-defense. "You wouldn't dare."

Chuckles shook his chest. "You know I would."

A fat drop of water struck her nose. "Joel, don't—"

He froze, his smile fading, replaced by a look of yearning so intense that she tilted her head to one side, wondering at the sudden change in him.

"I'm not interested in Nancy." His soft voice surrounded her as he lowered the sprayer and tossed it aside.

"Why not?" She rose up on her elbows, mesmerized by his clear blue eyes.

"She's not you."

Without another word, he turned and left her there, her mouth hanging open.

A happy feeling fizzed inside of Mari. Joel's confession pleased her and she didn't understand why. She didn't give a flying fig what he thought of her. And since when did she care if he preferred her to any other girl in the state?

The answer came on swift wings. Since Joel Hunter came home, that's when.

Chapter Eight

Mari stood beside the toolshed, holding a glass of fresh-squeezed lemonade Mom had just made for Joel. With the exceptionally warm weather, pink and white blossoms sprouted on the fruit trees. Breathing in their sweet fragrance, she studied Joel as he prepared to bunny-proof another greenhouse.

His rustic good looks distracted her, his faded T-shirt tight across his muscular chest. Since he'd come to work at the farm, his face, neck and arms had tanned into a healthy, golden brown. As he went to retrieve the wheelbarrow filled with rocks, he walked with a unique, confident swagger.

"You gonna just watch, or come and help?" he called without looking up.

She jerked, embarrassed to be caught staring. She walked over to him and handed him the glass of lemonade.

He removed his right glove before taking the glass. "Thanks."

Tilting his head back, he gulped the lemonade down in four swallows. Droplets ran from his mouth to his chin and corded throat. He wiped them away and took a deep breath before handing the glass back. As he smiled at her, his blue eyes sparkled. "Just what I needed. A beautiful woman to bring me something cold to drink."

His words brought a rush of heat to her face and she turned away so he wouldn't see. After she set the glass aside, she donned the pair of work gloves she always kept in her pocket. "What can I do to help?"

He nodded at a hoe. "You can help me dig a small trench around the length of the greenhouse."

She picked up the tool and dug into the soft soil, lifting it back to create a valley of dirt beside the edge of polyethylene. Next she helped him unwind a bale of chicken wire while he stapled it to the timbers. He wheeled a load of rocks in with the wheelbarrow. Together they laid the stones in the trench over the chicken wire, then they buried it with the dirt. Even if the rabbits dug through the soil, they'd be thwarted by the rocks and wire.

"This is quite ingenious," she admitted. "Where'd you learn this technique?"

He chuckled. "You know where. Your dad taught me. Hopefully it'll discourage the cottontails enough that they'll go somewhere else to find their food."

"I hope so. We've lost a lot of plants to those varmints. Livi loves them and thinks they're so cute. I even caught her leaving carrots out for them at night. To me, they're just pests who steal our livelihood."

"Even pests are God's creatures and need a home."

She laughed. "Just not here at Herrera Farms, I hope."

He stood to his full height and gazed down into her eyes. In the afternoon sunlight, his blue eyes looked beautiful and clear as Mom's expensive crystal. He reached out and brushed a strand of hair away from her cheek.

Startled, Mari stepped back. "What's next?"

"Another greenhouse. I plan to do them all. Then it'll be easy to police the perimeter and make sure a rabbit hasn't breached the barrier. If a bunny or squirrel breaks through, I can quickly repair the damage."

Mari breathed a sigh of relief. With Joel here to help, life seemed much easier. She could almost allow herself to sit back and let him take charge of what needed to be done. But that would be futile. He wouldn't stay long and then she would have to assume responsibility for the farm once more.

They worked in companionable silence for some time. Just before dinner, a chill wind blew past, carrying the scent of rain on the air.

"Storm's coming," Joel remarked.

"Thank goodness you got the cottage reroofed."

A deep laugh rumbled in his chest. "Were you afraid I'd have to stay in the house?"

"Of course not." Well, just a little, but she wasn't about to admit it.

"Don't worry, Mari. I'm not an ogre and I didn't come here to hurt you or your family."

"I know that."

He stood straight and dusted dirt from his big hands. His gaze locked with hers and she could tell from the solemn look in his eyes that he wasn't teasing anymore. "Do you really?"

His words sounded so forlorn that a lump of emotion formed in her throat. "Sure."

"I have friends here. Herrera Farms was the only place I could think of where I might find what I'm searching for. I never intended to cause you a problem."

She'd never thought of Joel being lonely, but she supposed the life he'd chosen didn't offer many real friends. "What are you searching for, Joel?"

"Peace." He didn't even hesitate.

"And you can't find that in Oakland?"

He shook his head. "I'm afraid not. Mom's gone now and

Oakland isn't who I am anymore. My friends there would try to drag me back into trouble, and I can't have that. I'm not proud of everything I've done in my life, but I don't want to hurt anyone, especially you."

Her throat tightened and a burning emotion she couldn't comprehend settled in her chest. "Joel, I—"

The bell up at the main house rang, heralding dinnertime. Mom always rang the bell so they would hear and know it was time to come in for a meal. Otherwise Mari tended to keep working and forgot to eat.

"Come on, I'm starved." Joel smiled as he brushed past her and reached for the staple gun to put it away with the other tools.

Mari drew away, her shoulder tingling where he had touched her. They walked to the house in silence. Though still early, the blue vapor lights came on, lighting the dim path as the sun slid behind the western hills.

When they arrived at the house, Joel jutted his chin toward the front porch. "You go on in. I'll be along shortly."

Without thinking anything about it, she stepped onto the porch and went inside, washing up for dinner. Joel soon joined her in the laundry room to wash his hands.

"I brought in the mail." He set a pile of letters and invoices on the washing machine beside the sink and Mari noticed the top envelope stamped "overdue."

She dried her hands and snapped up the mail, mortified that Joel had seen the overdue notice. She glanced at him, but found him staring at his hands as he lathered the bar of soap. He didn't acknowledge her, but his ears reddened and she knew he must have seen the late notice.

What business was it of his to fetch their mail?

"Why are you checking our mail?" She couldn't deny the demand in her voice.

"I'm expecting a letter."

"Oh." Why was she so testy? And why did it bother her so much that he'd seen the overdue notice? She didn't care what Joel Hunter thought of her and her family.

Yeah, right! And she didn't mind little cottontail rabbits eating all their plants, either.

Turning, she headed for the kitchen, barely noticing the pleasant aromas of homemade chimichangas and refried beans.

Dinner seemed a subdued affair. Elena offered a blessing on the food and they dug in, too hungry and tired to visit. Only Livi chatted nonstop, telling them about Jack Dalton, a boy from school who kept pulling her hair and trying to take her colored markers.

"Did you tell your teacher?" Mom asked.

"Nah, I don't want to be a tattletale." She looked at Joel. "I thought maybe you could come to school and make him stop. You chased off the boys who were bothering Mari."

"Um, I don't think that's such a good idea," Mari said. "Mom or I can go down to the school."

Joel cleared his voice and leaned an elbow on the table. "Usually when a boy picks on you, it's because he likes you."

Livi's mouth dropped open. "Really?"

Joel reached out and patted her cheek. "Sure. Try not to be so hard on him. He'll grow up and thank you for it some day."

Mari stared at Joel, hardly able to believe what she heard. Was this Joel's way of telling her that she'd been too hard on him when he'd yanked on her braids and tied her shoelaces together? Had he done those things because he liked her? What an odd way to show it, but who could understand the mind of a ten-year-old boy?

"Where's Matt?" Livi asked as she spooned beans and cheese into her mouth.

"Please don't talk with your mouth full. He's having dinner at Dallin's house and will be home later tonight," Mom said.

Joel peered at the door, his forehead creased with worry lines. Mari could tell that Matt's absence bothered him just as it did her.

Later they all pitched in to help with the dishes. Joel's deep laughter mingled with Livi's shrill screams as he playfully snapped a dish towel at her and chased her around the table.

Taking a jacket with her, Mari slipped outside to feed Max and sat in the swing on the porch. The cool air caused her to wrap her arms around herself as she inhaled the fragrant scent of damp sagebrush. A light rain began to fall and she zipped her jacket up to her chin before she curled her legs beneath her.

The porch light flicked on, gleaming dimly as Joel stepped outside. Mari bit back a sharp exhale of irritation, hoping he didn't notice her. With any luck, he'd just go out to the caretaker's cottage for the night and leave her alone.

He turned straight toward her, walking slow, his hands buried in his pockets. He leaned his hip against the porch railing, watching her. "Nice night."

"Uh-huh." She didn't want to talk right now.

"A bit chilly."

"Hmm."

"Mari, I don't mean to be nosy, but have you considered doing something about your financial problems?"

Yep, just as she thought, he'd seen the past due notice. Her face burned with anger and embarrassment. "No, I really like getting overdue notices in the mail."

Her voice sounded sarcastic and too sharp.

"I'm serious, Mari."

"So am I. It's none of your business, Joel. Leave it alone." She stood to go inside.

He blocked her path with his athletic shoulders and held out a hand, as if to placate her. "I know you're right. I don't mean to upset you, but hear me out. Have you considered a fundraiser of some kind?"

"A fundraiser?"

"Yeah, like the cookie dough or bars of chocolate the kids sell in the local schools to raise funds for new computers and basketball uniforms. Only we could do it with flowers. If you give the school a fair percentage, they'll be more likely to go for our fundraiser." His breath came out in little puffs of air as he spoke, indicating a drop in temperature.

She'd never thought of a flower fundraiser, but she had to admit the thought tantalized her mind. Her body relaxed as she folded her arms and prepared herself to listen to his idea. "What did you have in mind?"

"What if we call it the Herrera Farms Spring Flower Fundraiser? We could make up some order forms and flyers and take them to the local schools. You already know almost everyone in town and whom we should speak with. The kids could take the order forms home to their parents and friends, who surely plan to buy plants for their gardens. We could give the schools a cut of the profits and still make a truckload of money. As long as you think we can come up with the bedding plants in time."

Why hadn't she thought of this before? Joel had always been clever, though he'd wasted much of his intelligence by thinking up pranks to play on others rather than focusing on more productive endeavors. "You know, it just might work. It could turn us a tidy little profit to help get us out of debt."

"Yeah, and next year, we'd have more time to plan ahead. We could expand to the schools in Reno, if you like. By then, we'd need to hire more people to help with the project, but we'd be able to afford it. I think if we work hard, we could make it a great success." His eyes gleamed with the challenge.

Mari pinched her chin with her fingers as she thought this

over. It would take a lot of work to put it together, but the dividends could make the endeavor worthwhile. "Okay. Where do we start?"

"First thing in the morning, I'll get busy planting more seed cups of petunias, marigolds, pansies and tomatoes. Maybe your mom can help create some order forms and flyers."

And so they made their plans. Mari got a notepad and they stayed up late, estimating how many more bedding and vegetable plants they might need and planning delivery dates and inexpensive marketing strategies.

By the time they parted ways, Mari fell into bed exhausted, but exhilarated. Finally they had a plan of how to get themselves out of the mountain of debt that had plagued them since Dad died.

She wondered how she'd ever gotten along without Joel's help. The loneliness that had settled in her heart since Dad's passing seemed much lighter and she even felt excited about this new project. If Joel was right, their Spring Flower Fundraiser could make a big difference in their economic life. It might even earn enough money for her to pay tuition to take one or two classes at the university next fall.

Then another thought struck her. Could she trust Joel? He'd been arrested for shoplifting twice. Confusion filled her mind and everything within her rebelled. She'd learned from sad experience not to trust this man and to question his motives. But that was a long time ago when he was a kid. He'd never stolen from her father even though he'd stolen from the stores in town. Would he try to steal from her?

She lay awake, too tired to sleep. One thought tangled in her mind. What was so undesirable about Oakland that Joel didn't want to return? She understood about his bad crowd of friends and hoped it was that simple. And yet she couldn't shake the feeling he wasn't telling her everything.

Chapter Nine

"The high school hasn't changed much," Joel remarked as he pulled into the parking lot and killed the motor to the van. He gazed at the redbrick structure. A large marquee with a growling cougar leaping over the letter *G* sat in the middle of the front lawn.

"What did you expect? We're a small town and life plods along the same as always, most of the time." Mari reached for a packet of flyers and order forms for the flower fundraiser.

"Most of the time?" Joel pondered her profile. She'd pulled her hair back in a ponytail today. He studied the familiar slant of her jaw, the slope of her impertinent nose and stubborn chin. The fullness of her lips and eyelashes that needed no mascara to darken or lengthen them. And when she smiled, the sun, moon and stars all became one blinding light.

"Yeah, most of the time, until someone like you comes to town and disrupts everyone's routine." She gave him an impish smile so bright it made his jaw ache.

"What'd I do?"

Picking up the box of packets, she opened the door and got out. He followed, hurrying to catch up to her brisk stride as she walked toward the double doors at the entrance of the school. "Nothing. Let's just keep it that way."

He shook his head, wondering at her innuendo. "Am I being accused of something?"

"No, but you have a reputation to live down." She fumbled with the box as she reached to open the door. He tried to take the box from her arms, but she jerked it back. Instead, he pulled the door wide so she could precede him inside.

As she juggled the box, she dropped the envelope of flyers on the doormat and he picked it up. She reached to take it from him, but he held on tight, staring deep into her eyes. "I don't want a second chance. I want a first chance."

She paused, her eyes crinkling at the corners. "What do you mean? My father gave you hundreds of chances."

Joel thought of all the times Señor Herrera had bailed him out of trouble. The long drives home as the elder man talked about changing his life for the better. "But you never did."

She flushed a pretty shade of pink, her lips pursing with disapproval. "I never gave up on you, Joel. Neither did Dad."

She took the envelope before sliding it into the box. As she turned to continue down the hall, he clasped her arm gently, forcing her to meet his gaze. "I know you resented me at times because I took your father's time away from you. But if I hadn't had your dad, I'd have had no one, Mari."

"You had your mother."

He studied the dented trash can sitting beside the brick wall. "I let her down. I hurt her more than I can say. I always loved Mom, but she had no control over me. I never cared how much I hurt her, until—"

"Until what?"

"Until she was gone. I would have died without your father."

Her brow crinkled in confusion, her whisper echoing in the empty hallway. "What do you mean?"

A remorseful pain jerked at his heart. If she only knew how foolish he'd been after that last summer he'd spent working at the farm, or how much danger it had put him in. Danger that had cost another man his life. Joel longed to tell her about it. To confide in someone. Anyone. But he couldn't right now. Maybe never.

"Mari, do you realize almost every one of my Oakland friends who I ran with in the gang are now dead?" His throat ached with tears he couldn't shed. Tears for those friends he couldn't save. He'd been the lucky one...if you could call prison lucky. He'd had someone like Señor Herrera, sending weekly letters, calling to make sure he was okay. Reminding him that he had a Father in Heaven who loved him. His old friends had no one. Not one living soul who cared if they lived or died.

He turned and continued down the hall.

"Joel," she called and he paused, turning to look at her, his insides churning with tension.

"What aren't you telling me? What happened to you?" she asked.

He blinked, unable to meet her gaze. "There's nothing I want to tell you right now. Not until you trust me. But believe me when I say I've seen enough trouble to last a lifetime and I'd die happy if I never saw it again."

As he pivoted on his heels and walked away, she stood there staring after him. He could feel her eyes boring a hole in his back.

Mr. Thorndike, the school principal, greeted them in the main office. Dressed in a white shirt and tie, the man shook Joel's hand. Joel hesitated, surprised at the open smile on the man's face. He'd never gone to school here and so he'd never had any run-ins with the principal. It felt refreshing to meet the man's eyes without feeling a pang of guilt.

"Thanks for bringing the packets by," Mr. Thorndike said. "The coach just finished teaching his history class and is expecting you in the gymnasium. He's already told his football team about the fundraiser." He chuckled. "Having macho football players sell flowers didn't go over too well at first, but Coach helped them understand it'll mean new equipment they need."

Mari showed a smile of relief. "Thank you. We're glad to help out."

As Mari headed toward the school gym, Joel trailed behind, relying on her to lead the way. Again, he tried to take the box from her.

"No, thank you," she murmured.

"You're still stubborn as ever. Still determined to do everything on your own."

She shot him a glare to curdle blood, but made no response. From the tightening of her mouth, he could tell his words bothered her. Her independence and feisty spirit were just two things he loved about her, and yet he wished she'd soften a little and ask for his help now and then.

When they reached the gym, Joel pushed the exit bar and held the door wide for Mari. The door slammed behind them, echoing as they stepped inside. Vibrant red and green lines on the shiny floors marked the boundaries and key around the basket hoop. The air smelled of lacquer. The custodian must have refinished the floors recently.

A man with sandy brown hair stood on the opposite side of the gym, his back turned toward them as he jotted notes on a clipboard. Without hesitation, Mari walked past the bleachers. Joel followed. Hearing their footsteps, the man lifted his head and turned. Joel stopped dead in his tracks, a sickening thud pounding his chest.

Troy Banks. Mari's old boyfriend from high school. Now

the football coach at Gardenville High. Because of Mari, Joel and Troy had despised each other, which resulted in a fist-fight that left Troy laid out on the pavement and Joel with bleeding knuckles.

"Hi, Troy," Mari said. "You remember Joel Hunter, don't you?"

Joel contemplated the silver whistle hanging on a lanyard around Troy's neck. He felt like he'd just been sucker punched. How could Mari act so composed? Why hadn't she told him Troy was the coach and now worked at the high school?

"Uh, yeah. How could I forget? What's he doing here?" Troy's eyes narrowed and his mouth tightened.

"Joel works for us out at the farm. It was his idea to have the fundraiser, so I'm letting him head it up." Mari spoke rather fast, her voice elevated slightly. As if that would help Troy and Joel forget the bad blood between them.

Troy's mouth dropped open and he looked dumbfounded. Likewise, Joel stared at Troy, completely unprepared for the sudden fury that billowed up inside him like a storm cloud before a hurricane. This was his old nemesis and Joel's heart boiled with green envy. The anger took him completely off guard. The last thing he wanted to do was act like they were friends. Joel had made a vow to follow a path leading to the Lord, but now he couldn't quite remember that promise. He'd sought forgiveness from the Lord. Now he couldn't seem to grant the same concession to Troy. But he must! If he ever had any hopes of redeeming himself, he must.

Joel forced himself to extend his hand. "Hi, Troy. It's been a long time. How you doing?"

Troy clenched his jaw and diverted his gaze. He held the clipboard with his left hand, wearing a thick pinky ring. He brushed his free hand down the front of his white polo shirt, as if to wipe some invisible grime off his palm. "I'm fine."

Joel lowered his hand, rebuffed by a guy he'd knocked senseless nine years ago. For a fleeting moment, the urge to put his fist through Troy's teeth almost overwhelmed Joel, but he resisted. One of them had to take the first step to forgiveness. Why not him?

Feeling a surge of spiritual strength, Joel focused on the promise he'd made to Mari's father and to the Lord. Never again would he react with violence. Never would he allow himself to be in a situation he couldn't control.

"What are you doing with this convict?" Troy jerked his thumb in Joel's direction.

The blood drained from Joel's face, replaced by sickening rage. So fast and stunning that Joel almost reacted before he could stop himself.

This forgiveness thing was proving harder than he thought. He doubted Troy realized how close to home he'd come with his offhanded remark. Joel wanted to pound something. Troy's face would have suited fine. He clenched his fists and stepped forward, then clamped an iron will on his emotions.

Thankfully, Mari interceded. She thrust the box of packets at Troy, who dropped his clipboard with a clatter. Mari ignored Troy's startled expression and placed her hand on Joel's arm. Her gentle touch soothed him instantly, like a rainbow after a summer rain shower.

Mari glowered at the two men, her dark eyes flashing fire. "Knock it off, Troy. You two roosters never stop picking at each other. But it's time to put aside your differences and act like grown-ups."

Troy didn't seem cowed. He reached up and rubbed his chin, as if remembering the night Joel nearly broke his jaw.

"I think I'll wait over here while you two talk about the fundraiser." Joel stepped away, going to sit on the first row of bleachers. He leaned forward, bracing his elbows on his knees, his hands clasped together as he rested his chin against his knuckles. Even from this distance, the big, empty room carried Troy's harsh whisper like a shout.

"What are you doing with him, Mari? He's a loser. Why'd you hire him?"

Joel's insides clenched. He tried to tell himself that Troy was wrong. He wasn't a loser. Not anymore. But he had been. Now he wanted to be so much more. If people would just give him a second chance.

"That's not your business. If you don't want to participate in the fundraiser, we can take our business elsewhere." She reached to take the box of packets from Troy, but he pulled it back.

"No, we'll participate. But don't let that guy handle any of our money. You can't trust him, Mari. He'll steal you blind." Troy jutted his chin toward Joel.

Unable to sit there and listen to more slurs, Joel stood and walked out of the gym. When he hit the door, he heard Mari's stern voice behind him.

"Now you've hurt his feelings."

"Oh, the poor baby. I hurt his itty-bitty feelings," Troy quipped.

"You're not kids anymore. Try to act like a grown man, will you?"

The door slammed behind Joel, shutting off the sound of Mari's voice. Joel leaned against the cold stone wall, closing his eyes tight. Everything within him rebelled. He didn't like Mari defending him like he was a little kid who couldn't stand up for himself. Yet he was determined not to be baited into a fight by Troy Banks. For some reason, her words rankled inside him, leaving a bitter taste in his mouth. Then he thought of how much the Lord had come to mean to him and he let go of his rage.

Within ten minutes, Mari joined him. Joel pushed himself

away from the wall, feeling completely calm again. "Everything okay?"

Funny how his anger dissipated with his concern for her. He didn't like Troy upsetting her.

"Yes. Fine." Her clipped words invited no further conversation.

He watched over the top of her head as Troy exited the opposite door, tossing a glare at Joel before he sauntered down the hall in the opposite direction.

"I'm sure glad that's over with. So much for you no longer being a troublemaker." Mari breathed a giant exhale as she hurried toward the parking lot.

Joel followed, his long stride keeping up with her jog. "I didn't do anything wrong."

She didn't pause. "But you wanted to."

What could he say to that? It was true. Old habits were hard to break, and he'd been fighting all his life. "But I didn't. Give me some credit."

"You're right. You behaved better than Troy."

"Did Banks agree to have his team participate in the fundraiser?"

"Of course. He needs new football equipment and funds are tight with the school district."

Out in the parking lot, she slowed to a walk. Joel's arm brushed against hers. "Thanks for the warning."

"What warning?"

"Exactly. Why didn't you tell me that we were coming here to meet with Troy Banks?"

"Would advance warning have made it easier?"

No. "It might have helped prepare me more, so I didn't have the urge to knock the guy out again."

She snorted and shook her head. "Two roosters still picking at each other."

He opened his mouth to respond, but thought better of it. Nah! He didn't want to hurt Mari. More than anything, he longed to leave the past behind.

Without waiting for him, she jerked open the door to the van and climbed inside. Joel followed, snapping his seat belt in place before he started the ignition.

"You know, Joel, if you're going to live and work here in Gardenville, you're gonna come across a lot of people like Royce, Millie and Troy. People have long memories and they know who you are. You can't go around wanting to rip the heads off of anyone who brings up your past."

"I don't have a problem with most people, but Banks and I never got along."

"It's time to let your rivalry go."

Knowing she was right didn't make it any easier. "Still trying to save me, Mari?"

She screwed up her lips and crossed her eyes in a googly expression. "Sometimes I think you're beyond saving."

He laughed, glad to see she hadn't completely lost her sense of humor.

"At times, you make me crazy," she confided. "But don't let Troy get to you. He has his own demons to deal with."

She was right, of course. He was a man now, with a solid faith in God and clearly defined goals for his future. If only he could convince Mari that she should be included in those plans, he'd be the happiest of men.

He steered through traffic and drove downtown before pulling into the Hamburger Shack drive-in.

"What are you doing?" Mari asked.

"Getting us lunch. You must be hungry." He rolled down the window.

A teenage girl wearing a name badge that read "Jenny" and a red-and-white striped hat slid the drive-through window open and leaned her elbows on the ledge. "Hi. What can I get you?"

"We can't afford this, Joel," Mari whispered.

"Don't you worry about it," he returned. "I got my first paycheck today and I'm buying."

As he turned and smiled at Jenny, he hoped Mari didn't argue or take it personally. It'd been a long time since he'd had a burger or fry sauce and he wanted this simple pleasure. "We'll have two cheeseburgers, drinks and curly fries with fry sauce."

"Sure." Jenny cracked the gum inside her mouth, then slid the window closed.

"Thank you for not fighting with Troy."

Joel lifted one eyebrow. "You're welcome. You worried for me? Or for Banks?"

Her forehead crinkled. "I'm worried about my family."

"And here I was hoping you cared about me, too."

She threw him an impatient glare. "I really hate it when you make fun of me, Joel. Sometimes your sense of humor isn't funny."

He kept his expression completely serious. "I'd never laugh at you, Mari. I'd rather laugh with you."

"I'm not laughing, Joel."

He rested both hands on the steering wheel, squeezing hard. "It's obvious you don't laugh enough."

"I laugh."

"Not much since I've been here. You used to laugh all the time. Remember that last summer I was here when we found those baby kittens after their mother had been killed by a car on the freeway?"

Her lips curved in a smile. "How could I forget? You helped me bottle-feed them for several weeks so they wouldn't die. You were so kind."

Kind? He wasn't so sure about that, but he never meant anyone harm. He'd been so thoughtless with his life. Living on the edge of reason. No thought for the consequences of his actions or what the future might hold. "I'll tell you what. I'll continue to control my temper if you give me a little warning next time you know we're going to meet with someone I had trouble with in my past."

She bit her bottom lip and her face softened. "Deal."

Now! He should tell her about his past now, while she seemed in a forgiving mood. Maybe she'd understand. Maybe he could finally be at peace.

Jenny slid the window open and handed him two drinks. "You need napkins?"

"Yes, please."

The white paper sack crackled as the girl stuffed several napkins in and handed it to Joel. He passed it right over to Mari before shifting the van into gear and pulling forward. He parked at the side of the drive-through and killed the motor. While he waited, Mari dug into the bag and pulled out their food. She handed him a burger and they ate in stilted silence for several minutes. He'd been on the verge of telling her the truth, but now the momentum seemed lost.

A dribble of ketchup ran onto his hand and without a word, she handed him a napkin. He couldn't deny a feeling of comfort as she anticipated his needs and answered them without being asked. Whether she liked it or not, they often seemed to know what the other person was thinking.

"Thanks for defending me back there. With Banks, I mean," he said.

"Uh-huh."

"Why did you?"

She bit into her hamburger before releasing an exasperated sigh. "I don't know. Maybe I should go back and change my mind and tell Troy he's right and let you two fight it out in the school yard like a couple of thugs."

The vision of him and Troy Banks rolling around on the blacktop while they tried to knock each other's brains out made him laugh. Mari smiled, too.

"Ah, there you are," he said. "I knew you couldn't have gone far away."

He loved the way her eyes crinkled and lit up from inside. In response, she popped a curly fry into her mouth and shook her head. A perverse smile remained on her lips. As if she found humor in their conversation, but refused to admit it.

After they ate, they drove to the elementary school where they planned to meet with the principal. As they got out of the van and Joel pocketed the keys, he turned to Mari. "Anyone here from my past that I need to watch out for?"

"Yes. I think the head custodian is Malcolm Knight, the man who caught you painting graffiti on the school walls by the playground."

Joel resisted a cringe. "I was twelve years old. You think he'll recognize me?"

She shrugged. "Who knows? You've changed a lot over the years."

Great! More feathers to ruffle.

As they entered the school building, Joel peered around, hoping they didn't encounter Malcolm. They walked down the spacious hallway to the principal's office, passing classrooms filled with children sitting at their desks. A clatter caused Joel to turn and he saw an elderly man wearing olive green pants and shirt buttoned at the collar. The man dipped a mop into an industrial-sized bucket, sloshed it up and down twice, then lifted the mop and set it onto the floor with a wet slap.

"Here we go again," Joel muttered beneath his breath.

"What did you say?" Mari asked.

"Nothing."

Malcolm swirled the mop around on the floor, whistling as he worked. Joel urged Mari forward, hoping to bypass any confrontations.

Mari turned and saw the custodian and her eyes widened before she whirled and gaped at Joel in horror. "Joel—"

"Relax, Mari. There won't be any trouble."

And that's when Joel realized what he said was true. He'd made promises he intended to keep. He couldn't go back in time and undo all the wrongs he'd done. But with the Lord's help, he could overcome the past by making a more powerful present. In fact, he owed this man an apology.

Malcolm lifted his head, a smile on his face. "Hello."

"Hi there," Joel returned with caution, seeing the lack of recognition in Malcolm's eyes. Even so, a sick feeling of guilt washed over Joel. Sudden regret swamped him as he thought of the work he'd created for this man all those years earlier. Cleaning the brick walls of the school couldn't have been easy.

Joel stepped forward and Mari tried to pull him back. "Don't, Joel—"

He kept going, extending his hand to Malcolm, who took it. In a sincere voice, Joel reminded Malcolm of what he'd done and begged the custodian's forgiveness.

Malcolm rubbed his chin and shook his balding head in confusion. "Son, I forgot all about that. I can't tell you how many times I've had to clean that wall. But you're the first one to ever apologize for it. That alone has made my work worthwhile."

Mari's mouth dropped open in surprise. Joel felt as though a weight had just been lifted from his chest, lightening his step as they continued to the principal's office.

Mrs. Snider, the school secretary, had them wait while she informed Mr. Calder, the principal, that they were here. An elderly man with shocking white hair came out of the back office and greeted them.

"Hi, Mari. How's your mother doing?"

Mari shook Mr. Calder's hand. "She's fine. Thanks for agreeing to see us. This is Joel Hunter, my associate. The fundraiser is his project. He's got some great ideas we'd like to share with you."

Associate! She sounded so formal and businesslike, yet Joel couldn't help feeling pleased by her acknowledgment.

Mr. Calder gave Joel a friendly smile and shook his hand. "Come on into my office and let's talk."

He opened a door and indicated they should precede him. Inside the cramped office, they sat in front of a small desk cluttered with papers and waited for Mr. Calder to settle himself in his chair.

"We're interested in buying some new playground equipment. What's your suggestion for this fundraiser?" Mr. Calder clasped his hands and leaned forward on his desk, his gaze piercing Joel to his spinal cord.

Joel explained about the order forms. "Your students will take a packet home and sell flowers to all their family and neighbors, just like they would sell candy bars or cookie dough."

Mari handed a packet to Mr. Calder, who perused the order forms and brochures while he listened. Joel explained the pricing and percentages, his confidence increasing.

Mr. Calder nodded, his eyes lighting up with interest. "The percentage the school receives is quite generous. Usually we get quite a bit less on other fundraisers we participate in. And the children should be pleased by the incentives."

"We believe it's important to help our schools," Mari said.

Mr. Calder smiled wide. By the time Joel and Mari left the school, they had an agreement for participation from the school principal. Every child at Garden Elementary School was going to take home a packet.

As they climbed into the van, Mari let out a deep sigh of appreciation. "This has been a productive day. I think this idea of yours is actually going to work. Thank you, Joel."

Her gratitude caused butterflies to swarm inside his stomach. She gave him a smile so bright he had to swallow. He reached across the seat and squeezed her arm before he thought to stop himself. This time, she didn't pull away. "You're welcome, sunshine."

Sunshine. The name he'd called her throughout their teenage years. He half expected her to tell him not to call her that, but felt heartened when she didn't say a word.

Their gazes locked for several pounding moments. The silence lengthened and Mari's smile dropped like stone. She withdrew her arm. "We better get home. We've got a lot of work to do."

Her words broke the magic moment. A warm feeling that had nothing to do with the sunny day filled his soul. A feeling that he'd accomplished something wonderful and unique. For the first time in his life, he'd blessed someone else's life instead of causing them pain and anguish.

Fierce joy swept him and he couldn't explain the warmth engulfing his heart. Like coming home after being deployed to a war zone for eight years.

Chapter Ten

On Wednesday morning, Joel came into the house for breakfast at seven-fifteen, like any other day. With a rap of his knuckles on the front door, he entered the living room. The scent of chorizo and chili peppers filled the air. He hung his jacket on the peg by the door and turned.

"Happy birthday!"

Joel almost jumped out of his skin. Mari and her family stood in the kitchen, a pile of gaily wrapped gifts sitting in the middle of the table.

"Happy birthday to you. Happy birthday to you," they sang in unison. "Happy birthday, dear Joel. Happy birthday to you."

"Boom, boom, boom, and many more," Livi ended the song.

They all erupted into laughter.

"Wow! This was unexpected." The heat of pleased embarrassment flushed Joel's skin. When he awoke that morning, he'd decided to forget it was his birthday. For years, he'd had no one to remember, except Elena and Frank, who always sent him a card. No one else seemed to know he existed. Throughout his life, holidays had never been much fun.

"*Feliz cumpleaños.*" Elena hugged him.

His gaze rested on Mari and she gave him a dazzling smile. "Happy birthday, Joel."

"Thanks, sunshine." Three simple words and she'd just made his year.

Elena handed him a present. He stared at the big red bow, his pulse accelerating with anticipation. He couldn't remember the last time someone gave him a gift.

His voice roughened. "You didn't need to get me anything."

Elena squeezed his arm. "It's your birthday. You're part of our family and we always celebrate."

Part of the family. Just what he'd always wanted to hear. A place where people loved and accepted him, no matter his weaknesses and failings.

As he looked into Elena's eyes, he searched for condescension, but found only sincerity. She really meant what she said.

They sat at the table, everyone smiling and urging him to open his gifts. His hands trembled as he tore back the bright paper. Elena gave him a new pair of blue jeans and tennis shoes. The powerful scent from the rubber soles filled his nostrils.

"I hope they're the right size," she said.

He chuckled, thinking about the quarter-sized holes in the soles of his current pair of shoes. "They are. I sure need them. Thanks, señora."

"You're welcome, Joel."

"This is from me." Livi slid a small gift in front of him.

Everyone waited expectantly as he unwrapped the package. In his hand, he held a block of wood painted blue with Livi's school picture glued in the center and the words "I love you, from Livi" etched beneath in black magic marker.

"I sanded and painted it myself," she explained. "I made it so you'll never forget me, even if you leave us."

He froze. Leave them? The thought left him stunned. When he'd come here, he'd never expected to stay long. Never expected anything. He'd hoped for a fresh start and some peace of mind. That was all.

Or was it?

He glanced at Mari, wishing he could stay at Herrera Farms forever.

"I love it, honey. I'll keep it always." He hugged the girl and she beamed with pleasure.

"This is from me." Matt pushed a flat gift toward him.

The present had no bow, the wrapping taped with uneven edges. Joel held it up and chuckled. "I take it you wrapped this yourself."

"Yeah. Livi wouldn't wrap it for me." Matt tossed his sister a glare, then gave a sheepish smile.

Joel tore open an edge of the gift wrap and revealed a leather wallet and a CD of country-western music. He found himself wishing it were orchestra music instead. He'd come to love classical music. It reminded him of Mari and everything lovely and good life had to offer.

He blinked, thinking of the ragged wallet in his back pocket. Obviously Matt had noticed he needed a new one. The boy's thoughtfulness left him wishing he'd been as considerate when he'd been Matt's age. "Thanks, buddy. I'll put it to good use."

"And this is from me." Mari pressed a wrapped box with a white bow into his hands.

A feeling of exhilaration swept him. Mari had given him a gift. He didn't care what was inside the box. Just the fact that she'd given him something went straight to his heart.

He studied the blue paper for the longest time, soaking it in. Planning to remember this day as long as he lived.

"Aren't you gonna open it?" she asked.

His gaze locked with hers and he wished she could see the love in his heart. "Yeah."

He tore the wrapping away and lifted the lid with all the

expectancy of a kid on Christmas morning. A battery-operated quartz wristwatch with a silver expandable band rested inside. Not too expensive, but very useful.

"I noticed you didn't have a watch and figured you needed one as you went through your workday," Mari explained.

He loved it, for the simple reason that she had given it to him. A lump hardened in his throat. "It's great. Thank you so much."

"You're welcome." She stood and walked over to the kitchen sink, breaking the magical moment.

"Mari's gonna make a birthday cake today with vanilla ice cream for after dinner tonight," Livi said.

Mari was making a birthday cake. For him.

"That sounds great. Thanks so much."

Mari's lips curved in a genuine smile. "No problem. I just hope you like it. I'm not as good a cook as Mom."

"Nonsense," Elena objected. "I've taught you everything I know."

Listening to their friendly banter, a hollow ache settled in Joel's chest. How he wished this was his family for keeps. He'd do almost anything if he could make Mari love him. If only he could stay.

The next evening, Mari came into the house to help fix dinner. The tempting aroma of refried beans hung in the air. Even after all these years, Mom still made them from scratch, cooked in a pan on the stovetop.

"*Hola, niña!*" Mom greeted her with a wide smile. "How did it go with the meetings out at the schools?"

"Fine. They all agreed to participate." After Mari washed her hands, she reached into the cupboard for the dishes and set the table.

"Aren't you glad Joel's here?" Mom said. "He's helped out

so much around the place and came up with the fundraiser idea. Isn't he a blessing in our lives?"

"Yes, he's been a blessing." Which confused Mari. She couldn't get used to this new side of Joel. Maybe he really had changed.

As she compared the old Joel with the new, she poured milk into Livi's glass. And then a thought struck her. What did the Lord have in mind by bringing Joel here? She shook her head, wondering at the purposes of God. Was it possible that not only did Joel need them, but they also needed him?

"Where's Matt tonight?"

Mom sighed with resignation. "Doing homework over at Dallin's house."

Mari understood Mom's hesitation. Being with Dallin meant no homework would be done. Instead, she and Mom would be worried until Matt got home later that night, safe and sound. Mari remembered feeling this same way so many times when Joel came to stay with them in the summers. She'd watched her father pace the floor, making phone calls to find out where Joel might be. Now and then, the phone would ring and Dad would have to run out the door to the police station to pick up Joel for some illegal prank.

In spite of the past, Mari couldn't help being relieved Joel was here now. Before he'd shown up, she'd prayed to God for help. That some way they'd be able to pay their bills and keep the farm. That she'd have the strength to carry the workload in front of her.

And then Joel Hunter came to stay.

As if knowing she was thinking about him, Joel walked into the house. A burst of chilly air followed him. He closed the door and took a deep, relaxing breath. He'd doffed his muddy boots on the front porch and stood in the doorway in his stocking feet, his cheeks red from the cool night air. As his gaze rested on Mari, she dropped the forks to the table with a clatter, mesmerized by the crooked curve of his smile.

A smile for her.

Mari couldn't explain the sweet foggy feeling she felt at that moment or why seeing him made her unexplainably happy. As if her world were better and she and her family could handle anything life threw at them.

"Hi," he spoke softly.

"Hello," she returned, feeling silly for her fanciful thoughts. This was Joel Hunter, trouble incarnate. But even she believed people could change and deserved a second chance. Even people like Joel.

"Come in, Joel," Mom called. "It's a cold night. You must be frozen."

"You think we'll have frost?" Now why did Mari ask him that? She'd always handled such dilemmas on her own, but here she was consulting with Joel.

He removed his gloves and jacket, hanging them on the hook by the door. "The weather man predicts low temperatures tonight, but I checked all the heaters to make sure they're working properly. We shouldn't lose any of our plants."

Our plants. As if he had a vested interest in the farm. Part of her wanted to take offense, but she just couldn't. For so long, she'd wished someone would share the worry. As usual, he'd saved Mari some additional work. She wouldn't have to go out again tonight. "Thank you for doing that."

"My pleasure." He reached for a bowl of cherry tomatoes and popped one into his mouth.

"Joel!"

Livi came running from the back of the house and launched herself at him. He went down on his haunches, meeting her at eye level as she flung her arms around his neck for a tight squeeze. "Hi, sweetheart. How's my favorite girl?"

"Fine. I have two pages of math to do. You promised to help me with my homework." The child pulled away, showing a toothless grin.

"That I did." He stood and flashed a smile at Elena. "Have we got time before supper?"

"*Sí,* we're having tamales."

Joel's eyes locked with Mari's and his grin widened. He gave a short bark of laughter. Her cheeks burned like road flares when she remembered him calling her a hot taco.

Mom shot her a quizzical look, but Mari busied herself with setting the table. Taking Livi's hand, Joel walked into the living room and sat beside the child on the couch before bending his dark head over her homework.

As Mari sliced carrots for a salad, she heard the soothing tone of Joel's deep voice while he patiently explained division to her little sister. Before Joel, homework time used to be a yelling match.

Joel had, indeed, blessed their lives. Because of his efforts, he'd saved them thousands of dollars in repair charges. The minutes ticked by as she worked in the kitchen, feeling oddly calm and settled. Feeling as though Joel had fit the broken puzzle pieces of their lives back together.

"Dinner is ready. Come and eat," Elena called.

"Good timing," Joel said. "Livi's finished with her homework."

"Mrs. Jenkins is sure gonna be surprised when I get an A in math," Livi said as she ran to take her seat at the kitchen table.

The girl hummed to herself and Mari gave Joel a smile of thanks. "You sure work magic with her. Whenever I try to help with her homework, she usually ends up in tears."

"I'm glad to help."

The tantalizing aromas of tamales, beans and peppers filled

the air. After giving thanks for their meal, they dug in, the comfortable conversation turning to their activities that day.

The phone rang and Elena answered on the cordless. "Hi, son. We're just having dinner and would love to see you. I can save you a plate. You coming home soon?"

She paused for a few moments, listening to the receiver. "I see. Did you have something to eat?"

Another pause.

"Yes, Joel is here. Is everything okay?" She waited for his response. "Okay, let me get him for you."

She handed the phone to Joel. "It's Matt. He says he has a guy question for you."

Joel sat forward on his chair and took the phone before pressing it to his ear. "Yeah, what's up?"

Mari watched Joel's expression, straining to hear his conversation. He stared at the beige linoleum, not meeting her eyes.

"Is Matt coming home for dinner?" Mari asked her mother.

"No, he said he's already eaten with Dallin."

"Give me twenty minutes." Joel hung up the phone, set it aside, then picked up his fork to finish his dinner.

"What's going on?" Mari asked.

"Nothing much. He's just having some car trouble. I told him I'd drive into town and help." He appeared casual, but Mari couldn't help feeling that something wasn't quite right.

Joel scooped the last few bites of food into his mouth, then scraped his chair back from the table. As he reached for his jacket on the peg by the door, he regarded Elena. "Is it okay if I borrow the van for a while? Matt's truck is out of gasoline."

"Sure." Elena smiled as she took a bite of salad.

Wait a minute! Mari had given Matt some gas money this morning and he'd gone into town to fill up the truck. How could it be empty already?

"I think I'll come with you." Mari stood and followed Joel to the front door, grabbing her purse and jacket along the way.

He hesitated, a frown curving his mouth. "I think I can handle it. Maybe you should stay here and get some rest."

"Nope, I'd like to ride along."

He didn't argue, but took her coat and held it while she slipped her arms into the sleeves.

"Can I come?" Livi called.

"No," all the adults answered in unison.

"You can stay and help me clean up the dishes," Mom said.

"Ah."

Mom came from behind and wrapped her arms around the child to give her a big hug and kiss her cheek. "But now your homework is finished, you get to watch TV before bedtime."

"Hooray!" Live hopped up, then gathered her dishes to carry over to the sink.

"See you all later. Drive safely," Mom called.

Mari stepped out on the porch with Joel, the brisk night air cutting through her. She zipped her jacket up to her chin, able to see her breath on the air.

Joel stuffed his arms into the sleeves of his coat as they headed for the van. "You know you really don't need to come along."

Mari didn't break stride. "Cut the baloney, Joel. What's Matt done this time?"

They got into the van and Joel started the vehicle before turning the heater on high. "Okay, I'll tell you, but try not to get upset. Matt was drag racing, hit a neighbor's mailbox and put it through the windshield."

"What! Why didn't you say so?"

"I didn't want to upset your mom." He turned on the head-lights and pulled out of the dark driveway before heading toward the main road.

"Is Matt okay?"

In the shadowed interior of the truck, Joel's eyes gleamed with purpose. "Other than an attack of the stupids, he's just fine. No one was hurt, thankfully."

Mari groaned, covering her face with one hand. "Oh, Matt. How do you plan to keep Mom from finding out?"

Joel accelerated. "Right now, my goal is to get the mailbox out of the windshield and get Matt and the truck home safely without the cops finding out. They'll throw him in jail for drag racing."

"You mean the police don't know?"

"There's only one sheriff and deputy in town. They're probably safe at home with their own families, unless some-one heard the noise and called them."

"Whose mailbox did he hit?"

"The Sutherlands'."

Mari grit her teeth, trying to remain calm. On the graveled road, a rabbit darted in front of them, its eyes gleaming in the headlights. The animal scurried to safety in the sagebrush. Joel didn't even flinch. He kept driving, slow and steady.

In town, they passed down Main Street, the shops and gas station dark with not a single person in sight. As they headed toward the Sutherlands' house on the eastern outskirts of town, Mari fretted about her brother.

"When I get Matt home, I'm gonna let him have it," Mari steamed. "He's gonna get himself killed. He causes Mom and I nothing but heartache. He doesn't care who he hurts. I'm fed up with his nonsense. Maybe he should leave our house."

"Would you worry any less about him if he left?"

"No, in fact I'd worry more."

"Then stop that kind of talk. You can't ever give up on him, Mari. He's your brother."

She threw him an irritated glare. "I know, but right now, I'd like to strangle him."

"Maybe I can help."

"Strangle him?"

"No, I had something else in mind."

"I don't doubt it." Her voice sounded cynical. "This is just the type of trouble you used to get into. I'm sure you know just what to do to make the situation better."

A brief flash of hurt crossed his face. She stared out the window, feeling angry and childish. She had no right to take out her frustration on Joel. He hadn't done anything wrong. "I'm sorry, Joel. I just don't know what to do with Matt or how to help him."

"I have a suggestion." His soothing voice made her look at him.

"Okay, I'm all ears. Tell me what you have in mind." She couldn't believe she was asking his advice, but if anyone could understand Matt, it would be Joel.

"I know you're upset and you have a right to be. But right now, Matt needs us. He's on the edge of losing himself and he can't even see that he's about to fall and hit the cliffs. If we handle this wrong, we might give him the shove to push him over. But if we're careful, we might be able to make him see that it's not too late and he has a reason to turn his life around."

"I understand, but how? How can we make him see that what he's doing could ruin his life?"

His shadowed face tensed, becoming more angular, more solid and strong. "With all the things I've been through, I know I can scare Matt straight."

Mari wondered what Joel had been through to give him the experience to scare Matt. Part of her couldn't stand to let go and turn this situation over to Joel. There was too much at stake. And yet deep inside, she knew he could help. Peace of the Spirit told her if she let Joel handle this, everything would be okay.

"What are you gonna say to Matt?" She couldn't help asking.

"I don't know, yet. But I'll take care of it. I promise you that."

"Uh-uh. That's not good enough. I want to be there."

"I won't let you down, sunshine. I've never lied to you and I never will."

True. She could accept that. But only Matt could control Matt. Joel might try his best and still not get through to her brother, but it was worth a try.

When they arrived, the headlights outlined the truck, parked at an odd angle on the side of the lane leading up to the Sutherlands' house a quarter of a mile down the road. Matt sat on the back tailgate. When they appeared, he lifted an arm to shield his eyes from the bright light. He stood and waited, his hands sunk low in the pockets of his baggy pants.

Joel pulled over, the van scraping against the hollyhocks lining the side of the road. Mari lowered her window. It took every ounce of willpower to remain in the van while Joel got out and went to meet her brother.

The crisp air smelled sweet. Crickets chirped, the wind blowing a chilling breeze inside, but Mari felt warm with anger and shock. She couldn't believe this had happened, yet she felt grateful it hadn't been worse. No one had been hurt.

Matt gestured to the truck, but Mari couldn't hear his words. Joel placed his hands on his hips, his head bent as he listened to her brother. Then Joel started talking. The boy glanced at the van where Mari sat watching him, then he pondered the ground, nodding his head in contrition.

He helped Joel hook a towline from the truck to the van. Joel reached into the cab of the truck and lifted out the wooden pieces of the Sutherlands' ruined mailbox. Then he opened the van and reached into the back for a tarp.

"What do you need that for?" she asked.

His face tightened with a stern frown. "The mailbox went through the windshield. I'll spread this across the front seat for Matt to sit on and protect him from the shattered glass while he steers the truck home."

Maybe it was a blessing Matt didn't ride home in the van with them. Mari might say some things she'd regret later.

Joel joined Mari a few minutes later, pulling the van away from the side of the road, moving slow and steady. In the rearview mirror, Mari saw the towline tighten and Matt steered the truck, following behind the van as they drove home.

"Did Matt say what happened?" she asked Joel.

"Yes, but I'll let him tell you about it when we get home. Just relax for now, Mari. Everything's gonna be okay."

How could he say that? How could he be so calm?

Trust him. He will make this right.

The words filled her heart, as if someone were speaking to her from within. Although she was steaming mad, she also felt at peace. She remembered the story in the New Testament of when the Savior braided a rope before chasing the money changers out of the temple. No doubt the Lord had been angry, but he'd also prepared the rope and thought about what he should do beforehand.

They arrived at home and Joel tugged the truck down the dirt road to the caretaker's cottage. Mari went inside the cottage to wait while the boys pulled the truck inside the garage. Finally Joel opened the door, holding it wide as Matt stepped inside and sat on the sofa. Matt refused to meet Mari's eyes, staring at his shabby high-top tennis shoes instead.

"You want to tell your sister what happened tonight?" Joel sat across from Mari, reclining in the straight-backed chair as he crossed his legs and placed his hands on the arm rests.

Mari stared at Matt, biting her bottom lip to keep from speaking. Joel had cautioned her to handle this situation carefully, to keep from pushing Mateo over the edge. She loved her brother so much, but right now, she had to literally bite her tongue.

"I…I was drag racing, Mari. I lost control of the vehicle and…I'm sorry." Matt ducked his head in shame.

Mari shifted her weight, a deep breath whooshing out of her. "Who were you racing against?"

Matt shrugged. "Just some other guys."

"Were you in the truck alone?"

He shook his head. "No, Dallin rode with me."

"And where is Dallin?"

"He caught a ride home with Alan Smith."

"And left you alone to clean up the mess? Some friend he is."

"Your sister's right, Matt. If Dallin was any kind of real friend, he would have stayed with you, to make sure you were okay and that you got home safely."

Matt nodded, his face hardening with anger, at Joel or at Dallin, she wasn't certain.

"So what now?" she asked, hoping Matt might do the right thing and take responsibility for his actions and offer some solutions.

Cold disappointment swept her when Matt shrugged and didn't say a word.

Joel cleared his voice and looked at Matt, his brows lifted in expectation. Matt blinked and stared at the floor again. Mari caught the impression that Joel had already had this conversation with Matt and worked out a resolution.

"Um, tomorrow morning, Joel and I are gonna go over to the Sutherlands' and…and I'm gonna say I'm sorry and fix their mailbox."

Good! At least Joel was leading Matt to apologize and make amends.

"And what about the truck?" Mari asked. "It's still too cold to drive without a windshield every day and it might rain. We can't afford to get it repaired. We need that truck, Matt. We have a business to run and you've ruined one of our forms of transportation. If we put in an insurance claim, you could be arrested if we tell them it was damaged during drag racing. So what do you suggest we do?"

"I...I don't know." He shook his head, his eyes filling with tears.

Mari's heart wrenched. She hated hurting her brother, but realized the tears were part of repentance. He was still young, but he had so much potential. So many good things to live for. He needed to learn there were consequences to his actions. That it wasn't just his life to do with as he pleased when he had the power to hurt other people. That he must make restitution for what he'd done and learn to make responsible choices.

"You could have been killed, Matt. What if the mailbox had been a person? You could have killed someone."

"I know, Mari. I'm sorry. It won't ever happen again."

She wanted to believe him. She really did. But she'd heard these promises before.

She stood and went to her brother, pulling him into her arms for a long hug. "Do you know how much I love you, my dear brother? Do you know how much we depend on you? What would we do if something happened to you? Have you thought of what that would do to Mom? We've all lost Dad. We can't lose you, too. Mom deserves better than that."

He wept against her shoulder, his throat and chest making soft strangling sounds as he pinched the bridge of his nose.

She drew back and wiped the tears from her own eyes.

Joel stood and took a step toward Mari. "In addition to his normal chores, Matt's going to work off the damage to the truck here at the farm. Tomorrow after school, he'll be spending the afternoon working with me. We have extra plants we need to get started for the spring fundraiser and a shipment of manure to unload. But right now, he's going into the house to tell your mother what he's done and apologize to her."

Matt's head snapped up. "No, anything but that."

Maybe Matt wasn't too far gone after all. Not if he felt this worried about confessing what he'd done to Mom.

Joel put his hand on Matt's shoulder, his eyes filled with compassion. "Matt, when you hurt someone, you have to make it right. Apologizing can be the hardest thing of all, but it's also the most freeing thing you can do. You owe that to your mother."

Matt's eyes filled with true repentance and he nodded, turning toward the door.

"Wait, Matt," Joel stopped him. "There's one more thing I want to suggest. This is something I can't make you do, but you ought to do it just the same because it's right."

Matt hesitated. "Don't tell me I have to go to the police."

"No, I don't think that's necessary, but hanging out with guys like Dallin Keats isn't doing you any good."

"Then what?"

"You need to apologize to the Lord."

Matt pursed his lips and rolled his eyes before stepping to the door. Joel cut him off, forcing the boy to look him in the eye...not an easy feat considering Joel stood about six feet four inches tall.

"You may scoff, but there's no escaping the Lord. And you have to mean it. He's the one person who will never abandon you, and I guarantee there will come a time when you'll be alone in this world and need Him there for you. So, don't let Him down again."

There was no denying the fierce intensity in Joel's eyes. He meant every word. Mari couldn't have said it any better.

Matt nodded, appearing more humbled. "Yes, sir."

Joel stepped aside and let Matt pass.

If Mari doubted Joel's desire to do what was right, she no longer disbelieved it now. He'd surprised her. She never expected him to act and say the things he had to Matt or to Troy. Her respect for him grew by leaps and bounds.

Joel didn't return to the house with Matt and Mari. Livi had already gone to bed before Matt turned on the light and invited Mom to sit in the living room with him. Mari stood silently beside the door while Matt fidgeted with his hands. In a subdued voice, he told his mother what had happened and apologized. Mom didn't say a word, but her weeping spoke volumes.

"I'm sorry, Mom."

He turned to go to his room and Mom embraced him, her eyes closed as tears washed her cheeks. "I love you, son. I can't lose you, too."

The expression on Matt's face changed from shame to compassion. Tears filled his eyes as he whispered against her ear. "I love you, and this will never happen again. I promise."

Mari clenched her eyes closed. She realized what had happened tonight had cost them dearly, but it was worth it if Matt finally realized what he had done was wrong. For this, she owed a debt to Joel. Maybe it was time to view him in a different light and let the past heal at last.

Mari didn't sleep much that night. She tossed about, her mind in turmoil as she worried about so many things. Matt's troubles, Mom's health, their financial woes. She didn't dare even consider her schooling or the future and what it might hold for her. Though she longed for a life of her own, she deeply loved her family and determined to do everything possible to keep them safe.

The thought occurred to her to pray. In the dark, she knelt beside her bed and bowed her head before pouring her heart out to the Lord. Peace entered her soul, allowing her to rest.

The next morning, Joel arrived at the house bright and

early, before Matt had to leave for school. The boy didn't even grumble when Joel got him out of bed. They didn't wait for breakfast before they went to the toolshed, took a saw, some lumber, a hammer, nails and paint, then drove off in the van to go over to the Sutherlands'.

Mari didn't tag along. Without transportation, she planned to stay at the farm and work with Mom and Netta. Still Mari worried about Matt and what Mr. Sutherland might do when he found out about his mailbox. What if Mr. Sutherland reported the accident to the police? They didn't have money to pay a fine, much less get the windshield repaired. She decided to leave these concerns up to the Lord. He knew their needs and would help make this right.

Mari walked Livi to the school bus stop. "Where's Matt? Why isn't he here?"

"He had to take care of an early chore, but Joel is taking him to school. He'll ride the bus home with you later this afternoon."

"Okay." Livi smiled, swinging her blue lunch box as she walked.

Mari squeezed Livi's hand, loving her sweet innocence and trusting nature.

By nine o'clock, Joel returned to the house, having dropped Matt off at school. He smiled and nodded, giving her a thumbs-up that everything was okay.

"What did Mr. Sutherland say?" she asked.

"He was very decent and praised Matt for repairing the mailbox. You can rest at ease."

If only it were that simple. "Thanks for everything, Joel. You've been such a great help to all of us."

He touched her hand, his fingers warm against her flesh. "You're welcome, sunshine."

She watched as he returned the tools to the shed, wishing she dared to relax. Praying this didn't happen again. With Dad gone, Matt needed a man's influence in his life. He needed structure and someone strong to help give him direction and teach him how to be a good man.

Thank goodness for Joel. She might have fallen apart if she'd been left to deal with the situation alone. But what about Dallin Keats and the rest of the gang Matt had been running with? How could Mari be certain Matt wouldn't be influenced by them again? He'd gotten off easy this time. The next time, he could lose his life.

Chapter Eleven

On Thursday evening, Mari returned to the house to wash up for supper just as Joel and Matt got into the van and pulled out of the driveway. Mari stood on the front porch and placed one hand on her hip, watching them go.

Inside, Livi stood at the kitchen sink, slicing radishes under Mom's close supervision. The house smelled of cooking meat and onions and Mari's stomach rumbled.

"Where are the boys going?"

Elena shrugged. "I don't know. Joel just asked if he could borrow the van. I assume he's going to his usual Thursday night place."

Hmm. He'd done the same thing last Thursday and the Thursday before that.

"Why did he take Matt with him?"

Mom placed a bowl of homemade salsa on the table. The pungent aroma of garlic filled the air. "I don't know, but I can't think of anyone I trust more to send my son off with than Joel Hunter."

True. After all the changes she'd seen in Joel, Mari no longer questioned his motives. But she couldn't help being curious.

The next morning, she decided to ask him. He just shrugged. "I'm taking care of something I should have done years ago."

"And Mateo? Why are you taking him?"

He smiled and climbed onto the small forklift they used to carry heavy bales of peat moss. "Don't worry. It'll do Matt some good, too."

As he started up the forklift, the roar of the motor shut off further questions. His answers left her puzzled. Why so secretive?

Realizing she would get no information out of Joel, she went to Matt. But he would tell her nothing.

"I promised Joel I wouldn't tell anyone what we're doing," Matt said. "Joel says good deeds should be done in secrecy, not out in the open for everyone to see."

Good deeds? What kind of conspiracy was this? "But can't you even tell your own family?"

"No, I'm sorry. It's not bad, Mari. In fact, it's good. I have to make amends for some things I've done and Joel's helping me."

She opened her mouth to ask more questions, but he startled the words right out of her mouth when he wrapped his arms around her and gave her a big hug.

"Trust me, *hermana*. Trust me this once," he whispered against her ear.

Without waiting for her response, Matt turned and went outside to help Joel mow the lawns. More and more, the two seemed inseparable. When he wasn't in school, Matt always worked with Joel. Knowing her brother wasn't off with Dallin Keats brought her peace. At least here at the farm, she knew what Matt was up to.

A huge lump of gratitude clogged her throat. She told herself it wasn't important where the boys went on Thursday nights. Somehow it no longer mattered. What was important was the change in Matt. He spent more and more time at home, helping around the house, doing his homework and signing up for the track team at school.

She dropped the issue, but received an answer the next week after they picked up the truck from the repair shop. Finally, they'd scraped together enough money to get the shattered windshield repaired. Joel dropped them off, then returned home in the van. Mari drove the truck, taking Livi and Mom grocery shopping.

They stood in the checkout line, placing their purchases on the conveyer belt. Carl Hendry, the man who ran the homeless shelter in town, came inside the store. Seeing them, he swung by the counter, giving Mom a giant smile.

"Hi, Mrs. Herrera. I'm glad I finally get the chance to tell you what a fine boy you've raised." He reached out and squeezed Mom's hand with both of his. She almost dropped her purse and Mari caught it, looping the strap over her arm.

"Huh?" Mom looked dumbfounded.

"Joel Hunter's been bringing Matt over to help cook and serve meals at the shelter every Thursday night. They both sure hustle. Anything I ask them to do, they do it without question. They're both compassionate men and have made a difference. You've got a good son there and should be proud of him."

"Um, thank you," Mom gushed, her face suffused with pleasure.

"Have a nice day, ladies." Carl left them as the cash register chinged. Mom handed her debit card to the cashier and Mari packed the bags into the cart before taking Livi's hand and pushing the groceries outside. No one spoke. They moved as if in a fog.

At the truck, Mari stowed their bags in the back, then

climbed into the driver's seat. She started the engine, but didn't put it in gear, her hands resting on the steering wheel.

Livi sat on the seat between Mari and Mom, munching a bar of chocolate. "What's the matter, Mari?"

Mari turned and stared at Mom from over the top of Livi's head. "Did you know Joel was taking Matt to the homeless shelter to work each week?"

Mom shook her head, her eyes sparkling with tears. "No, but I can't think of a better thing for them to do."

As Mari put the truck in gear and pressed the accelerator, she couldn't have agreed more. This wasn't the Joel she'd known as a teenager. This Joel was a compassionate, hard-working, mature man.

After school, when she saw Matt, Mari told him about their visit with Mr. Hendry in the grocery store. "I think it's wonderful that you're working at the shelter each week."

He looked up from his homework and placed his pen aside, his dark eyes meeting hers without flinching. "I didn't want you to find out. I figured I could do my service in secret. The Lord knows and that's good enough for me."

His maturity astounded her. He'd changed so much so soon. Lately he said *please* and *thank you,* acting more respectful to Mom and more loving to Livi.

And all because of Joel.

That night at dinner, Matt said the *C* word for the first time. "I've applied to go to college in Reno."

Mom dropped her fork and it landed on her plate with a clatter. Mari choked on her glass of water and pressed a napkin to her mouth while Livi patted her back. They all stared at Matt like he'd just grown horns on top of his head.

"What's the matter?" He gazed at them all like discussions of college were a normal occurrence at the dinner table.

"That's wonderful, Mateo. Your father wanted you to get

the education he never had." Mom's face glowed and a knot of emotion settled in Mari's chest. It'd been a long time since she'd seen her mother this happy.

Joel didn't say a word, just continued munching his string beans. A slight smile curved the corners of his lips.

Matt reached for the milk and poured a second glass for Livi and himself. He set it aside and looked at Mari. "After Dad died, my grades fell, but I've been working hard to make it up. Mr. Thorndike says I might still be able to qualify for a scholarship. If not, do you think we can afford the tuition for me to go to college in Reno? They have a great geology program."

"Absolutely, Matt," Mari answered without hesitation. "Don't worry about the cost. You just keep your grades up and see if you can get that scholarship."

She smiled wide, having absolutely no idea how they would pay her brother's tuition. But she'd find a way, if she had to mortgage the house to do it.

Joel avoided her eyes. His lean jaw tensed as he chewed on a tortilla. Two questions circulated around her brain, but she didn't know how to ask him without sounding like she'd lost her mind.

Who are you? And what have you done with the real Joel Hunter?

That evening, Mari went out to the pepper greenhouse to tell Joel to come up to the house for homemade vanilla ice cream. Riding one of the quads, she turned on the headlights and drove slowly through the dark, wondering why he was working so late.

She found him sitting at a workbench, transplanting seedlings into four-inch pots. His hands moved so fast that she thought he worked like a pro. A watery glint of moonlight shimmered in his dark hair and she admired his handsome profile, so strong and stubborn, yet peaceful in his labors.

"You seem a natural at this."

He turned, looking startled by her presence. Seeing her in the doorway, he smiled. "I figure we'll need extra money to pay some college tuition this fall."

She came inside and rested her palms on the top of the rough bench. He nudged a high stool toward her and she sat down. "About Matt, I…I want to thank you, Joel. How can we ever repay you for what you've done for him?"

"Your thanks is enough."

She cleared her throat, feeling jittery inside. What was wrong with her? "You don't need to work this late, Joel."

"I don't mind. I love working with the soil."

She picked up a hand trowel and twirled it with her fingers. "You do?"

"Sure." He held up his hands, his fingers long and graceful, his fingernails filled with dirt. She knew he'd clean them with a brush when he washed up later. His eyes glimmered as he picked up a green seedling and cradled it on his callused palm. "I love the feel of plants and soil against my fingers. As I watch our work grow and blossom, the peace and beauty of God's creations astounds me."

"You're sounding poetic again." And she liked it. This gentle side of Joel Hunter left her feeling amazed and nostalgic. In all her life, she'd never met anyone like him. He was certainly not ordinary in any way. Her father had made the farm his life's work. How could she begrudge Joel for loving it, too?

He took her hand in his, then placed the seedling on her palm. "You asked me once why I would want to come here to work. I'll tell you why. I love Herrera Farms, Mari. I always have. The good, honest work. The nurturing of plants. The smell of rich, dark soil. Call me a wimp if you like, but I love watching our plants bloom, knowing they'll bring joy to others for Mother's Day, in a flower garden, at a wedding reception, or a senior prom. The work we do provides a living for your family, but it also brings people a lot of happiness. What could be better than that?"

She'd never thought of it that way. She surveyed the greenhouse, the benches lined neatly with colorful plants just starting to bud, and she realized she loved it here, too. But she loved nursing just as much. "I think that's why I've fought so hard to hold on to this place since Dad died. It's a lot of hard work, but I would feel so bad to let it go. It's just that—"

"What?" he urged.

He met her eyes and she bit her lip. "I want a little bit more."

"Your education and perhaps a family of your own?"

How did he always know what she was thinking? He listened and never made any judgments. She wished now that she could say the same thing.

"Why can't you do both?" he asked.

She couldn't, unless he stayed here. Without intending to, she'd come to depend on him too much. His strength and ingenuity. His calm support. But surely he'd move on soon. He had a right to a life and family of his own to love. But she couldn't grasp that right now. The thought of him leaving left her feeling bereft. She didn't know what she'd do without him.

She decided to change the subject. "Why didn't you tell me you were serving meals over at the shelter with Matt?"

He dusted off his hands and stood. "I didn't want you to know."

"Why not?"

He put his tongue in his cheek, hesitating before he answered. "I know what it's like to be hungry, and I'm hoping I can make a difference for someone else the way your father made a difference for me."

His words brought a thud to her chest. She'd always

thought he took her father's help for granted, never appreciating what Dad tried to do for him.

"Matt's so different since you came to stay," she said.

Joel stepped with her to the door, flipping off the light. They didn't take the quad back to the house, but walked instead. "Matt's a good kid. He was just deeply hurt when your father died and he felt very alone. He needed to know that someone cared about him."

"We've always cared about Matt. He could always come to Mom or me with whatever he needed."

Joel hitched one shoulder. "I don't think he felt like he could bother you. After your father died, Matt was the man of the house, and yet you were the strong one, carrying the family. How could he ask you for more help under those conditions? He had to figure it out on his own."

Mari stopped and considered Joel, amazed by his insight. These things had never occurred to her. She'd been so busy working, trying to pay the bills, suffering with her own grief, that she didn't realize how much Matt needed her, or that she needed Matt.

"I won't take him for granted again," she promised.

Joel draped his arm over her shoulder for a squeeze. "Yes, you will, but it's okay. We all take each other for granted at times. We just need to keep reminding ourselves not to forget what's really important."

The weight of his arm didn't seem to bother her like it used to and she didn't pull away. They continued walking down the lane, the evening shadows filled with moonlight, the mild breeze smelling sweet.

Maybe there was hope for Matt after all. And for Joel.

On Saturday morning, Mari dressed in blue capris and a matching shirt. As she walked into the living room, she struggled to comb the snarls out of her long, damp hair. She looked up and found Mom and Joel sitting on the sofa, talking quietly together.

They clammed up and drew apart too quickly. Their eyes widened, as if they'd been caught gossiping.

"What's up?"

"Nothing. We're just waiting for you." Joel stood and slapped his A's baseball cap against his thigh.

The sight of the cap brought a rush of memories to haunt her. They'd been twelve years old when he taught her the game of baseball, chasing her around the bases they'd drawn with chalk powder in the dirt of the wide driveway. She'd screamed like a total girl, knowing he could have tagged her out if he'd wanted to. Instead, he'd let her slide home, much to the disgruntlement of the other kids that had come to play with them that day.

"Good morning, *niña*," Mom said as she walked to the kitchen. "If we're going to the lake, I'd better get a lunch packed for us."

"What?" Mari stared at Mom as she opened the refrigerator and removed cheese, luncheon meats, tomatoes and lettuce.

Joel took the brush from Mari's hand and began to comb her hair. Too startled to object, she let him perform this service for her, enjoying the rare luxury of having such attention. He took her breath away when he leaned down and placed a gentle kiss on her forehead, then handed the brush back to her.

A wave of heat flooded her cheeks. He stood too close for comfort. She turned and stepped back, giving him a half smile. Like always, he wore faded blue jeans and a shirt, the long sleeves rolled up to his muscular biceps. His short hair had been lightly spiked with gel and he looked handsome in a casual sort of way.

She blinked her eyes. "I'd better get to work. I think we can assemble some hanging baskets today—"

"We're not working today."

"What?"

"We're going fishing. I'm making us a picnic lunch," Mom chimed in. As she laid out bread to assemble sandwiches, she hummed a lively tune.

"Oh, no. I don't have time to waste on such foolishness." Mari headed for the door, but Joel caught her arm.

"Mari, I've already loaded two four-wheelers on the trailer and hitched it to the van. I found your dad's old fishing equipment in the garage and stayed up late last night to collect a can of night crawlers. I remember once your father telling me there was no better way to build a close relationship with a boy than to take him fishing. It'd be good for Matt, and Livi and the rest of us, too."

Was he daft? How could fishing get through to Matt? What her brother needed was to learn to work and to serve others. "I don't go fishing when there's work to be done. I've got a zillion flowers that need to be watered."

Joel brushed his fingertips against her cheek, a fleeting touch that left her skin burning. "Relax, sunshine. I got up at four o'clock this morning to water the plants. They're fine. Netta and Tom will be working if any customers come in to buy some plants. Nothing is gonna happen while we're gone for one day."

She pursed her lips. "You stayed up late and got up early? You didn't get much sleep last night, did you?"

"It doesn't matter. What Matt needs is his father. It's not about the fishing, but rather the time he spends with his family."

"But you're not—"

"I know, I know—" Joel cut her off with a slash of his hand "—I know I'm not family, but I can help that boy, if you'll just let me."

"Actually, I was going to say you're not his father. But

you'll always be a part of our family, Joel. You're like Matt's older brother and you have every right to be here."

Okay, she'd done it now. Her words defied everything she'd believed…up until now. For so long, she'd tried not to include Joel in her family, but now she realized what Dad had seen in Joel from the beginning. The wonderful man Joel might become, if only he could see his own potential. He was like a prodigal son returned. Humble, thankful and repentant. An influence for good in all their lives.

An answer to her prayers.

"You think we can meet our deadlines if we take today off to go play?" She felt uncertain, but deeply longed to hear an affirmative response. Work had become a daily drudge and she needed some time off to laugh and enjoy being alive.

"Of course. What good is the family business if you lose your family?" He stepped in front of her, gazing down into her eyes as he rested his big hands on her shoulders. "You've forgotten how to enjoy life."

His words pierced her heart. She took a deep, settling breath and released it.

"We're going, Mari." Mom's voice startled her. She stood in the kitchen, holding an open jar of mayonnaise. "We've all been working too hard and we need a day off. Tomorrow, we're going to church. This family is gonna get back to what's really important and what your father always believed in. Family and God."

Mari laughed and held out her hands, as if to ward them off. "Okay, okay. I can't fight you both. Maybe we can catch some trout for dinner."

"Are we going fishing?" Livi stood in the hallway, wearing her pajamas as she rubbed the sleep from her eyes.

"Yes, we are, so get dressed," Mari told her.

"Hooray!" The girl scurried down the hall.

"And wake up Mateo," Mom called after her.

Livi ran into Matt's room and flipped on the light without warning. They heard her call to her brother. "Get up, Matt. We're going fishing."

A screeching yelp followed a grumbling from Matt. "Turn off that light and get out of my room, you little brat."

A muffled boom sounded against the wall, as if Matt had thrown a shoe at his sister.

Livi came scurrying out of his room and ran into her own. She called over her shoulder in a cheerful voice. "Matt's awake."

Joel chuckled. "That'll teach Matt to not stay up so late watching movies on TV."

Shaking her head, Elena headed down the hallway. "I'd better go talk to him. I don't like him calling his sister names."

Within an hour, they all piled into the van. Livi bounced on the backseat between Mom and Matt, a constant stream of chatter coming from her mouth. "Chrissy Taylor went fishing last weekend, but she didn't catch anything. I want to catch a fish, just so I can tell her I caught something."

"We'll work on that," Joel promised.

"What about you, Matt?" Livi asked. "You like fish, don't you?"

With no window to stare out of in the back of the van, Matt slumped against the seat, closed his eyes, folded his arms and pretended to sleep. "Yeah, sure."

The drive out to Turner Reservoir took thirty minutes. While Joel drove down the freeway, Mom sang a Spanish ballad. A love song about a girl whose wealthy father disapproved of the poverty-stricken young man who loved her. Contrary to other Romeo-and-Juliet type songs, this one ended happily as the two young people ran away where they married and lived a long and loving life together.

Joel and Livi joined in on the chorus, Livi's high, sweet trills mingling with Mom's husky alto and Joel's deep bass. The combined beauty of their voices raised a rash of goose bumps on Mari's arms. She found herself wiping her eyes and turned away so Joel wouldn't see how a silly love song could touch her heart.

She flinched when she felt his hand squeeze her fingers gently. When she glanced at him, she found him smiling as he watched the road. He seemed so peaceful, as if he were the head of the household. She longed to let Joel be strong for her.

He said not a word, but Mari couldn't help wondering if she had a single secret this man didn't know. The years since he'd become an adult seemed shrouded in mystery, yet she appeared to be an open book. As if he could see into her very soul and know her every thought.

Staring out her window, Mari folded her arms so Joel couldn't hold her hand. It was a method of self-preservation, to hide from his discerning gaze.

Mom filled the silence with a variety of happy, sad and ridiculous songs that got them all laughing. Even Matt perked up, opening his eyes and smiling when Mom sang his favorite tune about a squirrel chasing a leopard up a tree. By the time they arrived at Turner Reservoir, they all were in good spirits and everyone helped unload the fishing equipment and four-wheelers.

They found a shady spot near the dock where Mari helped Mom set up lawn chairs and a foldaway table for their picnic lunch. Near the shore, patches of dark green sedges mingled with light green grass. Trails for all-terrain vehicles surrounded the low hills around the reservoir. Dainty blue larkspur blanketed the open fields. Mari breathed in deeply, enjoying the warm sun on her face, thinking what a beautiful, perfect place.

"Let me help you with that, *Mamá*." Matt took the ice chest from Mom and set it beside the table.

Mari studied her brother. Matt rarely helped of his own accord and she couldn't believe her eyes.

Joel handed a fishing pole to Mari while he carried the can of bait and a fishing box. Mom sat in a chair and crossed her legs while the rest of them walked out on the dock. The sounds of their footsteps pounded the wooden planks. Livi's ponytail swayed as she skipped ahead.

"Lesson time," Joel called as he set the fishing box down. "Who knows how to bait a hook?"

Livi watched in horror as he opened a can of night crawlers and hooked one worm with short, efficient movements of his fingers. "Yuck! I'm not doing that."

"Neither am I. Dad never made us bait our own hooks," Mari said.

"Sissies." Matt dug his fingers into the can and pulled out a wriggling worm. He copied Joel's technique with his own fishing line.

"Good job, Matt," Joel said. "You think you can help Livi catch her fish?"

"Sure. Come take the fishing pole, Livi." The boy spoke with confidence as he handed his little sister the spinning rod.

Matt wrapped his arms around Livi to show her how to cast the line into the water. "Hold it right here with both hands."

Livi gripped the cork handle of the rod with both hands, then swung back and forward. Joel yelped with alarm when her fishhook clipped his baseball cap and jerked it off his head.

Matt crowed with gales of laughter. "Nice catch, Livi."

The cap dangled from the hook, bobbing in the air. Joel scrambled to retrieve his hat from the hook. Mari covered a giggle behind one hand, amused to see the big man scuttling around the dock.

As he unhooked his hat, Joel chuckled and rubbed the top of his head. "Hey, little girl! Aim for the water, not me."

Livi nodded, a solemn expression on her face. "Sorry, Joel."

He gave her long ponytail a playful tug. "Don't worry about it, sweetie. No harm done."

Mari cast off and their fishing lines whizzed overhead. They all sat down on the edge of the dock, their legs dangling over the side. Mari felt content, sitting beside Joel and her siblings.

Mom shouted encouragement from the beach. "We'll need several fish if we're to have enough for dinner, so catch some big ones."

It became a challenge to see who could cast out the farthest. As their lures hit the water, little splashes and ripples skimmed across the surface.

Mari didn't try to compete with the boys. Joel chuckled when Matt beat him time and time again. "Must be that great throwing arm of yours. You're good with a pole, but can you catch any fish? I'm planning on trout for supper."

At that moment, Mari's line gave a hard tug and the reel began to buzz. Taken off guard, she almost dropped the fishing pole. Joel grabbed the handle and pulled backward. "You can't let go, sunshine."

At that moment, Livi's line gave a sudden jerk and she squealed with delight. "I got something, too."

"Wonderful," Mom called. "Looks like we'll have trout for supper after all."

Matt scurried to set his rod aside and helped Livi hold on to the pole while they fought with the fish. The flexible pole arched with the added pressure.

"Jerk back hard, to set the hook," Joel told Mari as he helped her tug on her fishing pole. "You have to work the pole like this, or you'll lose your catch."

She gave a nervous laugh. "I guess I'm out of practice. I think I was Livi's age the last time Dad took us fishing."

He showed her how to rein in the fish, twirling the handle of the spinning reel. The whirring sound filled the air as the fish appeared, skimming just below the surface of the water.

Within minutes, they reeled in a seven-inch trout for Mari and a five-inch fish for Livi. The girl shrieked with joy as she clasped the slippery fish with both hands. "Take a picture, Mom. Take a picture."

Mom came running with the camera. "Crowd together. I want everyone in."

Joel stood behind Mari, his hand on her waist as Mom snapped a photo. They all smiled for the picture and Mari thought she'd never had so much fun.

Livi's fish flapped around in her hands, gulping for air. The child started to cry, thrusting it at Joel. "It's gonna die. Throw it back in the water. Throw it back."

"We can't have fish for supper if we throw it back, *hermana*," Matt explained in a gentle, reasoning tone. Mari liked this considerate side of her brother and almost wished they could go fishing every day.

"But I don't want to kill it." Livi's sobs turned to wails of misery.

"Mateo, toss it back in the lake," Mom called. "I'll fix tacos for dinner tonight."

Matt did as ordered, shaking his head, a frown of disapproval crinkling his brow. The fish splashed into the water and swam away. Livi's tears instantly dried and she flung her arms around Matt's waist. "Oh, thank you, Matt."

Matt rolled his eyes heavenward and muttered under his breath. "Women!"

A laugh rumbled in Joel's chest and he winked at Mari.

"Maybe we should find another spot where we can fish without bothering Livi."

"Livi, come here. You've caught your fish and have a picture to show Chrissy. No more fishing for you." Mom came to the dock and took the girl's hand, pulling her over to the ice chest where she retrieved a can of soda pop.

"Ah," the child grouched.

Joel nudged Matt's arm. "You want to drive one of the four-wheelers?"

"Sure!"

"Let's remember to be considerate. We can't rev the quads around our neighbors." He inclined his head toward a group of fishermen wearing waist-high waders and standing a hundred feet away in the water.

Mari liked how Joel spoke to her brother, teaching Matt to have respect without making it a big deal.

Joel picked up the can of worms, smiling at Mari. "How about if you ride with me? You remember the last time we went four-wheeling together?"

"How could I forget? I hope you're a safer driver, now." A vision of him racing through the canyon back home filled her mind. She'd held on for dear life, sitting behind him, praying he didn't get them killed. The reckless pace had both thrilled and terrorized her. But this time was different. No longer were they kids. Mari wasn't certain she wanted to wrap her arms around Joel's waist and hold on as they bounced over rough terrain.

"Don't worry, Marisol. You're safe with me. Come on." He tugged on her hand, pulling her with him to the quad.

Mari laughed at his exuberance and called over her shoulder. "Mom, you sure you're gonna be okay here alone with Livi?"

"*Claro, niña.* Of course. We'll take a nice long walk

together. Four-wheeling is for you younger kids." Elena waved her novel in the air.

"But I want to ride on the quads," Livi said.

"You will when they return. Right now, you can swim and look for shells." Mom held up a red bucket and small hand shovel.

"I'll be back soon to give you a ride," Joel promised as Mari climbed on behind him.

"Okay." Livi grasped the bucket and headed for the shore.

"Have fun," Mom called to the others.

Joel revved the motor of his four-wheeler. As soon as Mari sat secure behind him, he moved the quad at a slow pace, skirting around the other fishermen. Once they were clear of people, he took off like a shot, trying to catch up to Matt.

"Wooee!" he yelled with glee.

Mari laughed, unable to help herself. She held on tight to Joel's waist, the feel of the breeze in her hair so freeing as her spirits soared. Matt roared ahead of them, bouncing over the uneven hills, his deep laughter filling the air.

"He sounds so happy," Mari spoke into Joel's ear so he would hear her over the roar of the engines.

"Yes, I think my evil plan is working. This is just what he needed."

They rode the quads for some time, enjoying the freedom of the day. Finally, they located a sheltered spot and slowed the machines to a quieter pace. When they killed the motors, Matt discovered that his fishing pole had disappeared.

"I didn't even see it go. It must have flown off with that crazy driving of yours," Joel quipped.

He lifted his own fishing pole and handed it to Matt. "You can use mine. But I expect to eat trout for supper. And he who catches them has to gut them."

Matt chuckled. "Okay, okay. I can take a hint."

They doffed their shoes and rolled up their pants, dangling their legs over an outcropping of rocks while Matt cast his line. After a time, Mari laid back and dozed in the morning sun. Later, she sat up, stiff and sore. She walked along the beach, searching for unique rocks and fossilized shells that might please Livi. Even at this distance, the afternoon breeze carried Joel's conversation with her brother to her ears.

"I remember Dad used to take us fishing when I was little," Matt said.

"I know. He took me, too."

Matt watched the water, holding his fishing pole steady. "I miss him a lot."

"I know, so do I. You want to talk about him?"

Matt shook his head. "It's been only a year, but sometimes I can't remember him. Not even what he smells like."

Mari remembered like it was yesterday. Daddy smelled of rich loamy soil and peppermint on workdays, and spicy aftershave on Sundays. He had thick dark hair that had just started to gray at the temples and Mari had loved him with a devotion she could barely comprehend. Remembering her father caused her heart to wrench painfully.

She turned away, blinking tears from her eyes, but Joel's soothing voice carried on the breeze. "He loved you, Matt. You can remember that. He'd want you to be happy. He's a part of you that will never end. The important thing is to live a life that wouldn't disappoint him."

A long pause followed. "I guess I've kind of let him down lately."

"I think he'd understand. But you can start fresh today. Your father taught you what's right. You just need to have the courage to do it, even when your friends try to get you to do something else. If you ever find yourself in a situation you know isn't right, it's okay to say 'no, let me out of this car right now.'"

"They make it hard to say no," Matt confessed. "They'll think I'm a coward."

"The Lord never said it would be easy to do what's right. And in your heart, you know it takes more courage to say no than to follow along like a dumb sheep."

"I guess so."

Mari paused as she picked up a smooth black stone. She thought about Joel's words. What he said was good advice for her, too. Doing what she knew was right had proven to be the hardest thing she'd ever done. And yet even now, she knew the Lord was with her, giving her the strength to get her family through their current hardship. With Joel's help, she'd been able to accomplish so much more. Once again, she had to believe that God had sent Joel to help them. To help Matt. After years of knowing Joel Hunter, she'd never thought of him as more than an unwanted burden.

Until now.

Chapter Twelve

"What you got there?" Joel asked, startling Mari.

She whirled around, her cheeks flushed with fresh air, her hair windblown and attractive around her face. He admired her slender, athletic calves. The sight of her standing on the beach, clutching a handful of shiny rocks, made him forget to breathe.

"I hope that's not illegal." He inclined his head toward her hands and bulging pockets. She dropped several rocks and he quirked one brow.

She chuckled. "Only if they're diamonds. Livi collects rocks. I thought she might like these."

"I have no doubt she will. Here, let me help." He reached to take the mound of rocks from her hands. The breeze carried the light floral scent of her shampoo and he inhaled deeply.

"Thank you for today, Joel. It's been great."

He looked into her eyes and saw his own heart there. "Yeah, it sure has."

She tilted her face to the sun and closed her eyes. Watching her, he thought life could never get any better than this moment, right here and now.

"It's so lovely here," she said.

"Yes, it is. The day's nice, too." His gaze rested on her.

Her face flushed a pretty pink. "That's not what I meant."

"I know what you meant. But Mari, you need to realize I've thought you were beautiful since I was ten years old. In my eyes, you were never anything but stunning."

She gave a nervous laugh. "Sure! Even when I had braces and pigtails."

Shock waves of emotion bubbled inside him. He felt like he'd explode if he didn't tell her how much he loved her. Like he'd never get another chance. And right now, the moment seemed right to confide in her. But how should he begin? How could he tell her what he felt without also telling her the truth?

"Yes, even then. But I've also never felt like I was good enough for you."

She placed her hand on his arm, her touch sending electric currents through him. "Joel, that's not true. It's just that we're so different. We want different things."

"Such as?"

"Well, you've always been so outgoing and I prefer staying at home, reading a good book."

"You might be surprised to find that I'm also a voracious reader. I always have been."

"You have?" She eyed him with curiosity.

He longed to take her in his arms. Instead, he bent and picked up several flat stones. As he walked with her down the pebbled beach, he tossed the rocks, skipping them off the surface of the lake.

"Yeah, even when I was living here during the summer months. When your dad took me to town to make flower deliveries, I'd sneak over to the county library and check out a book or two. I hid them in my jacket so no one would see. At night, I'd take a flashlight and read until your father caught me and made me go to sleep. I think he's the only one who ever knew I read a lot of books. One night, he came out to the cottage and brought me a Bible to read."

Her mouth rounded. "I never knew. Why'd you hide the books?"

He shrugged. "I didn't want my friends to find out. Reading isn't cool."

She chuckled, covering her mouth with her hand. "Who's your favorite author?"

A blaze of embarrassment swept him. "You'll think I'm silly."

"No, I won't. Tell me."

"Jesus."

"Really?"

Feeling nervous with these confessions, he bent and picked up a stick, peeling the bark off with his fingers. "Believe it or not, I've read that Bible several times. I love the book of Matthew and the Sermon on the Mount. When the world gets too crazy and there's no one else I can talk to, I turn to the words of the Savior and it brings me peace that I can't find anywhere else."

"Wow! I never knew." Her eyes crinkled in confusion. "Then why did you always do such horrible things? I mean, the drag racing, the drinking and cigarettes, the tagging and shoplifting. Joel, you were a hoodlum."

A deep sigh trembled from his chest. "I know. Now I think back on my life, most of my antics were just cries for help. Your parents were the only ones who ever answered me."

"But Joel, after my parents answered, you went right out and did it over and over again. I remember once, after Dad went into town to bail you out of jail again, I heard him talking to my mother late at night. He'd paid every last cent he had. Mom didn't know how she was going to buy groceries."

"I know. I overheard that conversation, too. We ended up

eating refried beans for two weeks straight." A feeling of guilt swamped him.

"If you loved my father so much, why did you do such things, knowing how badly you would hurt him?"

"It took a long time for me to realize how much he loved me. It also took me a long time to trust him. I had to fit in with the gang I was running with. It's difficult for a parent to compete with peer pressure."

"Why? You had us, Joel. Weren't we more important than outsiders?"

"When you think about it that way, you're right. But when I was sixteen years old, I didn't see it quite like that. I was a stupid, foolish teenager, Mari, and I made a lot of mistakes. And I wish with all my heart that I could start over and take it all back."

Well, he'd done it now. Spilling his guts to Mari like a school kid. He'd be lucky if she ever looked at him like a normal man—

"There're things I wish I could take back, too," she said. "I haven't been very kind to you in the past. I've been too judgmental when I should have been supportive. Maybe if I'd been kinder, you wouldn't have felt the need to get attention by doing crazy things like tipping over all the porta-potties in town."

They both laughed at the memory. At the time, it hadn't been so funny, but now they could find humor in what he'd done and Joel was grateful for that.

The smile on Mari's face faded and her eyes grew serious. "I haven't treated you very well since you returned to Herrera Farms. I'll try to act nicer in the future. Is there anything I can do to make it up to you?"

Oh, wow! That opened the corral gate. He could think of only one thing he wanted from her right now. His mouth went dry and he tried to think of the best way to make his request without just blurting it out. "Go out on a date with me. I want to take you to dinner."

Her eyes narrowed, her expression skeptical. "A date? As in a real, holding-hands, mushy date?"

"Yes, a real handholding, mushy date. You know I don't have much money, but I can still afford to take you out and treat you like a lady." He was moving too soon, but his emotions warred inside of him. Didn't she understand? Couldn't she see it in his eyes every time he looked at her?

Her face stiffened, as if the thought of dating him repulsed her. Maybe she thought of him the same way she did Phil Taylor. Maybe he'd been too bold by revealing too much too soon. But the truth was, he'd been keeping his feelings to himself for years and he was tired of waiting. By some gift of providence, Mari had never married another man. If Joel didn't make a move soon and let her know how much he loved her, he might never get the chance.

"Joel, I don't know if that's such a good idea—"

He held up one hand. "Wait, Mari. Before you lock your mind against me, hear me out. All I'm asking is for you to see me as a man, not a hoodlum from your childhood. If it doesn't work between us, you'll still have a good dinner and I promise to make you laugh at least twice. Okay?"

He searched her face for the slightest inkling that she might acquiesce. In his heart, he prayed she said yes. And yet he also hoped she said no. If she agreed, it would simply postpone the inevitable. At some point, he would have to tell her the truth.

"Okay. You take care of dinner, but I have two tickets to the Sierra Philharmonic Orchestra on Friday night and no one to go with me."

He tensed. What did he really know about listening to orchestra music? Although Señor Herrera had earned his living from the soil, he'd been a dignified man. Mannered and refined.

Everything Joel was not.

"Mari, maybe you should go with someone else to hear the orchestra. I mean, I don't know much about it. I'm kind of gruff and—"

"You learn by doing."

"Your dad always said that."

She lowered her gaze, her voice sounding small. "You don't want to take me?"

"No, no! It's not that." He held up his hands to reassure her. "It's just that I'm not very cultured."

The admission came hard. He'd lived a lifetime of rebellion and acting like he was in control. On the streets of Oakland, his survival had depended on it. Who'd have ever believed he'd fall for a gardener who loved classical music and wanted to be a nurse?

She pursed her lips and angled her head to one side. "You learned quite a bit of culture. Dad taught you."

"That was a long time ago."

"It'll come back to you. And you're gonna need a suit."

Her insistence caused his heart to take flight. She wanted to go out with him. How could he fight her? He laughed, focusing on being happy for the first time in a long time. "I think I can manage that."

Maybe now was the time to tell her the truth. All of it. To get it out in the open and off his chest.

He took a deep breath. "Mari, there's something else I want you to—"

"Help! Someone help me."

A shrill scream penetrated his brain. Mari's expression changed to a deep scowl as she turned toward the lake. The wind had picked up and the sparkling waves undulated as she scanned the beach. A little boy about Livi's age lay convulsing on the slippery dock, his frantic mother standing over him screaming.

Without hesitation, Mari raced to the dock with Joel in hot pursuit.

"Someone call 9-1-1!" the mother screamed and several people standing nearby reached for their cell phones.

"What happened?" Mari knelt beside the child, holding him still. His arms flailed about, nearly striking her head.

The mother cupped her hands over her mouth, her eyes wide with fear. "I don't know. He just fell down and started shaking like that. Help him, please."

"What's his name?" Mari asked, checking his eyes and air passages.

"Tyson." The mother's voice vibrated with hysteria.

"Tyson, it's okay. Just relax." Mari turned him on his side, rubbing his back and jiggling him gently. The boy's glazed eyes stared wide, not blinking. Saliva ran from his open mouth as he continued to jerk and groan.

"What can I do to help?" Joel crouched beside Mari, helping her hold the boy so he didn't roll off the dock or do something to injure himself.

"I think he's having a seizure. If so, there's really nothing we can do until it passes."

"But he's not breathing. His face and lips are blue," the mother cried. "Please, do something."

"Give him a moment and I think he'll start breathing again." Mari spoke in a calm, soothing voice while she continued to rub the child's back.

"Are you a doctor?"

Mari shook her head. "No, I…I was a nursing student."

"What is it? What's wrong with my son?"

"I believe he's having an epileptic seizure. Has this happened before?"

"No, never."

"It usually lasts only a couple of minutes. The first one is always the most frightening, because you aren't sure what's happening."

People crowded around, offering suggestions. "Someone get a stick to put in his mouth."

"No! Absolutely not," Mari said.

"But he could bite his tongue off." Tears ran down the mother's face.

"No, we don't want to put any sticks or other objects in his mouth that he could choke on. Contrary to popular belief, it could do more damage than good. Back up everyone and give him room. This should pass quickly."

As if on cue, Tyson blinked and took a deep, wrenching breath. Again and again, his little chest heaved as he dragged in gulps of oxygen. He grunted, as though he wanted to speak, but his eyes had no focus.

Mari continued to rub Tyson's back. "He just needs time to reorient himself. There now. That's fine, Tyson. It's gonna be okay."

A man ran onto the dock, his eyes wide with alarm. He knelt over Tyson, touching the boy's face and arms. "Son, can you hear me? Are you okay?"

Tyson started to cry, confused and agitated. His parents knelt on the dock and cradled him in their arms, rocking back and forth.

Joel watched in awe, amazed by Mari's swift actions. She seemed to know instinctively what to do.

"Just keep him quiet for a few minutes and then take him to a hospital. You'll want to consult a doctor as soon as possible," Mari suggested.

"Oh, thank you!" the mother exclaimed. "If you hadn't been here, I don't know what we would have done."

"You're welcome. It was nothing, really."

"Mari!" Elena came running with Livi and Matt, no doubt

alerted by the screaming and commotion. Their pounding feet thumped against the wooden dock.

"What happened, Mari?" Livi asked.

Mari stood and staggered on the dock. Joel took her arm and led her to the shore with her family following behind. He helped her sit on a wooden bench.

"Are you okay, *mija?*" Mom asked, concern lacing her voice.

"Yes, I'm fine. My legs are just numb from kneeling too long on the hard dock." Mari gave a nervous laugh.

Elena breathed a sigh of relief. "I think it's time for us to go eat lunch."

"I agree." Livi rubbed Mari's arm, her little face contorted with worry for her sister.

"I'm fine."

"I'll pack up the fishing poles," Matt offered and took off like a shot.

Joel watched the boy go, realizing Matt loved his family very much.

"Do you think you can stand, now?" Joel asked Mari. He kept hold of her arm, fearing she might lose her balance and fall.

"Yes, the pins and needles have passed." She stood, seeming her old, confident self once more.

He sat her on the blanket while Elena served lunch. They talked about Tyson and Mari's heroics in saving him.

"I did nothing, just made sure he didn't hurt himself," she insisted.

No, she'd done so much more. Joel realized she had a gift and it'd be a terrible shame if she didn't pursue her schooling.

After they packed up their lunch, Joel opened the door to the van, ensuring Mari had her seat belt buckled before he closed the door. He went to climb into the driver's seat, but Elena gave him a quick hug.

"Thank you for this day, Joel. Our family has felt pretty

battered since Frank died. We needed this so much. Because of you, Mateo's with us and we're a family once more. We're happy again."

Elena's words humbled Joel right down to his toes. He'd never made anyone happy before. And there was no one he wanted to make happy more than this family. "You're welcome, *señora*."

"Call me Mom. Your own mother was my dearest friend, but I don't think she would mind if you call me *madre*." She patted his cheek, then climbed into the van.

Mom. Most people only had one mother, but Joel had two. He couldn't think of any sweeter name, except for Marisol.

On the drive home, Joel kept glancing at Mari, to make sure she was all right. She chatted with Matt and Livi about the fish they had caught, cleaned and stored in the ice chest.

"I'm not eating those fish," Livi exclaimed.

"You can eat peanut butter sandwiches," Mari said.

"You were amazing the way you helped Tyson," Joel told her when Livi finally dozed off. "You should finish nursing school. You were born to it just as I was born to growing things at the farm."

"That's what I keep telling her," Elena said. "She got perfect grades in science and math."

"She should go back to college and finish her education," Joel agreed.

"I know. I don't understand why she won't listen to me. She could get a scholarship or we could find the money somehow."

"Maybe she'll listen now."

"You know," Mari interrupted them, "it's rude to talk about someone like they aren't there listening to every word you're saying."

"Sorry." Joel chuckled at her perturbed look. "So why don't you listen to us and go back to school?"

In the rearview mirror, Joel saw that every set of eyes in the van rested on Mari, awaiting her response.

"I'm not having this conversation. Leave it alone." Mari slashed her hand through the air, her eyes narrowed, her jaw tense. She wasn't jesting.

She turned away and folded her arms. Joel stared out the windshield, maneuvering through the afternoon traffic as they sped along the freeway. He could take a hint. The conversation was over. But inside, he couldn't help wondering why Mari refused to go back to school. She loved nursing and had done well in her program. So, what was she afraid of?

Chapter Thirteen

"You picked a nice suit," Matt told Joel on Friday night. "A double-breasted suit looks good on tall men. At least that's what Mom said."

Joel stood in front of the full-length mirror Matt had borrowed from the main house and brought to the cottage. He wasn't about to tell the teenager that the white shirt, shiny black shoes and dark, pinstriped suit were all he could afford. He had to admit he looked good. He just hoped Mari liked it. She'd never been the type to quibble over proper fashion. In spite of her old work clothes, clean, modest and classic were her styles. Nothing contrived. No facades. That's what Joel loved about her. Hopefully she would see him the same way.

"Which tie should I wear?" Joel held up a red and a yellow tie, one in each hand. "It was a two-for deal, so I have a choice."

Matt pointed. "The yellow. It'll match Mari's dress."

"She's definitely wearing the yellow dress tonight?" Joel quirked his brows, glad to have Elena as an inside spy.

"Yeah, and she looks pretty, even if she is my sister."

"Your sister would look terrific dressed in a gunny sack."

A moment of panic climbed up Joel's throat. He hadn't

been on a date in years. And this date was the most important one in his life. What if he said something wrong? What if he blew it and Mari never wanted to go out with him again?

"You put the roses in the refrigerator, right?" Joel asked as he threaded his belt through the loops before buckling it.

"Of course. They're pretty. Yellow, to match her dress."

Joel flipped the tie around his collar. Señor Herrera had taught him how to tie one to wear each Sunday for church. The memory of how to form the knot came easy to him. "Mari didn't see the flowers, did she? She doesn't know about them?"

"No, and Momma will keep her away from the fridge." The mattress bounced twice as Matt sat on the edge of the bed. "Don't forget to open the door for her. And hold her chair for her when she sits down. Dad taught me that's how you treat a lady."

Joel picked up a pillow from the bed and tossed it at the boy. Matt caught it before it struck his head. "Your dad taught me the same things, remember?"

Matt chuckled and stuffed the pillow behind his head as he leaned back. "Then why worry? It'll be a piece of cake."

If only it were that easy. Joel felt like a space alien far from home. Normally, he had no problems talking to Mari. But on a date, he feared he'd become tongue-tied and not know what to say.

As he reached for a bottle of aftershave, he thought about possible conversations, just to be prepared. Somehow the weather didn't seem like a good topic. He wanted to share his deepest hopes and dreams with her.

Splashing a little aftershave on his palm, he rubbed his hands together before gently slapping his face. He cringed at the sting. With a final smooth of his hair, he picked up the keys to the truck and his wallet and headed for the door.

"Have fun, Joel. And have my sister home at a decent time tonight," Matt yelled after him.

"Yeah, right," Joel called back.

"Mari, Joel's here for you." Mom stood at the bedroom door, a big smile on her face. "You look beautiful."

"Thanks, Mom." Picking up a white lace shawl, Mari glanced at the clock radio. Four o'clock, right on time. Because they had to drive all the way to Reno to hear the orchestra, they'd decided to go to dinner early.

Mari tottered across the room on her ridiculous high heels, praying she didn't fall and break her neck. She much preferred her flats, but vanity did crazy things to a woman. She'd waited a long time to hear the orchestra and intended to wear her best and have the time of her life.

With Joel Hunter.

She stepped into the hallway and saw him standing in the living room. He wore a dark suit, the jacket cut perfectly for his broad shoulders and lean waist. He'd slicked his hair back, his high cheekbones showing a smooth, shaven face. She caught the spicy scent of aftershave and thought he smelled nice. For a careless kid from the wrong side of town, he looked good. Too good. She didn't understand the funny churning in her stomach or why she couldn't take her eyes off him.

His blue eyes gleamed with a hint of a smile as she walked toward him. In his hands he held a bouquet of yellow roses.

Her heart melted.

"Hi." Okay, not too original, but the sight of him stole her breath. In that moment, she realized Joel Hunter was an incredibly handsome man. Not a boy. Not a troublemaker, but her date tonight. The thought of going out on his arm made her feel all warm and fuzzy inside.

"Hi there," he returned, his gaze traveling over her yellow silk dress. "You look stunning."

"Thank you. So do you."

He reached out and fingered one of the long curls cascading over her shoulder. Mom had helped with her makeup and pulled her hair up in a pretty, but simple, style. From the gleam in Joel's eyes, he liked the effect.

"Wow, Mari. You look great." Livi stood beside Mom, clapping her hands.

Matt sat forward on the sofa and gave a low wolf whistle. "You sure do."

A smile came unbidden to Mari's lips and she silently thanked them all with her eyes. Dating at the Herrera house wasn't a simple matter. All of them stood around gawking, all of them had a say in what she wore. Now she understood Matt's insistence that she wear her best yellow dress. She matched Joel.

"This is for you." He held out the roses.

The delicate green paper around the flowers crackled as she took them from him. She buried her nose in the smooth petals, breathing in their sweet fragrance. "They're beautiful, Joel. Thank you."

Flowers! He'd bought her flowers. Other than her senior prom, the only time a boy had given her flowers was when they handed her a four-pack they wanted to purchase from the greenhouse.

"I wanted to get you roses since you missed your junior prom because of me." Joel shuffled his feet, his ears turning slightly red.

The burn of tears caught Mari by surprise and she pondered his shiny wingtips. His kind gesture touched her like nothing else could. The prom no longer seemed to matter. Nothing mattered except this moment, here and now. "It was just an old prom. No harm done."

A long, swelling silence followed.

"I can put these in water for you. I'll put them in a vase in your bedroom for you to enjoy later." Mom took the roses and gave Mari a gentle shove toward Joel. "You two go and have a nice time."

Joel opened the door for her, then took her arm as she walked down the porch steps. The afternoon sun gleamed golden, the weather perfect for a lovely evening.

Max came running from around the side of the house, barking, tail held high. Mari tensed, prepared to fight off the exuberant dog in order to protect her delicate dress.

In one graceful step, Joel placed himself in front of Mari. "Down!"

Max came up short and whined pathetically, his ears and tail lowering in submission.

"Stay!" Joel commanded as he escorted Mari to the truck.

Mari noticed the spatters of mud that usually covered the vehicle had disappeared. "You washed the truck?"

"Yep. And cleaned out the inside of the cab, too. It needed it. We work this truck hard. I didn't want anything to dirty your pretty clothes."

Again, his consideration surprised her. He opened her door and helped her step up on the foot rail. He waited while she buckled her seat belt, then closed her door and went around to the driver's seat.

As he inserted the key in the ignition, he gave her a lopsided smile. "My limousine is in the shop, so I borrowed your truck. Hope you don't mind."

She giggled. A real, silly, girlish giggle. "Of course not. This is preferable to the van."

He started the engine and orchestra music came softly from the CD player. Mari blinked, more than charmed.

"I didn't know you were such a romantic," she observed.

He reached across the seat and took her hand in his. "I'm glad I surprised you. And the evening is still young."

She laughed, her heart light as the fluffy clouds resting in the blue sky above.

"Aha! That's one," he said.

"Hmm?"

"I told you I'd make you laugh at least twice tonight. That's number one."

She laughed again. "I'm glad you've achieved your mission."

"Oh, no, sunshine. Making you laugh brings me joy, but it's not my mission tonight."

"Oh? That sounds rather ominous." She studied his serious expression.

"Not at all. I intend to ensure you have the best time of your life this evening. That's one of my goals for tonight."

She tightened her fingers around his, enjoying their comfortable chatter as they drove down the narrow road. "And what are your other goals?"

"Ah, *that* you're just gonna have to wait for, my girl." He grinned, putting on the blinker and watching as he pulled onto the freeway.

My girl! Like a pointed dart, his words went straight to her heart. She'd never expected to hear him say such a thing to her. Not in a million lifetimes. And yet it seemed so right.

As they drove along, they talked about everything and anything. Finalizing the fundraiser in another week, plans to build another greenhouse in the fall, how they might produce more plants more efficiently.

"We need a good winter crop. Have you thought about planting poinsettias in August so they bloom in time for the holidays?" Joel asked.

Again, his business sense amazed her. "That's a great idea. We could make enough to carry us through until spring. Do you know anything about growing poinsettias from scratch?"

"Quite a bit. I've been reading up on them and called a grower in California to talk about techniques. With Matt in school, we might need to hire another full-time person to help with the work, but I think it'd be worth a try."

She nodded in agreement. "Where did you say you got your college degree from?"

He looked away and cleared his throat. "Topman University."

"I've heard of them. Dad had some brochures lying around the house, telling all about the various programs they offer. They're national and accredited and you can get your degree completely online."

"Yes, that's what I did." He watched the road ahead.

"Taking online courses requires a lot of self-discipline. There's no professor standing over you to make sure you do your work."

He shrugged. "I would have preferred going to a classroom. I had so many questions I couldn't ask as effectively because I was doing it all online."

"You must have worked hard, putting yourself through school."

"I had a lot of help. People I can never repay or thank enough."

She twined her fingers with his. "Your mother must have been so proud of you. Maybe I should look into Topman. I doubt I could get a nursing degree online, but I might pursue another program."

A pained expression crossed his face. "But you always wanted to be a nurse, Mari. I recommend you go to Reno and take your nursing classes there."

She didn't respond. They drove through Topaz Canyon, the shadowed mountains rising up on either side of them, layered with alternating formations of pink, gray and orange volcanic tuff. Clusters of tall cottonwood grew along the Turner River as it wound its way beside the road. The late afternoon sun warmed the day. Splashes of yellow veronica, red Indian paintbrush, and delicate purple Penstemon dotted the hills. Midway down the canyon, Joel pulled into Hartman's Steak House. The restaurant sat off to the side of the road, built to appear like a giant log cabin. Mari knew the locals from all around came here when they wanted good food.

"Joel, this is too expensive."

"It's our first date and I'm giving my girl the best I can afford tonight. Didn't anyone tell you it's rude to ask your date about the cost?" He smiled to soften his reprimand as he got out of the truck and came around to open her door. Clasping her waist, he lifted her down and set her to her feet on the pavement.

"I won't bring up the cost again, Joel." She hated making him feel small and wished she'd kept her big mouth shut. Something had changed between them and she couldn't figure out how or what. She longed to protect him, but she wasn't sure what she wanted to protect him from. Since when did she care about hurting Joel's feelings?

Standing there in the parking lot, he cupped her cheek with his palm, his warm smile easing her mind. "We're an odd pair, you and I. We've known each other for so long that we feel comfortable speaking our minds, and yet we know so little about each other's dreams. I'd like to change that, if we can."

"What do you mean?" Hearing her own thoughts voiced made her uncomfortable for some reason.

"I'd like to know everything about you, Mari. And I'd like to win your trust."

Trust. When he'd first returned to the farm, she hadn't trusted him one bit. Now the old Joel seemed long gone and she not only trusted him, but she also depended on him. As she gazed into his eyes, she considered his words.

"Come on, let's not be so serious tonight, okay? Let's enjoy ourselves." He smiled and wrapped her hand around his arm before leading her inside the restaurant.

The hostess showed them to a table covered with white linens and drippy candles. Joel held Mari's chair while she sat. Support beams of knotty pine lined the center of the room and pictures of cattlemen and sleek horses graced the rough wooden walls.

The rustic surroundings gave no indication of the excellent fare. Joel ordered them rib-eye steaks with fat baked potatoes, garden salads, fresh bread and cherry cobbler à la mode. While they ate, they talked about their lives and laughed at some of the antics from their childhood. The drama of the past faded as they talked of the future.

"I'm stuffed," Mari confessed. "I don't think I can eat another bite."

He reached across the table, holding her hand. The candle glow glimmered off his dark hair. She couldn't remember seeing a more handsome man. The realization that this was Joel left her stunned. She couldn't get over the change in him, or the change in her feelings toward him.

The drive to Reno didn't take long. A feeling of excitement speared Mari when they went inside the Heritage Theater and were seated in the VIP section.

Joel bought a program and handed it to her. With their heads bent close together, they studied the list of musical numbers. When the production began, Mari's heart pulsed with the smooth rhythm of the violins, then throbbed with the beat of the bass. During a particularly emotional piece, Joel took her hand and she thought she was as close to heaven as she could possibly be. Sharing this evening with Joel made her feel close to him and special. As if they were more than two kids who had known each other all their lives. In spite of past problems, she now felt as though they were dear friends, which left her confused.

Back at home, Joel dropped her off at her door. Holding her arm, he walked her to the front porch. She felt jittery, wondering if he might try to kiss her and hoping he would.

"I had a wonderful time tonight. Thank you so much for a beautiful evening," she whispered.

"You're welcome, sunshine. I enjoyed it, too. More than I can say."

He took her hands in his and stepped near. As he looked down into her eyes, he kissed her gently and she closed her eyes. She absorbed the warmth of his fingers twined around hers like rays of sunshine. The evening had been more than magical and her mind spun with the realization that she cared for Joel. A lot.

The front porch light came on, breaking them apart. Livi burst through the screen door. "Hi! What you doing?"

"Olivia! Come back here." Mom rushed after the girl, a deep scowl on her face.

"Hi, kiddo." Joel chuckled and ruffled Livi's long hair before Mom latched on to the child's arm and dragged her back inside.

"But I want to talk to Joel. How was the orchestra? Did you have good seats?"

"Don't you have any manners? They're on a date," Mom scolded. "If this is how you're going to act, it's the last time I let you stay up late watching movies on a Friday night."

"What'd I do?" Livi whined as Mom closed the door and turned off the porch light.

Joel chuckled and stuffed his hands in his trouser pockets. "I guess I better be going before your little sister gets grounded for the rest of her life."

Mari laughed. She couldn't imagine Troy Banks or any

other man she knew being as easygoing as Joel. He seemed to take everything in stride. And he didn't mind her family's odd idiosyncrasies. He'd always fit in well with her family, which endeared him to Mari.

"Good night, Joel." She wrapped the lace shawl around her shoulders and folded her arms, watching as he walked down the steps.

"Good night, sunshine." With a last wave of his hand, he turned and disappeared around the back of the house as he headed for the cottage.

After he'd gone, Mari stood there in the dark, trying to sort out her feelings. Trying to understand.

She had told herself Joel was just a kid she once knew and their date tonight meant nothing more than having fun together. But somehow, she no longer felt the same. She looked forward to seeing him tomorrow. Working with him, planning and scheming as they found better ways to produce bigger, brighter blossoms on their chrysanthemums.

She turned and went inside, discovering the living room empty. Mom must have put Livi to bed.

Mari went to her bedroom and closed the door, not wanting to talk to Mom just now. Wanting to keep these new and funny feelings to herself. She didn't understand them, but realized they were unique and special. Emotions she'd never felt before.

She just didn't know what to do about them.

Chapter Fourteen

Joel didn't cut through the field to the caretaker's cottage on his way back to his place. Instead, he trailed the dirt lane, walking in the dark, enjoying the crisp damp air. He breathed in deeply, catching the sweet fragrance of apple blossoms. In the fall, they would pick the apples from the orchard and Mari would help Elena bottle applesauce. In the past, Joel had returned home to Oakland in the fall and never got to enjoy the bottled fruit during the winter months. Maybe this time would be different. Maybe this time, he could stay.

As he stepped inside the dark cottage and flipped on the light, he thought about being with Mari tomorrow. The thought of seeing her again lit up his soul from the inside. How had his love for Mari and her family grown so powerful? He thought love was finite, not this unlimited emotion that expanded his heart.

A heavy weight rested on him. Finally, he'd convinced Mari to go out with him and they'd had a great time. As long as he lived, he would cherish this evening. He was so close to getting the desire of his heart. So close to reaching his greatest dream. In his mind, he envisioned more dates with

Mari. Taking her to the movie theater in Reno, maybe another picnic and fishing trip with the family. Going to church. Falling in love.

He shook his head, knowing it might never be. He'd tried to tell Mari the truth several times, but never quite got it out. He hated to damage the fragile truce they'd found together. Maybe he should keep the truth from her and never tell her what he'd done.

No. Lying to the woman he loved wasn't in keeping with the promise he'd made to the Lord.

His emotions waged a battle within. He couldn't stand the thought of seeing the loathing that might come into Mari's eyes. Yet he couldn't live a lie with her, either.

He wondered if telling her how he'd paid for his stupidity would make a difference. Someone as pure and sweet and good as Mari might not understand how he'd fought so hard to make restitution for his crimes. How he'd spent hours on his knees begging the Lord to forgive him. And even then, he doubted he could forgive himself.

No, there was no way around his dilemma. Before they could move to the next level in their relationship, he'd have to tell Mari the truth. And every bit of his future happiness was riding on her reaction.

Four weeks before school ended for summer vacation, Mom went with Mari to collect the fundraiser packets. Joel stayed behind at the farm. They had two slim weeks to get the plant orders together and deliver them to the schools on the appointed day for pickup.

Joel hired extra help for the work. Three men from the homeless shelter who'd lost their construction jobs, due to the poor economy.

"Do you trust these men?" Mari asked as she sprayed soft

jets of water onto rows of yellow and orange marigolds. Rivulets ran from the wire mesh racks, dripping to the graveled ground beneath before running to the French drains underground.

He paused in his chore of cleaning out the overhead watering system. Standing on the ladder, he loosened a sprinkler head, then inserted a toothbrush to scrape out the mineral deposits. "They're not criminals, Mari. They're just out of work. The economy is tough right now. Why not help them out while they help us?"

Doing more good deeds. He'd never cared about homeless people before.

"Can we afford it?" Mari asked, knowing they could. She'd tallied the fundraiser orders and made a run to the bank to deposit all the checks and cash first thing that morning. Their earnings had exceeded her expectations and she just wanted to enjoy this moment by hearing him tell her again.

"You know we can." Joel grinned and blew on the sprinkler head before repositioning it and tightening it back into place.

"Thanks to you. There's no way we could have done this without you." She twisted the knob to the faucet and the flow of water stopped.

What she said was true and she no longer withheld her thanks from Joel. Because of him, they could now pay off the new tractor and bring all their bills current. The knowledge that they had enough money to meet their needs brought her a feeling of incredible relief. And she had Joel to thank for it.

After draping the hose over the hook, she came to stand beside the ladder, gazing up at him. He climbed down and stood in front of her, his face tightened into a serious frown. He opened his mouth, as though he had something to say.

"You okay?" she asked.

"Yeah, there's something I need to—"

"Hey, you guys! The McQueary truck is coming in for that pickup order. Do one of you want to handle it? Or should I call Elena?" Netta stood in the doorway, jerking her thumb toward the dirt road.

Joel stepped back and clamped his mouth tight. "I'll take care of it."

He walked the length of the greenhouse and followed Netta outside. Mari remained behind, finishing the watering. A nagging uncertainty kept her mind busy. Joel had been about to say something. Maybe he wanted to tell her how many bushels of hothouse tomatoes they'd picked yesterday, or when he predicted the new crop of azaleas might bloom.

It must not have been too important. Shrugging it off, she focused on her work.

The day before the scheduled delivery of the fundraiser flowers at the school sites, everyone at the farm worked hard. Joel and his three helpers from the homeless shelter watered all the plants heavily. Livi helped Mom sort the order forms. Matt rode into town with Mari to rent another big truck to haul the plants. Then Matt worked with Mari, Netta and Tom to fill the vegetable orders while Joel and his crew handled the flower orders. Joel ran the forklift, picking up heavy pallets of plants in the greenhouses and driving them out to the vans.

Happy voices rang out as the work crew turned the farm into a beehive of activity. Mari felt a poignant sense of nostalgia, remembering harvests like this when Dad had lived.

"I can't tell you how grateful I am for this job," Hank Ridley told her when they took a break.

Standing in the front yard, Mari reached into the ice chest and pulled out two bottles of water. She smiled and handed one to Hank, a middle-aged man with thickly lidded eyes and a heavy lower lip that jutted forward when he talked. "You're welcome. You've worked hard and we've been glad to have you here."

He popped the lid and took a long drink of water before he spoke. "Is there any chance you'll need me to stay on once the fundraiser's finished?"

His voice held a hint of hope. She wished she could hire all three of the men full-time, but couldn't support that large of a payroll. She needed to consult with Joel. "Possibly. Joel has an idea about growing poinsettias for the holidays, but it'll be an experiment this year. I need to speak with him about it first."

"Sounds good. I'd love to help out. Well, I'd better get back to work." He jerked on his work gloves as he jogged back to the truck.

Mari watched him go. Joel saw her and waved. She smiled back, thinking how funny that she'd become accustomed to talking everything over with him. After Dad died, she started making all the decisions on her own. But Joel knew instinctively when to plant, when to water, how many plants to grow and what technique to use. He even seemed able to predict the weather. She realized he was a much better gardener than her and it didn't bother her to admit it.

As she sipped her bottle of water, she walked to the house and sat down on the porch swing, resting a few minutes. They were winding down for lunch and Mom would soon take Livi inside to make sandwiches for all of them.

"Mari, you have a letter."

Scanning the top of the road where their mailbox stood, Mari saw Mom bustling down the lane, waving an envelope in the air.

"Don't run. Slow down," Mari yelled so Mom would hear.

Mom reached the expansive driveway and walked quickly to the house. She stepped onto the porch, breathing hard, her round face flushed with excitement. As Elena shoved the envelope into her hands, Mari noticed Joel reaching into the ice chest for a bottle of water. He had the longest legs she'd ever seen and looked great in a pair of blue jeans.

"Open it," Mom said, her voice quivering.

Mari scanned the outside of the envelope with curiosity. "It's from the university in Reno. Why would they be sending me something?"

Mom gave a little giggle, crushing the rest of the mail to her chest. What was going on?

Mari tore open the envelope and read the pages inside. Her mouth dropped open and her knees went weak.

"What does it say?" Mom asked, waving at Joel to join them.

"I've been admitted to the nursing program."

"I knew it. How wonderful." Mom hugged her, laughing with delight.

Joel stepped onto the porch, holding his work gloves in one hand, the bottle of chilled water in the other hand. "What's up?"

Mari held the paper in front of his nose. "Did you do this?"

His gaze scanned the first page. "Congratulations, Mari. They've given you a small scholarship that should help with the tuition. You should be proud of yourself—"

"Did you do this?" she interrupted.

"I submitted your application, if that's what you mean."

"Why?"

"You want to go. I know you do. Even you said—"

"You had no right." She jutted her chin.

His broad shoulders sagged. "I thought I was helping. I thought you just needed a nudge."

"I can't go to school right now."

"Why not?" Joel and Mom asked simultaneously.

"There's too much work. I don't have time."

"You have to make time for your dreams, Mari," Joel told her. "What are you afraid of?"

Ah, now he had her. She couldn't bring herself to tell him

that she was afraid of failure. Afraid she'd return to school and Mom would have another heart attack and the farm would start to go downhill and they'd lose everything Dad had fought to build throughout his lifetime.

She was afraid Joel would leave and she'd have to carry everything alone again. And she couldn't do that. There just wasn't enough of her to go around. Not without failing something.

"Look who's talking." She turned and walked into the house, letting the screen door slam behind her.

She thought she'd closed the door on more conversation, but then she heard the creak of hinges and turned, expecting Mom.

Joel stood in the doorway, his jaw clenched. "What do you mean by that?"

She cocked a hand on her hip. "Is this your dream, Joel? To work at Herrera Farms the rest of your life?"

His jaw tightened as he met her eyes. "Yes, it is."

She snorted, glaring at him with disbelief. "You've got to be kidding."

His eyes hardened. "Maybe we can talk later, when you've decided to be reasonable."

He pushed the screen door wide and stepped outside. She yelled after him. "That's just great. You accuse me of walking away from my dreams. You criticize me, but you're nothing but a coward yourself, Joel Hunter. And a hypocrite."

He didn't say a word, but returned to the truck and started working again.

A heavy weight settled on Mari's chest as she watched him. She longed to call him back, to apologize. But the words froze in her throat. Again, she had the fierce notion that he was keeping something from her. Neither one of them trusted each other enough to speak the truth.

She sat on the sofa, staring at the admission acceptance in

her hand. Feeling as though she stood upon a precipice of jagged rocks far below.

The screen door creaked and Mari turned, ready to tell him how much she needed him in her life, but not knowing how to get the words out. Instead, she found Mom leaning against the wall, her arms folded as she stared at Mari.

"Don't you think you were a bit hard on him?" Mom asked.

"Perhaps, but he overstepped the limits."

"He did it because he cares about you and he knows how much you want to be a nurse."

Mari indicated the envelope. "Did you know about this? That he applied for me and registered me in the nursing program?"

"Yes, I knew."

A conspiracy! She didn't know what to make of this. "He must have falsified my signature to do this, Mom. He had no right."

"Actually he got the forms and completed them and I signed the application on your behalf."

Unbelievable! Mari crinkled the envelope in her fist and tossed it across the room where it pinged off the wall. "Matt will be going to college soon and we'll need every extra penny for him. Joel is egotistic and selfish and—"

"Mari." Mom stepped over to the couch and sat beside her. "Joel paid your tuition himself."

Silence filled the room as Mari absorbed this bit of information. "He what?"

"You heard me. He's been saving his paychecks since he arrived. If he's so selfish, why would he pay for all your books and fees himself?"

That was the question burning through Mari's mind. Why? Why did he care so much? A sense of exhilaration warred with absolute terror. She wanted to go to school and now was her chance, but what if—?

"I'm worried about you, Mom. If I go to school, that will mean more work for you. We have limits on our man power and financial resources. It would push us too much right now."

Mom smiled and placed her hand on Mari's arm. "I'm not going anywhere, *niña*. The doctor told me yesterday that I'm doing fine. None of us knows the day or hour when we might be called home to our Heavenly Father. But we can't give up our lives by living in dread of what might happen. I thought I taught you to have more faith than that."

Faith. Oh, how she longed to cast her burdens on the Lord, but she didn't know if she could.

If not now, then when?

Mom hugged her. "We'll find a way to do the work around here while you go to school. Joel's not going anywhere and he can do the work of several people."

Mom's reassurance didn't make Mari feel better. "Joel won't stay here indefinitely. Eventually he'll leave. And then what?"

Mom shrugged. "We'll face that if the time comes. In the meantime, your life is passing you by, *mija*. If you don't live it now, you'll regret it forever. You owe Joel an apology."

Mari shook her head, overwhelmed by this development. She couldn't think clearly, not with all the work they had waiting for them outside. "I've got to get back out there. We've got to get all those plants in the truck."

Mari stood and went outside, standing on the porch, feeling the warmth of the sun on her face as she stared across the driveway at Joel. He stood beside the truck, holding a clipboard while he counted off flats of marigolds. When he reached the end of the tally, Hank and the other men picked up the flowers and carried them into the rented van.

He turned and saw her there and waved, but his smile seemed a bit sad. She hated the barrier that had gone up between them. And she couldn't help feeling that she had put it there. But she couldn't help being cautious. He'd never stayed with them permanently before. What kept him from leaving again? Nothing!

Right now, she wanted to run to him and apologize. To thank him for what he'd done. But something held her back.

Perhaps her own pride. And fear.

She'd have to speak with him eventually, but she didn't know what to say. She had a lot to think about. And a lot to reconcile within herself.

By late Saturday afternoon, the flowers for the fundraiser had been delivered to the schools. Joel paid the work crew with a promise to call them next week about other possible jobs. At the last school, Mari sent Elena and Livi home in the van. Then Matt helped her and Joel clean up the empty pallets and stack them in the truck.

"Can I take off, now?" Matt jerked his thumb toward a light post in the school parking lot. Alan Krueger sat in the driver's seat of his mother's green minivan.

"You going somewhere with Alan?" Mari asked.

Matt hunched his shoulders. "Nowhere special. We thought we'd hang out for a while."

Alan was a good boy who never got into trouble. "Okay, but be home by curfew."

"Thanks, sis!" Matt trotted off to join his friend.

"Nice to see him hanging out with better friends," Joel said. He stood beside Mari, enjoying the contented smile on her face.

"Thanks to you."

"Me?"

"Yeah, you've done wonders with him, Joel. Mom and I are very grateful."

Her words speared his heart like beams of sunshine and he opened his mouth to discuss their recent conflict over her college registration. She must have sensed his frame of mind because she walked to the truck in a brisk stride where she retrieved a stiff-bristled broom.

Maybe he could talk to her later, when she wasn't so tired. They'd worked hard over the past weeks and would now enjoy the fruits of their labors.

In silence, they swept the dirt out of the rental van. Then Mari got into the truck and followed Joel while he drove the van to the rental office. They returned the vehicle clean and in good order just before closing at seven o'clock.

Joel waited outside while Mari went in the office to deliver the keys and sign the final paperwork. When she returned, she climbed into the driver's seat of the truck.

Okay, she wanted to drive. Without argument, he sat in the passenger seat. When she drove directly to Troy Banks' house, Joel got a little anxious.

"Why are we stopping here?" He tensed, an automatic response conditioned by years of dislike for Troy.

Mari reached for an envelope on the dashboard and handed it to him. "This needs to be delivered to Troy."

The envelope hadn't been sealed and he opened it, finding a check made out to the high school football team. "I don't understand."

"I figured after your last conversation with him, you might like to deliver it yourself."

And possibly get slugged in the process. "I thought you already gave him the money his team earned for the fund-raiser."

"No, I was waiting for the plants to be delivered and all the orders finalized."

Great! Just what he needed. Another angry confrontation. He didn't mind apologizing to the other people he'd offended, but this was different. He hadn't just disliked Troy, he'd carried a deep and abiding hatred for the guy most of his life. When he'd promised God he'd do everything in his power to make amends for the things he'd done, he never realized it might be this difficult. The Lord said to love his enemies, but how could he love this particular enemy?

With misgivings weighing him down, Joel reached for the doorknob. Stepping out of the truck, he hesitated, staring back at Mari. Her face remained passive, as if completely unaware of the turmoil spinning around in his mind. "You're not coming in?"

Okay, coward. He didn't want to do this alone, but he knew he must if he wanted to be square with the Lord.

She leaned one forearm against the steering wheel, not meeting his eyes. "Nope. I think you should deliver this all by yourself. Troy might think twice before accusing you of anything dishonest again."

If only she knew how her confidence in him provided the catalyst he needed to walk up to Troy's house. No easy task, even knowing she waited for him.

As he sauntered up the front sidewalk, he noticed Troy's red sports car parked in the driveway. Joel walked slowly, every step heavy as lead. Why did he have to make the first move? Why couldn't Troy apologize to him?

By the world's standards, Troy was educated and had a successful career, but his personal life was in tatters. Troy's wife had left him and Joel couldn't help feeling sorry for the guy.

A thought occurred to Joel, as if the Spirit opened his mind and quickened his understanding. Maybe Troy was just like him. He'd made some serious mistakes in life and caused a lot of tears to the people he cared about the most. But if Joel could change and make things right, then Troy could, too. Someone had to take the first step. Why not Joel? He'd become too comfortable with his hate. It didn't matter if Troy apologized to him. But Joel had to forgive Troy. He had to do what he knew was right. And he had to do it now, before he lost his courage.

As he rang the doorbell, Joel glanced over his shoulder at Mari. She sat where he'd left her, her gaze pinned on him, watching his every move.

Don't be home. Don't be home.

The litany of words went through Joel's mind over and over again.

He was just about to turn away when Troy answered the door. He gaped at Joel, his face darkening, his words belligerent. "What do you want?"

Joel forced a smile and handed him the envelope. "I'm dropping off your check. Also, I wanted to tell you I'm sorry for hitting you all those years ago. I wish we could have been friends instead of fighting. I hope you'll forgive me."

Troy's eyes narrowed with suspicion and he peered inside the envelope, then craned his neck to look at Mari. "Is this a joke?"

"No joke. I'm dead serious." Joel reached out and clasped Troy's hand. Troy tried to pull away, but Joel held tight and Troy had no choice but to shake.

A long, swelling silence followed as Joel stepped back and waited for a response.

"No hard feelings, I hope," Joel said.

Troy's mouth hardened and he didn't say a word. Joel turned and walked away. The click of his steady footsteps rang through the air. Somehow, his legs didn't feel as heavy anymore. When he opened the door and climbed inside the truck, he contemplated the house. Troy went back inside and slammed the front door. The gesture saddened Joel's heart, but he felt oddly content. Gone was the loathing he'd felt toward the other man, replaced by a hope that one day they might be friends. He hoped one day Troy might find the same healing peace within his own soul.

"You look pleased with yourself. Is everything okay?" Mari asked.

He twisted sideways in his seat and smiled. "Yeah, everything's great."

"You gave him the check?"

"Yep."

She blinked. "And what did he say?"

"Thank you." No way was he going to tell Mari the details of his conversation with Troy. It'd just upset her and Joel figured it was time to put the past behind them.

A flash of relief lit up her eyes. She turned on the ignition, shifted the truck into gear, then pulled away from the curb. "I saw you shaking Troy's hand. He looked like he'd rather slug you."

Joel chuckled. "I didn't give him the opportunity."

"I'm really proud of how you handled him, Joel. You've come a long way. What changed you?"

"Your dad never gave up on me. I don't know where I'd be today without him fighting for me. But I also came to realize that God loves all his children, even Troy Banks."

As they skirted through traffic, she adjusted the rearview mirror. "You're very forgiving, considering all the animosity between the two of you."

"I don't want to be angry anymore, Mari. It doesn't do any good except make me bitter and old inside. Also, I've learned that if I want to be forgiven, then I need to forgive others."

Her brow crinkled with thought and he could see her contemplating his words. He hoped he hadn't said too much.

She took a deep, relaxing breath and let it go. "I'm sure glad this day is over with."

"You've earned it. Maybe we can go fishing again." He eyed her, trying to pick his words carefully. He wondered if he told her how much he loved her if it might make a difference.

Instead, he tried to act casual. No easy accomplishment with his heart slamming against his chest. "If I can just convince you to forgive me for going behind your back to register you for school, I'd be a happy man. I was only trying to help."

Her eyes snapped with fire. "I don't want to discuss it. I need more time to think. I don't know if I'm going back to school yet and I just can't have this conversation right now."

He nodded and sat back, resting his hands on his thighs. "When you're ready to talk, let me know. I'll be right here waiting."

Until she didn't need him anymore or asked him to leave. And he prayed that day never came.

Chapter Fifteen

Eating humble pie would be difficult, but that was exactly what Mari must do.

As she stepped outside on the front porch, she fixed her gaze on the star-laden sky. A warm breeze caressed her arms, but she still shivered. Something hardened inside of her. She felt as cantankerous as a porcupine and wasn't sure why. She hated the wall of animosity sitting between her and Joel like a giant blockade. And what was worse, she had put it there. She'd come to cherish her camaraderie with him, to trust him. And when he did something kind and generous for her, what did she do? She threw it back in his face.

As she walked to the greenhouses, she thought of what she should say to him. She'd overreacted and been too hard on him. And yet he had to learn not to interfere in her personal affairs.

The tall, mercury-vapor yard lights bathed the rows of greenhouses in a blue glow, making her hands appear mottled with splotches. She felt old and ungrateful. For the past few years, she'd gone through the motions of her life, doing what everyone expected of her. Somehow she'd forgotten her own dreams, her own hopes and joys.

She found Joel in one of the greenhouses, the wooden tables devoid of flowers since they'd carted them all off and sold them at the schools. He'd turned off all but the light hanging directly over the workbench. As he knelt on the damp concrete beside Max, watery moonlight trickled through the polyethylene, glinting off his dark hair. His strong profile showed a blunt jaw with a shadow of a beard. Resting back on his heels, he scratched the dog's ears.

"Yes, that feels good, doesn't it, Maxie? You're so picked on. No one pays enough attention to you, do they? You've been so busy today, eating, barking and lying sprawled on the floor sleeping."

Mari chuckled and he lifted his head. Seeing her, he stood and walked the length of the greenhouse, leaning his hip against a long table. From the tidy appearance of the greenhouse, he'd swept up the dirt, rinsed the filters and taken out the trash. Tomorrow, they'd start planting poinsettias. By November, the greenhouses would be aflame with fire-red blossoms in time for the holidays. What would she do without Joel?

"Hi there." His voice sounded low and husky, his dark gaze resting on her with the weight of an anvil.

"Hi. Can we talk for a few minutes?"

"Sure. Actually I was meaning to come up to the house to see you, so your timing is perfect. Maybe we can be alone for a few minutes." A bent metal chair leaned against the workbench and he folded it out for her. He half sat on the table, one leg braced against the ground, his other leg dangling over the side of the bench.

"You want to go first?" he asked.

His eyes didn't waver and she felt the heat of nervousness climb up her throat. He seemed so calm while she felt as though every nerve in her body might explode.

"Yes, I want to apologize. What you did in registering me

for school was very generous and I wasn't very grateful. It's just that…"

He tilted his head to one side. "What?"

"I don't think I can accept it, Joel. You came here to work. You need to keep your money for yourself."

"I don't need anything, but you do."

"But you have a life to live. Surely you have your own plans and goals."

"Everything I want is right here at Herrera Farms."

Oh, boy! She wasn't sure what to make of that. The air surged with energy. She felt it like a tangible thing. A complete awareness of Joel as a grown man who had his life under control and knew what he wanted.

"You can go to school, Mari. You have no excuses not to go."

She rested a hand on her hip. "I'm not making excuses."

"What's really bothering you? What are you afraid of?" He lifted one dark eyebrow. Just that single gesture told her he wasn't buying anything she was saying.

"I'm not afraid." Or was she? It'd been five years since she went to school. What if she couldn't cut it anymore? What if she couldn't keep up with the workload and the younger students?

"I know you too well for that nonsense. I think you're scared of failing."

He'd always seen right through her, never letting her get away with anything. But she supposed she did the same to him. Maybe that was why they were such good friends.

Good friends. Yes, and so much more.

"Okay! I'm afraid. Does it make you feel better if I admit it?" It did no good to deny it. No one but the Lord knew her like Joel did. Not even Mom.

She stood and turned away, pressing her hands against her heated cheeks.

"Mari." Joel placed his hands on her shoulders and she flinched.

She swiveled around to face him, stepping back. Wishing he'd hold and comfort her and keep her safe, but at the same time longing to run to the house and hide. "There's only so many hours in the day. I can't run the farm, keep Mom safe, chase Matt and Livi around, and go to school all at the same time. I can't do it all."

He smiled gently, lovingly. "You can with help."

"And what about when you leave? You've always left before."

"Not this time. Have a little faith."

Now that he had confronted her with it, she realized she hadn't exhibited a lot of faith in God. She prayed often enough, asking for His help. But then she doubted and withheld her trust.

"And why aren't you going anywhere, Joel? You talk about faith and living my dreams, but what about you? This is a dead-end job."

He shook his head. "It's the best job in the world."

She shook her head, unable to believe what he said. From his steady gaze, she realized he was completely serious. "You're not being honest with me. I feel strongly that there's something you're not telling me."

A shuddering breath whooshed from his chest. "Yeah, that's what I wanted to talk to you about. You really want to know why it's so important to me that you realize your dreams and go to school?"

She nodded, and a queasy feeling settled in her stomach. Like she was about to learn she had terminal cancer.

"Your father paid for my education, Mari. Every bit of it."

Mari felt dizzy. Dad hadn't told her this and she wondered now if she'd ever really known her father.

"Your dad wanted you to go to school," Joel said. "When he became ill and you dropped out, he was very upset about it."

"Yes, he tried to get me to go back, but he needed me here. He needed help to run the farm."

Tenderness filled his eyes. "I understand your reasons, but I promised him that I'd make sure you went back to school. You're not gonna make a liar out of me, are you?"

She staggered against the wall. "So, that's why you're here? To make me a charity case because my father helped you so much?"

"No, Mari. Absolutely not." He held out his hands to make his point. "I'm here because I want to be here. Because I love you."

Her head started spinning. He turned his hands palms up and waited for her reaction. She felt completely washed out, physically and emotionally. She cared for this man, but she'd never seen a future with him.

Until now.

"Is that what you wanted to tell me? That you love me?" She wasn't sure she believed him. This was Joel, the boy from her childhood. Always teasing, never serious.

Or was he?

"Yes, in part. But there's more, and I'm afraid you won't like it."

Oh, this was just getting better and better all the time. Her legs wobbled and she sat down, folding her hands in her lap. "Okay, I'm listening. Tell me everything. I just want the truth."

"The truth. I've carried the shame with me for so long, I'm not even sure I know what to say anymore." He spoke as if to himself.

"Just tell me, Joel. Tell me and get it over with."

Shoving his hands in his pants pockets, he began to pace the length of the cement walk path. He spoke slowly, as though he picked his words with care. "After that last summer I spent here at the farm, I returned to Oakland and got involved with my cousin, Bobby, and some of his friends. I was a foolish seventeen-year-old and discovered too late that I was riding in a stolen car. Bobby was being initiated into a gang."

Mari tensed, wondering if she wanted to hear this. It didn't sound good.

"It was late at night and we pulled over. I thought Bobby was going into a convenience store to steal a box of doughnuts and candy bars. A stupid kids' prank. I didn't know he was gonna shoot the store clerk."

Mari gasped. "Oh, Joel!"

He faced her, his eyes filled with anguish. "I didn't know he was gonna do it, Mari. I couldn't do anything to stop it. If only I'd gone into the store with him, I might have been able to save that man's life." His voice cracked and so did her heart. He dropped his head forward. When he lifted his face again, tears shimmered on his cheeks.

"What happened?"

He swallowed hard and his voice trembled. "Because he was eighteen, Bobby was tried as an adult along with the other guys in the car. Bobby may spend the rest of his life in prison. Even though I didn't know what was happening until it was over with, I was still there with them. I was considered an accomplice and found guilty and convicted as a minor. I spent the next eight years incarcerated in the juvenile justice system. I had a lot of time on my hands and your dad convinced me to get an education. He paid for it and I worked hard, so I wouldn't let him down. When I got out, I returned to Oakland. Some of the old gang from the neighborhood started to hassle me. They wanted me to join their gang again, but I couldn't. I'd made a promise to the Lord that if he'd give me a second chance, I'd do everything in my power to make amends. To live a good life and be the kind of man your father would be proud of."

She sagged back on her chair, staring at him, not knowing what to say. Part of her felt compassion for what he must have gone through. The guilt. Being locked away for so many years. Wondering if he'd ever have a normal life again.

Another part of her felt anger over his thoughtlessness and the needless loss of life. He hadn't pulled the trigger, but he'd been there, running with a gang of thugs who didn't care who they might hurt. "Oh, Joel. You really messed up your life, didn't you?"

His eyes filled with such deep remorse that she couldn't help feeling compassion for him.

"Yeah, I messed up big-time. My conscience told me not to go that night, but I didn't have the courage to say no, or to ask Bobby to stop the car and let me out. I can't tell you how that night still haunts me. If only I could go back in time. Just a few minutes is all I need to make it right. I'd do anything to stop what happened."

"Like what? Do you really think you could have stopped your cousin?"

His face creased with grief. "I don't know, but I should have tried. If only I'd known what was going on. I was so stupid, putting myself in that situation. Being there made me a part of it. Mom asked me not to go with them. I'll never forget the look on her face when she came to the jail to see me. I broke her heart, Mari. Because of what I'd done, I couldn't even be there when she died."

The emotion of his words overcame him and he ducked his head, wiping his eyes and nose with his hands. She waited, giving him time to gain his composure, trying to ignore the burn of tears in her own eyes. She wondered at her own emotions waging war inside her heart and mind. Outrage and sympathy. She wanted to scream at him for what he'd done. For what he'd been a part of. Yet she also wanted to hug him and tell him it was okay. How could he have been so stupid and naive?

"I've paid my debt to society, Mari. I'm a free man and I intend to keep it that way. But I haven't been able to let it go in here." He touched his chest, just over his heart.

She wanted to comfort him and tell him to let it go, but she couldn't. For her, it had just happened and she needed time to sort it out in her own mind.

"I came to Herrera Farms to escape Oakland and all the trouble awaiting me there. I can't go back. Even with an online degree from an accredited college, not many people will hire a jailbird like me. I know what I did was wrong and I have to live with that the rest of my life."

Everything made sense, now. Him showing up here at the farm unexpectedly. The secretive exchanges he shared with Mom. "I suppose my mother knows about this?"

"Yes, she offered me a job, so I could get out of Oakland and start a new life."

Mom had known and not told her. Mari could understand how her parents had tried to protect Joel, but it didn't stop the waves of emotional pain from washing over her. She bit her lip, wishing they had trusted her more. And then she realized if she wanted to be trusted, then she needed to be forgiving.

Joel came to her and knelt beside her chair, his eyes red. "When I got out of jail, all I could think about was you, Mari. I've always loved you. I want so much to be a part of your life, but I want complete honesty between us. I may not deserve it, but can you forgive me, Mari?"

"I don't think—"

The dinner bell interrupted her, ringing loud and clear. Both Mari and Joel stood, spinning toward the door.

"Why would your mom ring the dinner bell at this time of night?" Joel asked.

"I don't know."

The ringing persisted, an urgent *cling, cling, cling.*

Joel took a step. "You think Livi is playing a practical joke?"

"No, Mom would ground her for a month if she did that. Something's wrong."

They left the greenhouse, sprinting up the road. Max ran beside them, panting. Mari's lungs burned and she struggled to keep up with Joel's brisk stride. As they raced into the front yard, Mom and Livi stood on the porch. The outside light cast a pale glow over them. Mom stood ringing the bell, her face ashen.

When Mom saw them, she let go of the bell rope. "Thank goodness you're here."

Mari pounded up the steps behind Joel. "What's wrong?"

Tears streamed down Mom's face and she pressed a hand to her chest. "It's your brother. He's been in a terrible accident. The hospital in Reno just called."

"Is he okay?" Joel asked.

Mom shook her head, her voice cracking. "No, it's serious. He's lost a lot of blood, but that's all I know. They've taken him to the emergency room. They don't know if he'll live through the night."

Mari's heart wrenched. Matt might die? This couldn't be happening. Not now. Not ever.

"Dallin Keats is dead." Mom brushed the tears from her cheeks, her shoulders shaking with sobs. "He was driving when he rolled his truck and was killed instantly. Mateo was in the passenger seat, but he was wearing his seat belt. They believe that's the only reason he's still alive."

"No! I thought Matt was with Alan. When did he hook up with Dallin?"

"I don't know," Mom cried, her face a mask of agony.

The ramifications washed over Mari with sickening force.

Dallin Keats was dead. Her brother might die. Tears washed Mari's cheeks as she hugged her mother tight. She'd never liked Dallin, but she'd never wished for his death. How horrible for his family. They must be stricken with grief. And what a waste of his life.

Mom pulled back and took a halting step. "Joel, would you drive us to Reno, please? I've got to get to my son."

"Of course. I'll do anything to help," Joel said.

Livi threw her arms around Mari's legs, sobbing. Mari bent down and picked the little girl up, trying to comfort her. "Hush, sweetie. It's gonna be okay."

"Matt's hurt, Mari. He might die." The child shuddered and buried her face against Mari's neck.

Mom reached for her purse and green sweater, which had been flung over a wicker chair on the porch. As she thrust her arms into the sleeves, she spoke over her shoulder to Mari. "I need you with me tonight, *niña*. I need all of my children."

Joel gave Mom a comforting hug, his eyes glistening with emotion. Mari set Livi down. "Don't worry. We'll say a prayer for Matt. We just need to have faith in the Lord."

"Yes, faith." Mom gave a half smile, but her eyes filled with fear.

In her heart, Mari realized she did believe God could heal her brother. She just needed to trust in the Lord. She must have faith. But when she thought of Matt lying in the hospital, possibly dying, a feeling of dread gripped her heart.

Please, God. Please help my brother. Watch over my family tonight.

As they piled into the van and put on their seat belts, Livi curled against Mom on the backseat. Mari wouldn't consider taking Livi to stay with a friend tonight. If they never saw Matt alive again, they must be together as a family.

Joel didn't speak as he started the van and flipped on the

headlights. As he pulled out of the yard, Mari's stomach churned. An urgency built within her, to get to the hospital as fast as possible. To talk with the doctors and find out exactly what they were dealing with.

"Did the hospital tell you what happened?" Mari twisted to look back at Mom.

"Just that it was a car accident. I hope he wasn't drag racing again."

Joel shook his head, staring straight ahead. "He promised me that he'd never drag race again."

A harsh laugh slipped from Mari's throat. "This wouldn't be the first time Matt didn't keep his word."

Joel pinned her with a quiet gaze. "No, Mari. He gave me his word and I trust him."

A feeling of shame swept over her. Joel's faith in her brother made her feel disloyal and small for doubting Matt.

How had this happened? How could Matt be so foolish to get himself in this predicament?

What if her brother died? Mom had already had one heart attack and the stress could cause another. They just couldn't lose another member of their family. Not now, after everything they'd been through.

Please, Lord. Please keep us safe.

Chapter Sixteen

"Your son is still in surgery. He's hemorrhaging internally and they're trying to stop the bleeding. Follow me." The nurse at the front desk of the emergency room led them down a long hall to an empty waiting room.

The smell of antiseptic and bleach burned Joel's nose. Mari walked with Elena, her arm wrapped around her mother's shoulders. Livi reached up and took his hand, her small bones feeling fragile in his grasp. He gave her fingers a gentle squeeze of reassurance.

"The doctor will come visit you as soon as he's out of surgery," the nurse said before departing.

Elena huddled on the hard couch with her daughters. Joel sat opposite them, not knowing what else to do. Livi sniffled. All of their eyes reddened from crying, their faces pale.

Joel picked up a magazine from an end table, but then tossed it aside. He focused on the raised TV set, a late-night movie he didn't recognize. His neck knotted with tension and he wished there was something he could do. He loved Matt like his own brother. He felt so helpless. Maybe he couldn't do anything about this situation, but the Lord sure could.

"In situations like this, Frank always gathered us together for family prayer," he suggested.

Elena nodded. "Yes, would you lead us in prayer, Joel?"

In the quiet of the waiting room, they bowed their heads and Joel spoke reverently, asking the Lord to heal Matt and bring them comfort. He also asked the Lord to console Dallin's family in their grief. When he finished, they each wiped their eyes.

"Thank you," Mari said.

She dug through her mother's purse, searching for something. "Joel, will you get Mom some water, please? I want her to take her pills."

"Sure. Do you want anything?" He came to his feet and stepped toward the door. He'd seen some vending machines out in the hallway.

"No, thanks." Mari's voice cracked and so did his heart.

Livi shook her head, her eyes wide as moons.

Out in the hallway, Joel dug into his pocket for some change. He got a bottle of water and a chocolate bar, then returned to the waiting room. He handed the water to Elena and set the candy on the table. "For anyone who wants it. We can break it up and all have a piece, if you like."

Elena's pills rattled as Mari opened the bottle and poured one onto the palm of her hand. Elena took it, then popped it into her mouth and took a gulp of water. The candy remained untouched.

For three hours, they stayed in that stifling room. All alone, as if they were the only people on earth, with only the sounds of the TV to keep them company. The silence lengthened with each of them lost in their own thoughts. No one spoke. Joel found it difficult to breathe.

By two in the morning, Livi fell asleep. Elena eased the child into a more comfortable position on the couch and Joel covered her with his jacket.

Looking up, he caught Mari watching him, the corners of her eyes creased with uncertainty. Under the circumstances, he wished he hadn't told her the truth tonight. He should have waited, but he hadn't known about Matt at the time.

Her silent, brooding expression kept his insides tied in knots, filling him with doubt. She couldn't forgive him for what he'd done. He had no future with her here at Herrera Farms. He'd asked too much from her.

"I think I'll stretch my legs. I'll be back in a few minutes," he said.

Elena nodded, but Mari barely spared him a glance. With dark circles of exhaustion beneath her eyes, she looked worn out. He thought about suggesting she lay back and get some sleep, but knew the futility of such a request. All of their thoughts were consumed with concern for Matt. None of them except little Livi would rest until they heard some news.

As Joel walked out of the waiting room, he felt a sinking of despair. He'd tried to help Matt. He loved every member of this family and felt protective of them. Like they were his own. There wasn't anything he wouldn't do for them.

One thing he knew for certain. He and Mari couldn't continue as they were now. He loved her. More than his own life.

And she didn't want him.

His heart ached with the thought of her eventually finding someone else to love. Someone to marry and give her a family.

The thought made his heart jerk painfully. Watching her fall in love with someone else would rip him to shreds.

He couldn't stand to leave, but neither could he stay.

Mari watched as Joel left the waiting room and her throat went bone dry. Gone was his confident swagger, replaced by a sadness she could only define as grief.

She longed to call him back, to ask him to stay with her,

but she let him go. He'd laid a lot on her mind tonight and she needed time to think. To sort things out.

Alone in the waiting room, she faced Mom. "Joel told me about his incarceration in the juvenile justice system."

Mom lifted her head from the back of the sofa, her eyes widening. "And?"

"He asked for my forgiveness."

"That's generous of him, considering it's not your place to condemn or forgive him."

Mari stiffened, realizing she was right. "He also told me he loved me."

A slow breath eased from Mom's lips. "What are you going to do?"

"I don't know. Mom, why didn't you tell me?"

Elena shrugged. "It wasn't my place. Joel's paid for what he did. Now it's between him and God."

"But he was involved in the killing of another human being."

"Nonsense. Joel would never hurt a fly. He stayed in the car. He didn't know that man was going to be killed. He'd never sit by and allow a man to be killed if he knew what was going on."

Mari inclined her head. "He sure knocked Troy flat."

Mom gave a sad smile. "That was different. He did it to defend you."

"But he lied to me."

"Mari, he's been trying to tell you the truth since he arrived, but you make it kind of difficult. You expect absolute perfection from everyone, even yourself. And nobody is perfect, except the Lord. You need to lighten up a little bit."

Lighten up? If she did, she feared all the balls she was juggling in the air might hit the floor, and then what would they do? They could lose the farm and their livelihood. She couldn't afford to lighten up, and yet being so uptight wasn't doing her or the family any good, either.

Mari paused, remembering several times in the past weeks when Joel seemed rather pensive and said he had something he wanted to talk to her about. They always seemed to be interrupted. "Dad never would have condoned what Joel did."

"No, he didn't condone it, but why do you think your father took Joel under his wing? Joel's done the same for Mateo. Should we give up on your brother?" Mom's voice sounded thick with emotion.

"Of course not."

"Your father refused to give up on Joel, either."

"But Joel wasn't in trouble with the law when he was young. Why did Dad bring him here every summer?"

She tried to stand, but Mom held on to her arm, pinning her to the sofa. "Do you really want to know why your father loved Joel so much?"

"Yes." Mari brushed a length of hair back from her face, amazed at the vehemence in her mother's voice.

"Because he saw himself in Joel. Just like Joel sees himself in Mateo. They've mentored one another because they knew what they were each going through. Because they cared for each other."

"I don't understand." Mari sat forward, listening intently.

Mom sat back against the couch and inhaled a deep breath. "When your father came here from Mexico, he was young and wild. He moved to Los Angeles and joined a gang of bad kids. He got into so much trouble with the law. When the authorities released him from jail, he—"

"Wait a minute! Dad was in jail?"

Mom nodded, her eyes glimmering with tears. "Yes, several times. When he got out the last time, he knew he must change or spend the rest of his life in prison. He met a kind man who offered him a job working for a landscaping company here in Nevada. Your father came to Reno to get away

from the gangs and he met me. We married and worked hard
and soon started our own business."

"Herrera Farms."

"Yes, your father promised himself he would see each
and every one of his children educated, no matter how hard
he had to work. He did everything he could to help Joel,
because someone was kind enough to help him when he
needed it so badly."

Mari froze. She couldn't move. Couldn't breathe. As the
shock ran through her, she clasped a hand over her mouth.
"Mom! Why didn't you or Dad tell me this before?"

"Your father didn't want you to think less of him because
he'd been in jail. He loved you kids so much, Mari. But he
loved Joel, too. He believed he was doing a good thing by
helping Joel. I agree. Seeing the good man Joel has become, I
have no regrets in helping him. Not one. It's all been worth it."

Mari couldn't absorb all of this fast enough. To complete
the blow, Mom's next words left Mari speechless.

"Everyone deserves a second chance, Mari. You, me and
Mateo. Even Joel. The Atonement isn't just for the righteous.
It's for the sinners of the world. Those who need God's redeeming love the most. The Lord will forgive whom He will
forgive, but we must forgive all men. Who are we to judge
others when we walk so imperfectly?"

Mom stood and reached for her purse. "Can you stay with
Livi? I need to get some fresh air."

Without waiting for Mari's reply, Mom left her sitting there
in a daze. Several minutes passed as Mari listened to the
sounds of the hospital, the muted beep of a monitor going off
in another room, the clatter of a cart being pushed down the
hall. Such normal sounds. And yet Mari felt as though her
world had turned upside down.

All her life, she'd adored and idolized her father. Discovering he'd been in jail, she didn't know what to think. It made Dad seem so—

Human.

She considered Joel's many good qualities. His strong work ethic and sense of humor. His kindness toward Matt and Troy Banks. His take-charge manner and willingness to make amends with those people he'd hurt. His help around the farm. His generosity in paying her tuition to nursing school. She couldn't deny that Joel had become a remarkable man.

Maybe she had judged Joel too harshly when she had no right to judge him at all. Not if she hoped for mercy from God for her own weaknesses.

At five in the morning, a doctor wearing a blue smock and a surgical mask dangling around his neck walked into the waiting room. "Mrs. Herrera?"

Mari blinked her eyes, weary with fatigue. Both she and Mom came to their feet, facing the doctor. Joel hovered beside the TV where he'd been pacing for the last hour. Livi sat up and rubbed her sleepy eyes.

"I'm Mrs. Herrera," Mom said.

Finally! Finally some news. Mari braced herself for the worst and wrapped her arm around Mom's waist to lend her support.

"I'm Dr. Linton, your son's surgeon." He gave them a warm smile, which Mari took as a good sign. Surely he'd be frowning if he had bad news.

"How is Mateo?" Mom's voice wobbled.

"I won't lie to you. It was touch and go for a while, but we stopped the bleeding. I'm pleased to say he's now stable. I think the worst is over with."

Mari released a shuddering laugh.

"Oh, thank you!" Mom hugged the doctor, a spontaneous gesture.

"Can we see Matt?" Livi asked.

"Maybe later, once we're sure he won't have a relapse. He's still groggy, but he's been asking for someone named Joel. Is that you, by chance?" The doctor's gaze rested on Joel.

"Yes, sir." Joel stepped forward, looking quizzical and uncertain.

"Let's give it a few more hours and then you can go see him. Unfortunately, the child won't be able to go in until he's out of intensive care."

Livi gave a low moan of distress.

"Don't worry, sweetie. He's gonna be fine," Mari said.

They waited three more hours and a nurse came for them. "Mrs. Herrera, would your little girl like to stay with me while Anne takes the rest of you to visit your son?"

"I'd appreciate it," Mom said.

The nurse smiled at Livi. "How about some breakfast? Are you hungry?"

Livi nodded and stifled a huge yawn, completely worn out.

"Come with me."

While the nurse took Livi, they trooped after Nurse Anne, walking down the hallway, pushing past two sets of double doors before they were asked to put on sanitary gowns and masks. Then Anne led them into the ICU.

Draped in white blankets, Matt lay on his back, his face pale, both arms tied down with IV drips. Equipment and monitors stood at his head, blinking with a variety of buttons.

"Mijo," Mom whispered as she bent low and caressed his face before kissing his forehead.

Matt blinked his eyes open and gave his mother a wan smile. *"Mamá."*

They crowded around the bed, smiling with tears of joy. Careful of the IV lines, Mari hugged Matt. "I'm so glad you're gonna be okay. I love you so much."

"I love you, sis." His voice sounded weak.

As she drew back, tears dripped from Mari's eyes. She couldn't remember the last time her brother told her that he loved her. It'd taken a near tragedy to remind her family how much they all meant to one another.

She gave silent thanks to the Lord for His mercy. God had heard their prayers and spared her brother's life. Nothing else seemed of importance right now. The farm, the bills, the laundry. All of it faded away. Her family was all that mattered.

"Joel." Matt lifted one hand, his voice hoarse from the tube they'd put down his throat.

"I'm here, buddy." Joel stepped near and squeezed Matt's hand.

"I'm sorry," Matt croaked. "I tried to keep my promise. I remembered what you told me about being in a car and wanting to get out. You said you'd come get me, no matter where I was. I told Dallin to let me out, but he wouldn't stop the truck. He wanted to race. I tried to keep my promise. I'm so sorry and now…now he's dead."

Matt's chest heaved with sobs, deep and wrenching. Mom stood on the opposite side of the bed, resting one hand on Matt's shoulder, her other hand clutching a tissue to her nose as tears ran down her cheeks.

Mari's heart broke and she wished she could ease Matt's pain. In Matt's eyes, she saw Joel there. Surely he'd felt the same all those years ago when he'd been part of that horrible tragedy that landed him in the juvenile correction facility.

"Hush, *mijo*. Everything will be all right." Mom tried to comfort Matt, but it did no good.

Joel placed his hand on Matt's shoulder as he responded in a quiet tone. "You kept your word, Matt. You're a better man than me. I never asked to get out of the car."

Mari blinked, her eyelashes spiked with tears. She didn't know how much Joel had told Matt about his past and it didn't matter. She'd learned in the past few months that Joel performed acts of service in silence. Serving food at the homeless shelter. Planting pumpkins for Millie Gates. Repairing the van. Mentoring Matt. Paying Mari's tuition. Not once had Joel asked anything in return.

Except for her love and forgiveness.

The nurse brushed back the curtain and gave an apologetic smile. "I'm sorry, but he needs to rest, now. His mother can stay with him, if she likes."

"Yes, I'll stay." Mom gave a teary smile.

Mari walked out into the hallway before turning to face Joel. "I'd like to remain here at the hospital, in case Mom needs anything. Would you be willing to take Livi home? I called Netta on the phone earlier and she said she'd watch her."

"Sure." He smiled, a curving of his lips that eased the harshness of his face.

"Thank you."

He reached out and touched her cheek, the warmth of his fingertips tingling across her flesh. In his eyes, she saw tenderness. "You're welcome, sunshine."

They went to find Livi, reassuring the girl that Matt was fine and she'd see him soon. Mari watched as the child followed Joel out to the parking lot without complaint. The automatic doors whooshed open as he took Livi's hand. He looked at Mari over his shoulder and his expression tightened, his eyes filled with an emotion she didn't understand. She waved, longing to speak with him, but thinking now wasn't the time. Maybe later, when they could be alone.

She returned to the waiting room where she dozed off. At noon, she was able to visit with her brother again as he sat up and ate a few spoonfuls of cherry gelatin. Then Mari took her mother to the hospital cafeteria, where she made sure they both ate a turkey sandwich and Mom took her pills.

When Netta showed up with Livi at the hospital late that afternoon, Mari didn't think much about it.

"Did Joel stay behind to plant the poinsettias?" she asked.

Netta shook her head. "No, Mari. He's not at the farm."

"Where is he?"

"He's leaving, Mari." Livi sniffed, wiping her eyes. "He's not coming back. Can't you do something?"

Netta squinted her eyes. "I thought you knew. He rode with us to Reno and I dropped him off at the bus station."

Leaving? Without even saying goodbye?

White-hot panic peppered Mari's skin. "When? When is he leaving?"

"I don't know. He just asked me to drop him off and said goodbye."

"Can I borrow your car?"

"Sure. It's parked right out front." Netta handed her the keys.

"Tell Mom I'll be back." Whirling about, Mari raced for the door. In the parking lot, she sprinted for Netta's green compact car.

Don't leave, Joel. Please, don't leave.

The words zipped through her mind over and over again. This was her fault, she knew it. He'd asked for her forgiveness and she hadn't offered it to him. So much had happened since then, but she should have found a moment to tell him everything was okay. Who was she to forgive him when she had so many faults of her own? Forgiveness was for the Lord to offer, not her.

As she jerked open the door and climbed into the car, one thought pounded her brain. She loved him. When faced with the possibility of never seeing him again, she realized she couldn't stand to lose him. Not now, when she finally understood how much he meant to her. She loved him, more deeply than she'd ever loved anyone on earth. If only she could reach him in time. If only he could forgive her.

Chapter Seventeen

"Where you going?"

Joel froze, recognizing the mellow voice behind him. He knew Mari was there even before he turned and saw her.

Standing next to the ticket counter, he dropped his duffle bag on the floor and slowly pivoted on his heels. At first sight of her, his heart gave a giant leap. He thought when he'd left Herrera Farms that afternoon that he'd never see her again. And now, here she was, in the flesh. Looking more beautiful than ever before. He blinked, almost unable to believe his eyes.

She stood just inside the automatic double doors of the bus depot. Afternoon sunlight fought its way through the dingy windows, glinting off her dark hair as it lay in waves around her shoulders. Her lavender shirt accented her brown eyes. Her pink-painted toe nails peeked at him from her dainty sandals. Dressed in faded blue jeans, she slung her thumbs into her belt loops and took three steps closer. The thought of leaving her shredded his heart.

"I bought a ticket to Sacramento. My bus leaves in twenty minutes," he said, not recognizing his own clogged voice.

Her unwavering gaze pierced him to the bone, burning his heart to cinders. "You're leaving without saying good-bye?"

He lifted one shoulder. "It seemed the right thing to do. I thought it'd make things easier on all of us."

"You think you can get your money back?"

His pulse tripped into double-time. "I can try. But why would I want to do that?"

She stepped forward, her polished toes touching the tips of his pointed boots. So close he could see the golden flecks of light in her brown eyes and smell her clean, floral scent.

"Because I want you to stay."

His throat closed and he could barely speak. "You want me to stay? Or the business wants me to stay?"

"Me. I want you." She shot him a sideways glance, resting her hand on his chest. Beneath the cotton fabric, his skin burned.

"Why?"

She released an impatient huff. "You're not gonna make this easy on me, are you, Joel?"

"Sorry, sunshine. But this is too important. Why do you want me to stay?"

Her bottom lip quivered. "Because I love you. Is that a good enough reason?"

Firecrackers went off inside his brain, making him feel dizzy with joy. "Yes, that's a pretty good reason, if you really mean it."

"Oh, yes. I mean it. I love you, Joel. So much."

Did he dare believe her? "Really?"

She gave him a playful swat. "Yes, you dunce. I want you to stay with me always. Can I say it any more simply?" Her laughter surrounded him.

He covered her hand with his, gazing into her eyes. "Oh, Mari. I love you so much."

"Don't leave me, Joel." Her voice softened to a whisper as she gazed up at him with glistening eyes.

"I'm sorry, but I feel like I've let you down. I've done and seen so many ugly things in my life. I've tried to erase it all from my mind, but sometimes it returns when I least expect it. I don't know if I can be the man you deserve."

She shook her head. "Because of how you've changed your life, you are the man for me. And I don't want to hear any more about who deserves what. This is a partnership."

"You mean you can forgive me? For everything I've done?"

"Only if you can forgive me. I have so many of my own faults. We all do. No one's perfect, Joel. That's why we have the Atonement. The Lord knew we'd need it every day of our lives."

"If you can forgive me, maybe the Lord can forgive me, too."

"Absolutely. We need to fear God less and trust Him more. I believe He's a loving Father who wants us to succeed. He doesn't want us to live in misery. He wants us to be happy."

Joel wrapped his arms around her, pulling her close. Breathing her in. "Mari, I've been so lost."

She kissed him tenderly and murmured against his lips. "Not anymore. I've found you. Are you sure you know what you're signing on for by staying?"

"I'm signing on for forever and nothing less."

"Yes, but I've made a decision about school."

"You have?"

She twined her fingers with his, the tip of her nose touching his as she gazed into his eyes. "I'm gonna use the tuition you paid for the fall. I've decided I can go to school and still keep the farm going."

Laughter trembled in his chest. "I'm so glad to hear that."

"But I'm gonna need your help. I want you to stay with us permanently."

He lifted his brows. "As your husband, or as your hired help?"

She grinned up at him. "What kind of proposal is that?"

"Just asking where I stand."

She made a tsking sound, shaking her head. "I hope you'll stand beside me, but I expected more."

"Such as?" He couldn't help teasing her a few moments more.

"Such as kneeling and taking my hand as you gaze into my eyes with adoration and ask me to be your—"

He knelt so fast, his knees popped. Her laughter rang throughout the depot and strangers stopped to stare. When he pulled a simple gold band with a modest diamond from his pocket and held it up for her inspection, her eyes widened and her smile faded to tears of joy. The small gem glittered beneath the fluorescent lights.

"Marisol Herrera, I love you more than life itself. Will you be my wife and make me the happiest man on earth?"

"Joel! Where did you get that?"

"I've been saving every dime. I paid your tuition, bought a suit and paid for this ring. I'm dead broke, so I hope you'll marry me for my good looks and not my money."

"Yes, oh, yes!" She pulled him up and he swung her around in his arms.

He held her tight, just because he could. Just because she was his and he wanted to enjoy this sweet moment a little while longer. He'd come to Nevada, hoping to make her his own, begging the Lord for a second chance. And he'd just been granted the wish of his heart. It couldn't get better than this.

As he slid the ring on her finger, her eyes gleamed with love. For him.

"Come home. The family is waiting for us," she said. "Matt's sitting up and asking for something solid to eat. We've got to get those poinsettias planted, if we plan to have a winter crop."

"Yes, ma'am." Her words left him weak-kneed and delirious with happiness.

As he lifted his duffle bag onto his shoulder, he smiled. With his free hand riding the small of her back, he escorted her over to the ticket counter to see about getting a refund.

Home! His family. A place of contentment, love and acceptance. He wanted nothing more.

* * * * *

Dear Reader,

Forgiving others can be easy when the offense is simple, but sometimes the hurt cuts deep into our souls. It can be very difficult to forgive a painful offense. It can be an even greater challenge to forget and never bring it up again.

Likewise, when we have offended others, we might yearn for their forgiveness. None of us are without faults. When we are called to forgive others, we need to ask ourselves if we would want their forgiveness if the situation were reversed. Truly, the principle of forgiveness is a two-way street. In order to be forgiven, we must also be forgiving.

In *The Road to Forgiveness,* both the heroine and the hero learn this lesson the hard way. According to the Gospel of Luke, we must "judge not" so that we will not be judged, "condemn not" so we will not be condemned, and forgive so that we may be forgiven. These instructions carry an awesome and fearful consequence for each of us. This includes forgiving ourselves. Guilt can destroy us when we are unable to allow the Lord's redeeming love to cleanse our soul with forgiveness. The legal courts of our land endeavor to provide justice. God provides the ultimate justice, but His court is also filled with mercy. He knows each of our hearts and can judge with perfect fairness. Is it any surprise that He asks us to forgive one another, so that we then do not fall into the sin of judging others?

I hope you enjoy reading *The Road to Forgiveness,* and I invite you to visit my Web site, www.LeighBale.com, to learn more about my books.

May you find peace in the Lord's words!

Leigh Bale

QUESTIONS FOR DISCUSSION

1. In *The Road to Forgiveness,* Mari Herrera feels torn between her duty to her family and her desire to go to school and meet her own goals. Have you ever made sacrifices for other people in your life? Have other people made sacrifices for you? How can you find ways to meet your own goals while still caring for the people in your life?

2. Joel Hunter spent years incarcerated in the juvenile justice system. Do you believe people like Joel should be given a second chance to change their lives? Or should they remain isolated from society?

3. Guilt can help us make good changes in our lives. Joel has paid his debt to society, yet he still blames himself for the death of an innocent man. Have you ever blamed yourself for something you had no control over? How can God's love ease our guilt?

4. At the end of the story Mari learns that her beloved father had been in jail numerous times before he finally changed his life. Do you have people who are important in your life who have made poor choices? How have you loved these people without becoming drawn into their bad lifestyle? How have you tried to help them change? Is there a point when you must withdraw yourself from such people because they are damaging your life, too?

5. Matt is a teenager running with a wild crowd of kids and making poor choices that could destroy his life. Joel sees himself in Matt and endeavors to help the boy change. Do

you have rebellious teenagers in your life that you love and want to help? How can you work with these teens to help them change their lives around? Should we ever give up on them?

6. Mari has been extremely judgmental of Joel most of her life. Now that Joel is a grown man, why is it so hard for Mari to trust him and believe that he really has changed? Do you think Mari is too hard on Joel? Why or why not?

7. During the eight years Joel was incarcerated in the juvenile justice system, Mari's father called and wrote to Joel each week. Why was this contact so important to Joel? Do you think Joel would have been able to change his life without this contact from Mari's father?

8. Forgiveness is a process, both for people who are seeking forgiveness and for people who want to forgive. Joel recognizes what he has done wrong and humbles his heart before God, asking forgiveness and promising the Lord that he will forsake his bad lifestyle. Why is this such an important first step in the process of forgiveness? Have you ever had to seek God's forgiveness?

9. Throughout the story Joel endeavors to apologize and make amends to the people he has offended. Why are these important steps in the process of forgiveness?

10. During his teenage years Joel detested Troy Banks. Although Joel wants to make amends to the people he has hurt in the past, he finds it especially difficult to apologize to Troy. Why do you think that is?

11. Gradually Joel comes to realize that in order to be forgiven, he must also be forgiving of others. Do you agree?

12. When Joel apologizes to Troy, he is not fully surprised when Troy does not return the concession. Do we need to be forgiven by others in order to apologize and make amends? Have you ever apologized to someone who has refused to forgive you? How did you then forgive that person and reconcile the problem between yourself and God?

13. Has someone ever offended you and then come to you to apologize and make amends? Did you forgive them and forget the offense? Or did you withhold your forgiveness? If we forgive someone and then remind them of the offense later on when we are angry at them, have we truly forgiven them?

Here's a sneak preview of
THE RANCHER'S PROMISE
by Jillian Hart
Available in June 2010
from Love Inspired

"So, are you back to stay?" Justin's deep voice hid any shades of emotion. Was he fishing for information or was he finally about to say "I told you so"?

"I'll probably go back to teaching in Dallas, but things could change. I'll just have to wait and see." The things in life she used to think were so important no longer mattered. Standing on her own two feet, building a life for herself, healing her wounds—that did.

"And this man you married?" he asked. "Did he leave you or did you leave him?"

"He threw me out." She waited for Justin's reaction. Surely a man with that severe a frown on his face was about to take delight in the irony. She'd turned down Justin's love, and her husband of five years had thrown away hers. If she were Justin, she would want her off his land.

"You were nothing but honest with me back then." He leaned against the railing, the wind raking his dark hair, and a different emotion passed across his hard countenance. "I was the one who never listened. I loved you so much, I don't think I could hear anything but what I wanted."

"I loved you, too. I wish I could have been different for you." Helpless, she took another step toward the driveway. She didn't know how to thank him. He could be treating her a lot worse right now, and she would deserve it. "Goodbye, Justin."

"I suppose you need a job?"

"I'll figure out something." Need a job? No, she was frantic for one. How did she tell him the truth?

Find out in THE RANCHER'S PROMISE
Available June 2010 from Love Inspired

Love Inspired

Bestselling author

JILLIAN HART

brings you another heartwarming story
from

the
**GRANGER
FAMILY
RANCH**

Rancher Justin Granger hasn't seen his high school sweetheart
since she rode out of town with his heart. Now she's back, with
sadness in her eyes, seeking a job as his cook and housekeeper.
He agrees but is determined to avoid her...until he discovers
that her big dream has always been him!

The Rancher's Promise

*Available June
wherever books are sold.*

Steeple
Hill®
LI87601

www.SteepleHill.com

The Great Adventures of Sherlock Holmes

Sir Arthur Conan Doyle

Academic Industries, Inc.
West Haven, Connecticut 06516

ISBN 0-88301-712-1

Published by
Academic Industries, Inc.
The Academic Building
Saw Mill Road
West Haven, Connecticut 06516

Printed in the United States of America

ABOUT THE AUTHOR

Sir Arthur Conan Doyle, an English novelist, was born in 1859 and knighted in 1902. He was educated at Stony-hurst College in Germany and at Edinburgh University. He received an M.B. in 1881 and M.D. in 1885. He was a practicing physician in Southsea, England prior to his career as an author.

In 1891 he attained immense popularity for *The Great Adventures of Sherlock Holmes*. These stories follow the capers of Sherlock Holmes who detected crime and untangled mysteries with an uncanny talent.

Although his stories were often imitated, none were as successful as the Sherlock Holmes stories. In his later years, Doyle was a convinced spiritualist, and he wrote and lectured on spiritualism.

Sir Arthur Conan Doyle
The Great Adventures of Sherlock Holmes

Helen
Stoner

Dr. Watson

Sherlock Holmes

James
McCarthy

Miss
Turner

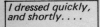

I dressed quickly, and shortly. . . .

Good morning, madam. My name is Sherlock Holmes. This is my friend, Dr. Watson, before whom you can speak freely.

I'll order some coffee, Holmes. The young lady is shivering with cold.

It is not cold which makes me shiver, sir. It is terror!

When she raised her veil, we could see she was indeed very much afraid.

You must not be afraid. We shall soon set matters right. You have come in by train, I see.

You know me then?

No, but I see the second half of a return ticket in the palm of your left glove. You must have also had a good drive in a dog-cart.

There is no mystery, madam. The left arm of your jacket has mud on it. Only a dog-cart throws up mud that way.

That is correct. I had no one but you to turn to.

My work is its own reward, madam. Now please tell us what brought you here.

Alas! The worst part of it is that my fears are so unclear.

But I have heard that you can see deeply into the evils of the human heart. . . .

Please go on.

My name is Helen Stoner. I live with my stepfather, who is the last living member of one of the oldest Saxon families in England, the Roylotts of Stoke Moran.

I know the name.

The family was at one time among the richest in England. But now nothing is left but a few acres, the 200-year-old house, and many bills to be paid.

The last squire, lived the life of a highborn poor man. His only son, my stepfather, managed to become a doctor, and then went to India, where he started a large practice.

But in a fit of anger, he beat his native butler to death. He served a long term in prison. When he returned to England years later he was a bitter man.

Please, no master!

When Dr. Roylott was in India, he married my mother. She was the young widow of Major-General Stoner. My sister Julia and I were twins. . . .

Mother left her money—a considerable sum to Dr. Roylott while we lived with him, but with the understanding that a certain yearly amount should be given to each of us if we got married.

Shortly after our return to England, eight years ago, my mother died in a railway accident. Dr. Roylott then gave up his medical practice.

We lived on the money mother had left—happily at first. . . .

We'll live together here, girls, in the old family house.

But a terrible change came over our stepfather. He began to quarrel with anyone who crossed his path.

Get out of here. . .and stay out!

Last week he hit the town blacksmith.

Out of my way!

What?

He had no friends but the gypsies who sometimes camp on the estate. . . .

He would go away with them sometimes for weeks at a time.

He has an interest also in Indian animals, which are sent over to him. . . .

Indian animals? What kind?

He has a cheetah and a baboon.

11

They wander freely over his land and are feared by the villagers almost as much as their master.

What do you think of it, Holmes?

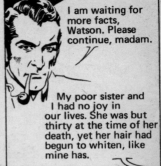

I am waiting for more facts, Watson. Please continue, madam.

My poor sister and I had no joy in our lives. She was but thirty at the time of her death, yet her hair had begun to whiten, like mine has.

Your sister is dead then?

She died two years ago. That is what I wish to speak to you about!

Holmes now showed his interest.

Living as we did, we were not likely to see anyone our own age. But we had an aunt, living near Harrow, whom we visited now and then.

At Christmas, two years ago, Julia went there and met a major in the marines whom she wished to marry. My step-father did not object, but shortly before the wedding day, the terrible event occurred.

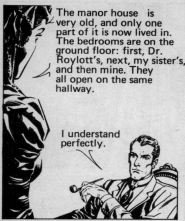

The manor house is very old, and only one part of it is now lived in. The bedrooms are on the ground floor: first, Dr. Roylott's, next, my sister's, and then mine. They all open on the same hallway.

I understand perfectly.

The windows of the three rooms open out upon the lawn. That night Dr. Roylott had gone to his room early. We knew he was not asleep because my sister could smell the strong Indian cigars he smoked.

My sister had come into my room, where we sat talking about her wedding. Then, as she rose to leave. . . .

Helen, have you ever heard anyone whistle in the middle of the night.

Never. Why?

Because these last few nights, I have heard a low whistle. I cannot tell where it came from, perhaps from the next room, perhaps from the lawn.

It must be those gypsies.

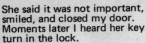

She said it was not important, smiled, and closed my door. Moments later I heard her key turn in the lock.

Did you always lock yourselves in at night?

Always. I told you about the cheetah and the baboon. We did not feel quite safe.

Of course.

That night a feeling of danger kept me from sleeping.

My sister and I were very close. . . . It was a wild night, the wind howling outside, the rain beating against the windows.

Something terrible is going to happen. . . I know it.

Suddenly. . . .

Good heavens! It's my sister!

Ai-eeee. . . .

As I opened my door I heard a low whistle, such as my sister told me about, and a few moments later a clanging sound as if a large piece of metal had fallen.

Ai-eee— help!

I'm coming, Julia!

The Great Adventures of Sherlock Holmes

As I ran down the hall, my sister's door was unlocked and slowly opened. I stopped, afraid of. . . .

Good heavens!

My sister came out of her room, her face white with terror, reaching out for help, moving backward like a drunk. . . .

Her knees gave way and she fell in terrible pain.

Julia!

Ah-hh! Oh-hh!

Julia! What is it?

Then in a voice I shall never forget she screamed. . . .

My God, Helen! It was the band! The speckled band!

W-what?

Her finger pointed toward the doctor's room, but she started to choke. She could no longer speak. My stepfather was running from his room in his bathrobe.

But I knew it was too late. . . .

I'm afraid it's no use.

Julia! Speak to me!

She died within a few minutes. . . .

Are you sure about this whistle and clanging sound?

The coroner asked me at the investigation. I thought that I heard it, but because of the sound of the storm, I may have been fooled.

Was your sister dressed?

No, she was in her night-gown. In her hands she held a burnt match and a match box.

Showing that she had lit a match when alarmed. That is important. What did the coroner find out?

He was unable to find the cause of her death. The door was locked on the inside. The windows were blocked by shutters with iron bars. The walls and floor were found to be solid. I am sure my sister was alone when she met her end. There were no marks of violence upon her.

What about poison?

The doctors found no trace of it.

What do you think your sister died of then?

Pure fear and shock, but I cannot imagine why.

Were there gypsies on the land at the time?

Yes, There usually are.

Hmm—most puzzling. . . .

What did you gather from this speckled band?

Sometimes I thought it was the wild talk of a high fever or perhaps that it meant the band of gypsies.

Perhaps it referred to the spotted hand-kerchief some of them wear.

I think there is something missing. Please continue.

Two years have passed since then, and my life has been lonelier than ever. A month ago, however, a dear friend asked me to marry him. . . .

My stepfather agreed to it. . . .

His name is Percy Amitage, father. We hope to be married in the spring.

Spring, eh? That's good news.

Two days ago, repairs were started on the house, and my bedroom wall was broken through.

Now where shall I sleep?

Good work, lads!

17

Now I have had to move into the room in which my sister died. . .to sleep in her bed.

Imagine, then, my terror last night when. . . .

That low whistle. . .the one I heard when Julia died.

My lamp showed nothing. I dressed, and at daylight got a dog-cart at the Crown Inn nearby, and drove to Leatherhead.

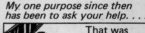

My one purpose since then has been to ask your help. . . .

That was wise. But have you told me all?

Y-yes.

I think not. You are protecting your stepfather.

These marks— four fingers and a thumb! Your stepfather's no doubt!

Ohh!

W-what do you mean?

18

He is a hard man. He does not know his own strength.

This is serious business! Could we see these rooms without your step-father knowing it?

He was coming into town for the day. There would be nothing to disturb you.

Good! You are not against this trip, Watson?

Not at all.

I shall return by the twelve o'clock train, so that I will be there when you come. I feel better already since I have told you.

After Helen Stoner had gone....

What do you think of it all, Watson?

It's an evil business.

Evil enough. Whistles at night, a band of gypsies on friendly terms with this doctor. . .And he has every reason to try to stop his stepdaughter's marriage.

What do you make of the strange words of the dying woman?

I do not know.

If the flooring and the walls are indeed solid, and no one could come in through the door, window, or chimney, then her sister must have been alone when she died.

And adding the fact that Helen Stoner heard a clanging sound, which might have been caused by a metal bar falling into place....

This makes me think the barred window may be the key.

But what did the gypsies do?

Suddenly Sherlock Holmes turned as the door flew open.

I don't know. That is why we are going to Stoke Moran today.

What in the name of the devil!

He threw down the poker and walked out of the room.

Don't you dare interfere in my business!

A friendly person.

As he spoke, he picked up the steel poker, and with a burst of strength. . . .

There!

My word, Holmes! And you are not half his size!

We must get to the bottom of this, Watson! I only hope our young friend will not suffer because he followed her here.

What now then?

Now, our breakfast! Afterward, I shall walk down to the courts, where I hope to get some facts to help us.

It was nearly one o'clock when Holmes returned. . . .

I have seen the will of the girl's mother, Watson. The total income is not more than 750 pounds. Each daughter will get 250 pounds when she marries. . . .

Why, that means. . . .

Exactly! The marriage of each daughter would cost Dr. Roylott a third of his income!

This proves that he has good reason to prevent their marriages.

You really think. . . .

Come! We must not delay. . . .

Holmes called a cab to take us to Waterloo station. . . .

Of course. . . .

And, Watson, you might take your pistol. It's a good argument against gentlemen who can twist pokers into knots.

At Waterloo we caught a train for Leatherhead.

There's our train! We'll take a cab at the station when we arrive!

You do work fast, Holmes!

As we rode through the country later. . . .

Look there, Watson.

Eh, what?

At the highest point ahead we could see the towers of a very old house. . . .

Driver, is that Stokes Moran?

Yes, that's it.

To get to the house you may follow the footpath. There, where the lady walks. . . .

Yes, we'll get off here then.

We sent the cab back on its way. . . .

Good afternoon, Miss Stoner. You see that we have kept our word.

Splendid. Dr. Roylott has gone to town and will not be back before evening.

We have already met. . . He followed you to our door.

Good heavens! I never know when I am safe from him. What will he say when he returns?

The Great Adventures of Sherlock Holmes

Don't Worry, Miss Stoner. You must lock yourself up from him tonight. If he becomes dangerous we will take you away.

Now we must use our time well. Please take us at once to the rooms which we must look at.

Follow me, then.

Although the house was being repaired, there were no workmen present. Holmes studied the window carefully. . . .

This, I believe was your old bedroom, the center one your sister's, and the one next to the main building was Dr. Roylott's bedroom.

Exactly. But I am now sleeping in the middle one.

I see no real need for repairs at that end wall.

No. I believe it was an excuse to move me from my room.

At the back runs the corridor on which these three rooms open. Are there windows?

Yes, but they are too small for anyone to pass through.

Asking Miss Stoner to close the shutters from inside, Holmes tested them with his magnifying glass.

Well, we shall see if the inside throws any light upon the matter.

I see. That presents some difficulties.

Watson, there is no way these shutters could be forced open from the outside.

So we went into the room in which Miss Stoner was now sleeping and in which her sister had met her death.

We must take in every detail, Watson.

Then pointing to a thick bell rope which hung beside the bed. . . .

Where does that bell ring?

In the housekeeper's room. It was only put there a few years ago.

Did your sister ask for it?

No, she never used it. We always got things for ourselves.

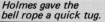

Holmes gave the bell rope a quick tug.

Why, it's a fake!

By jove. It won't ring?

No, it is not even attached to a wire, but only to that hook just above the little opening for the ventilator.

I never noticed that before.

Very strange! Why would a builder open a ventilator into another room, when it would make more sense to open it to the outside.

That was done about the same time as the bell-rope.

Holmes went into Dr. Roylott's bedroom.

What's in here?

My stepfather's business papers.

Not a cat? Why else this saucer of milk?

We don't keep a cat. But there is a cheetah and a baboon.

Well, a cheetah is just a big cat. Yet a saucer of milk would not be enough to feed it.

A small dog leash, with a loop at the end, caught Holmes' eyes. . . .

Look at this. A common dog leash tied in an uncommon manner. Ah, me! It's a wicked world.

Never have I seen my friend's face so sad or his brow so dark. . . .

You must do exactly as I say, Miss Stoner. Your life may depend on it.

I will.

Then, first, my friend and I must spend the night in your room!

W-what. . . .

I believe your windows can be seen from the Crown Inn?

Yes. . . .

You must lock yourself in your room when your step-father returns. When you hear him retire for the night, unlock your window and open the shutters.

Put your lamp there as a signal to us. Then go into your old room. The rest you will leave to us.

The Great Adventures of Sherlock Holmes

But what will you do?

We shall try to find out the cause of this noise which has bothered you.

I believe, Mr. Holmes, you already know it. Please tell me the cause of my sister's death.

I would like to have more proof before I speak. We must go now. Be brave.

Sherlock Holmes and I then took a room in the Crown Inn. At nightfall. . . .

Look, Watson. Dr. Roylott is driving up.

So he is!

Perhaps I should go alone tonight, Watson. It could be dangerous. . . .

Pooh! If I can help, of course I shall come. I saw nothing so dangerous.

You saw all that I did, but I fancy I may have figured out a little more.

I saw nothing remarkable except the bell rope, and I don't know what it meant.

You saw the ventilator, too?

Yes, but I do not think it so strange. It was so small—a rat could hardly pass through. What harm can there be in that?

A ventilator is made, a cord is hung, and a lady who sleeps in bed dies. Does that not strike you?

I don't see the connection.

The bed was nailed to the floor. Have you even seen such a thing before?

No, I haven't.

The bed must always be in the same place under the ventilator and the rope—which was never meant for a bellpull!

And at last I began to see what Holmes was hinting at. . . .

By Jove! We are only in time to stop some horrible crime!

When a doctor goes wrong, he is the worst of all criminals.

We waited for the lights to go out. . . .

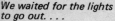

We shall have horrors enough tonight. Let us turn our minds to something more cheerful for now.

About nine o'clock, the lights went out, and the Manor house was all dark.

Now to wait for Miss Stoner's signal.

Then, at eleven o'clock. . . .

That's it, Watson. A light in the middle window!

A moment later we were on the dark road, with one yellow light leading us through the dark to the house. . . .

Suddenly, out from behind a clump of bushes, there darted what seemed to be an ugly and bent child.

My God, Holmes! What is it?

For the moment, Holmes was as jumpy as I. . . .

Great Scott!

You saw it too?

But soon he broke into a low laugh. . . .

My dear Watson, that is the baboon.

My word, so it is!

I had forgotten the baboon and the cheetah.

Enough worries, Watson. We're going inside.

Then Holmes whispered softly. . . .

The least sound would be the end of our plans. . . .

We climbed in the open window and slipped off our shoes. Quietly Holmes closed the shutters and looked around the room. . . .

All is as it was this afternoon.

We must sit without light. He would see it through the ventilator.

Yes, of course.

Do not go to sleep; your life may depend on it. And have your pistol ready.

I will sit on the bed, and you in that chair.

Holmes had brought a cane which he placed upon the bed beside him, along with some matches and a candle. . . .

Then he turned down the lamp. . . .

We wait now, Watson. This man is a quick thinker, but we shall think even more quickly. . . .

We waited then in complete darkness. . . .

The village clock struck one and two and three, and still we sat waiting for whatever might happen.

Bong! Bong! Bong!

Ow-w! That cat-like cry outside. . . it must be the cheetah!

Suddenly, there was a beam of light. . . .

That light. . . coming from the ventilator. . . .

Then the smell of burning oil and heated metal. . . .

Someone has heated a dark lantern. . . .

I heard a sound of movement. . .then all was silent again.

That smell. . . It's growing stronger!

For half an hour I sat with straining ears. Then suddenly I heard another sound—like that of a small jet of steam from a kettle. . . .

What is that?

Instantly, Holmes jumped from the bed and lit a match, hitting quickly at the bellpull with his cane. . . .

Do you see it, Watson?

W-what?

I heard a low, clear whistle. . . .

That light. . . I cannot see what it is. . . .

Agh!

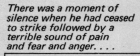

While I could not see what my friend hit at, I could see his face, deadly pale and filled with horror.

There was a moment of silence when he had ceased to strike followed by a terrible sound of pain and fear and anger. . . .

Ai-eeeee!

What is that?

Holmes, what can that mean?

It means that it is all over, Watson. Take your pistol and follow me.

He led the way to Dr. Roylott's room. Twice he knocked at the door.

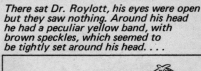

There is no sound from the room, Watson. . . .

Right, Holmes. I hear nothing.

He entered the room. . . I at his heels.

There sat Dr. Roylott, his eyes were open but they saw nothing. Around his head he had a peculiar yellow band, with brown speckles, which seemed to be tightly set around his head. . . .

How strange he looks. . . .

The speckled band, Watson!

Suddenly, his strange headband began to move. . . .

A snake!

He died seconds after he was bitten!

A swamp adder, Watson, the most poisonous snake in India.

Murderers often die the very way they have planned for someone else! Let us put this creature back into its den.

He threw the noose around the reptile's neck. . . .

Careful, Holmes!

carried it away from him to the open safe. . . .

Ah! He is safely put away now!

and closed the safe upon it.

We can now get Miss Stoner and notify the police.

The Great Adventures of Sherlock Holmes

After breaking the sad news to the terrified girl, we took her to her aunt's home at Harrow.

I'm certain, Miss Stoner, that the coroner's inquest will find that the doctor was killed accidentally by a most dangerous pet.

Oh, how awful!

But thanks to Holmes, you are safely out of it.

As we traveled home next day, Holmes told me a few points I had missed. . . .

It is always dangerous to reason without enough data. . . .

But soon it became clear that whatever danger threatened, it could not come from either the window or the door. . . .

The gypsies and the use of the word "band" by the poor girl put me on the wrong track entirely. . . .

Quite understandable, my dear fellow.

Quickly, Holmes explained why he changed his mind.

The ventilator, the dummy bellrope, and the bed being nailed to the floor made me think that the rope was a bridge for something passing through the hole to the bed.

Hmm, yes. . . .

The idea of a snake came to me at once. And I knew that the doctor had a supply of animals from India. . . .

Ah, quite so.

And the idea of using a poison which could not be traced would occur to a doctor who had been trained in India.

It would take a sharp-eyed coroner to find the tiny holes left by the poison fangs. Then there was the whistle. . . .

Yes, that rather puzzled me. . . .

He had to be able to get the snake back. He trained it, using the milk we saw, to return to the sound of the whistle.

Tweet-tt!

Hisss!

He would put it through the ventilator late at night, knowing that it would crawl down the rope and land on the bed. . . .

It might or might not bite the sleeper. . . .

She might escape every night for a week. . .but sooner or later she must be bitten.

He stood on the chair to reach the ventilator. The clanging sound was caused by his closing the safe when the snake returned.

I heard the snake hiss and instantly attacked it!

So that was the sound I heard!

So that it went back through the ventilator?

. . . .And bit its master.

My cane blows hurt it and made it angry so that it went for the first person it saw.

Agh! No—

In this way I was the cause for Dr. Roylott's death, but I cannot say that it will bother me very much.

Good to be back at Baker Street, eh Watson?

I thought we might never see it again, Holmes!

THE END

40

A telegram from Sherlock Holmes to my house was how I first learned of the Boscombe Valley Mystery. . . .

Telly for you, sir.

I wonder who that can be from?

Open it, dear, and you'll soon know.

The message from Holmes, although short, sounded interesting. . . .

Have just been sent for from the east of England to solve Boscombe Valley murder. Will you come along? Air and scenery perfect. Leave Paddington station by the 11:15 train.

You'll go, of course. You are always so interested in Mr. Sherlock Holmes' cases.

And so shortly. . . .

Glad you could come, Watson. I like having someone with me whom I can count on.

Nonsense, old chap. Glad to be of service.

And as our train passed Reading. . . . The London newspapers have not told the full story. I think it is one of those simple cases which are always so very difficult. But they have a serious case against the murdered man's son.

Is it a murder, then?

We shall see for ourselves.

The largest landowner in the Boscombe Valley is Mr. John Turner. He had made his money in Australia. One of his farms was rented to a Mr. Charles McCarthy, also an ex-Australian. . . .

The men had known each other in Australia. Turner was the richer man, but when McCarthy rented part of his property, they stayed friends and were often together.

I see.

McCarthy had one son, a lad of eighteen, and Turner had a daughter the same age, but neither of them had living wives. McCarthy kept two servants—a man and a girl. Turner had some half-dozen. . . .

Last Monday, June 3rd, McCarthy left his home about 3 P.M. and walked down to the Boscombe pool, a small lake. He had told his servant he was to meet someone there. He never returned!

From McCarthy's farmhouse to the pool is a quarter of a mile. Two people saw him passing: an old woman and William Crowder, Mr. Turner's gamekeeper. Both witnesses say McCarthy was alone.

The gamekeeper adds that just after seeing Mr. McCarthy pass he had seen his son James going the same way, carrying a gun. He thought the son was following his father. He thought no more of it until he heard of the murder.

The daughter of the lodge-keeper was in the woods picking flowers. She saw Mr. McCarthy and his son having a violent argument near the pool.

She was frightened by their yelling, and ran away, afraid they were going to fight. She had just finished telling this to her mother when young McCarthy ran into the house, saying he had found his father dead. He was very excited, he didn't have his gun or hat, and his right hand and sleeve were stained with blood.

Good heavens! And then what, Holmes?

They followed him back and found the dead body beside the pool. The head had been beaten with something heavy and blunt, such as the butt-end of the boy's gun which was found on the grass within a few feet.

So the son was arrested?

Yes. He's accused of murder in the first degree.

All the evidence points to young McCarthy as the guilty one.

This kind of evidence is very tricky. It may point straight to one thing, but if you shift your point of view a little it may point to something different.

There are several people in the neighborhood who believe young McCarthy didn't do it, and among them Mr. Turner's daughter. She has hired Inspector Lestrade of Scotland Yard, and he asked me to work on the case.

I am afraid that the facts are so clear that you will find little to do in this case, Holmes.

44

Consider this, Watson. When young McCarthy was arrested, he said he was not surprised to hear it and that it was just what he deserved.

A confession!

No, he then said that he was innocent. Had he acted surprised at his own arrest, I would have suspected him right away.

No, Watson, the fact that he let himself be arrested so easily makes me think that he may be innocent. The way he blames himself seems to me to be the signs of a healthy mind, not a guilty one.

Well, men have been hanged on far less evidence.

So they have, and wrongly, too.

Holmes then handed me a copy of the local paper containing the young man's story. . . .

You may read for yourself. . . .

Hm. . .I see the coroner missed nothing in his questioning. . . .

As I read the story I could picture young James McCarthy telling his story to the coroner.

I had just returned from three days at Bristol when I saw my father walk quickly out of the yard. Not knowing where he was going, I then took my gun and walked towards the Boscombe Pool. . . .

". . . .thinking I would try to shoot a rabbit for dinner."

"On my way I did see William Crowder, the gamekeeper; but he is wrong in thinking that I was following my father. I didn't even know that he was in front of me."

"As I came near the pool I heard a cry. . . ."

Cooee!

That was dad's signal for me!

"Hurrying forward, I found him by the pool. He seemed surprised to see me."

What are ye doin' here?

What d'ye mean, dad? I heard you call. . . .

"We were arguing and almost began to fight. . .My father had a bad temper. . . ."

Go on about yer business. I've no use for ye now!

You think you can talk to me that way?

"Not wanting to fight my father, I started back for the farm. . . ."

Go on, get away! Off with ye!

Might as well. He's too angry to talk reason to!

"I had not gone far, when suddenly I heard. . . ."

Agggghhh!

It's dad! I'd better go back.

"And found my father lying upon the ground, with his head badly cut. . .I dropped my gun and held him in my arms. . . ."

What happened, dad?

Sighhhh!

He died almost instantly. I then ran to the lodge keeper's house for help. I saw no one near my father when I returned and have no idea how he was killed. I never knew of him having any real enemies.

Hmm. . . .

47

Did your father say anything before he died?

He spoke a few words. There was something about a rat.

What did you think he meant by that?

Nothing. I thought he was out of his mind with pain.

What did you and your father argue about?

I cannot tell you. I can only say that it had nothing to do with the murder which followed.

It will be bad for your case if you refuse to answer. You say the cry of "Cooee" was a common signal between you and your father?

It was.

I do not know.

Then why should he use this signal, before he knew you had come back from Bristol?

Didn't you see anything when you returned and found your father dying?

I thought I saw a gray coat lying on the ground, but when I rose from my father it was gone.

Do you mean it disappeared before you went for help?

Yes.

How far was it from the body?

About a dozen yards or so.

And how far from the edge of the wood?

About the same.

Having finished reading the newspaper story of the murder. . . .

The coroner points out that it was odd that McCarthy signaled to his son before seeing him. Also that James refused to tell what the quarrel was about, and his strange account of his father's dying words. It looks bad for him, Holmes.

Perhaps. But I shall start this case from believing that what this young man says is true.

Inspector Lestrade of Scotland Yard was waiting at the station and had us driven to our rooms.

I knew you would want to see the scene of the crime, Holmes.

It was very nice of you, Lestrade.

We entered our room, then suddenly. . . .

Oh Mr. Holmes! James could not have done it! We've known each other since childhood. . .he's too tender-hearted.

I hope we can clear him.

I'm sure the quarrel with his father was about me. That's why he won't speak about it to the coroner.

In what way?

His father wanted us to marry. But we love each other as brother and sister. Also, he is young and does not wish to marry yet. So there were quarrels.

Did your father want this marriage too?

No. Mr. McCarthy was the only one who really wanted it.

Thank you for telling me this. I'd like to see your father.

I'm afraid the doctor won't allow it. This has upset my father very badly. Mr. McCarthy was the only man who knew dad from the old days in Australia.

In Australia! At the gold mines, I suppose, where your father made his money.

Yes. If you are able to see James, please tell him I believe in him.

I will, Miss Turner.

After the girl had left, Inspector Lestrade argued with Holmes. . . .

With that Holmes headed for the next train to Herford to see the prisoner.

Shame on you, Holmes. Why do you raise her hopes when there is no hope.

I think I can clear James McCarthy.

See you in a couple of hours, Watson.

Yes, you and Inspector Lestrade go. I'll wait here.

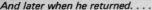

And later when he returned. . . .

I have seen young McCarthy, Watson, and learned nothing. But we must go over the ground at Boscombe Pool before it rains!

You really learned nothing by your visit?

Well, there was James' reason for not wanting to marry Alice Turner. He is really in love with her, but two years ago before he really knew her, he married a barmaid in Bristol.

My word.

No one knows about this. You can imagine how hard it is for him.

That was why he threw up his hands when his father kept talking to him about proposing to Miss Turner.

It was with his barmaid wife that he spent the last three days in Bristol. And his father did not know where he was.

And Holmes shocked me when. . . .

Fortunately, however, the barmaid found out that he is in serious trouble. She wrote to him to say that she already has a husband in Bermuda.

Then there really is no tie between them!

Quite so! I think that has made young McCarthy feel a little better.

But who is the murderer then?

We know that the murdered man was supposed to meet someone at the pool, and that could not be his son because James was away and his father did not know when he would return.

We also know that the murdered man was heard to cry "Coeee!" before he knew his son had returned. The case rests upon those two points.

Hmm. . .Yes. Quite so, old boy.

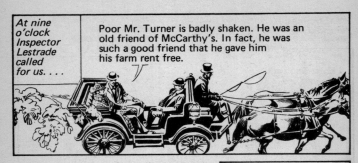

At nine o'clock Inspector Lestrade called for us. . . .

Poor Mr. Turner is badly shaken. He was an old friend of McCarthy's. In fact, he was such a good friend that he gave him his farm rent free.

And as we rode toward the Boscombe Valley pool. . . .

It seems strange that this McCarthy, a poor man, should talk of marrying his son to Turner's daughter, who will some-day get all her father's money.

And he talked about it as if Miss Turner and her father were sure to agree if only his son wanted to marry her.

It is even more strange since Miss Turner herself told us that James does not want to marry her, at least not now. Can you not figure something out from that?

Listen, Holmes. I find it hard enough to get the facts without going after guesses.

The Great Adventures of Sherlock Holmes

At Hatherly Farm, Holmes picked up a pair of McCarthy's boots and a pair of his son's.

I hope these will help you, sir.

They will do nicely, thank you.

Having measured the boots Holmes went to the court-yard.

Ah! From here we can follow the path to Boscombe Pool.

Remember, Holmes, I still think young McCarthy must have done it.

Swiftly and silently, Holmes went to the pool.

Ah, good! There are many marks here!

And as Lestrade pointed out the spot where the body was found. . . .

Ah. . .Three different tracks of the same feet. . .young McCarthy's I should think.

Amazing how he goes at it!

Holmes ran up and down carefully tracing the tracks until. . . .

Aha! This may interest you, Lestrade!

Indeed, Holmes? Why?

This stone could have caused the injuries. It is the murder weapon, I'm sure!

So you say! And who might the murderer be, Holmes?

Quite a tall man, left-handed, limps with the right leg, wears thick-soled shooting boots and a gray cloak, smokes Indian cigars, uses a cigar holder and carries a blunt pen knife.

I am still not sure, Holmes. Who was the murderer?

Surely, the man I describe can be found.

Holmes, I would be the laughing stock of Scotland Yard if I went about the country looking for a left-handed man with a lame leg.

Very well. Come along, Watson.

We dropped off Lestrade and returned to our hotel. . . .

Let us review the facts, Watson. We know that McCarthy cried, "Coeee!" before seeing his son. And also that he said something about a rat as he died. . . .

Well, what of it?

The call was not meant for his son, because he thought the lad was in Bristol. But "Coeee" is an Australian cry. . . so the person McCarthy was looking for at Boscombe Pool must have been an Australian.

What of the rat, then?

Sherlock Holmes took a folded map from his pocket.

This is a map of the colony of Victorian Australia.

Yes, I see that.

If I cover this part with my hand, what do you read?

ARAT!

And as Holmes removed his hand. . . .

And now?

Ballarat!

Quite so! Ballarat was the word! McCarthy was trying to name his murderer. . . so and so of Ballarat!

Wonderful, Holmes!

It is clear! Now taking the son's statement, we have the fact of an Australian from Ballarat with a gray cloak!

You said he was lame as well. . . .

The footprint made by his right foot was always less clear than his left. Why? Because he limped. . .he was lame!

But his being left-handed?

The blow was struck from behind and yet on the left side. It can only have been a left-handed man!

And as Holmes talked, suddenly the hotel waiter announced. . . .

He stood behind a tree during the father and son argument. There I found a stub of a cigar. He used a cigar holder with the tip of the cigar cut by a dull pen knife.

Holmes! I see. . .the murderer is. . . .

Mr. John Turner!

I was a hot-blooded young man then at the gold mines. I had no luck with my claim and met some bad friends. I became a highway robber.

"There were six of us, sticking up a station from time to time, or stopping wagons. I was called Black Jack of Ballarat, and we are still remembered in Australia as the Ballarat gang. . . ."

Turn over your gold or you're dead.

"One day we attacked a gold shipment and killed four of the six troopers, losing half of our own men before we got the gold. . . ."

"This man McCarthy was the wagon driver. I let him live though I saw his mean eyes study my face very carefully."

Make one move and you're dead!

We got it, Jack! Let's go!

We were now wealthy men. I left my pals and returned to England and settled down to an honest life. My wife died leaving me to bring up Alice.

All was going well until one day. . . .

Here we are, Jack! There's me and my son. If you don't take care of us we'll tell the police.

The driver! I should have killed him.

Later he saw I was more afraid of Alice knowing than the police. I gave him land, money, houses. . .but finally he asked for what I could not give. He wanted Alice for his son!

I did not dislike the boy, but I would not have his bad blood mixed with mine. When McCarthy promised to tell, I agreed to meet him at the pool.

I waited until he finished with his son, telling him to marry her. I knew I was a dying man, but I hoped I could save her if I could silence him. . .and I struck him down when his son left. His son came back, but didn't see me. I then picked up my cloak. That is the truth, gentlemen!

It is not for me to judge you. If young McCarthy is not found guilty, your secret is safe with us. . . .

James McCarthy was found not guilty because of the testimony of Sherlock Holmes. Old Turner died shortly after. The son and daughter are now happily married knowing nothing of the black cloud of the past.

Ah, it's good to be back at Baker Street, Watson.

You've done an amazing job, Holmes!

END

COMPLETE LIST OF POCKET CLASSICS AVAILABLE

CLASSICS

C 1 Black Beauty
C 2 The Call of the Wild
C 3 Dr. Jekyll and Mr. Hyde
C 4 Dracula
C 5 Frankenstein
C 6 Huckleberry Finn
C 7 Moby Dick
C 8 The Red Badge of Courage
C 9 The Time Machine
C10 Tom Sawyer
C11 Treasure Island
C12 20,000 Leagues Under the Sea
C13 The Great Adventures of Sherlock Holmes
C14 Gulliver's Travels
C15 The Hunchback of Notre Dame
C16 The Invisible Man
C17 Journey to the Center of the Earth
C18 Kidnapped
C19 The Mysterious Island
C20 The Scarlet Letter
C21 The Story of My Life
C22 A Tale of Two Cities
C23 The Three Musketeers
C24 The War of the Worlds
C25 Around the World in Eighty Days
C26 Captains Courageous
C27 A Connecticut Yankee in King Arthur's Court
C28 The Hound of the Baskervilles
C29 The House of the Seven Gables
C30 Jane Eyre
C31 The Last of the Mohicans
C32 The Best of O. Henry
C33 The Best of Poe
C34 Two Years Before the Mast
C35 White Fang
C36 Wuthering Heights
C37 Ben Hur
C38 A Christmas Carol
C39 The Food of the Gods
C40 Ivanhoe
C41 The Man in the Iron Mask
C42 The Prince and the Pauper
C43 The Prisoner of Zenda
C44 The Return of the Native
C45 Robinson Crusoe
C46 The Scarlet Pimpernel

COMPLETE LIST OF POCKET CLASSICS AVAILABLE (cont'd)

C47 The Sea Wolf
C48 The Swiss Family Robinson
C49 Billy Budd
C50 Crime and Punishment
C51 Don Quixote
C52 Great Expectations
C53 Heidi
C54 The Illiad
C55 Lord Jim
C56 The Mutiny on Board H.M.S. Bounty
C57 The Odyssey
C58 Oliver Twist
C59 Pride and Prejudice
C60 The Turn of the Screw

SHAKESPEARE

S 1 As You Like It
S 2 Hamlet
S 3 Julius Caesar
S 4 King Lear
S 5 Macbeth
S 6 The Merchant of Venice
S 7 A Midsummer Night's Dream
S 8 Othello
S 9 Romeo and Juliet
S10 The Taming of the Shrew
S11 The Tempest
S12 Twelfth Night